NINE ELEVEN TWO

A Novel by

COLIN HESTON

HARROW AND HESTON
Publishers

New York

Cover design by Gary Chung

Cover photographs by permission of 123RF

TABLE OF CONTENTS

9/11 TWO

1. Commencement

Mrs. Kohmsky leaned her head against the cold window of the Amtrak train. She was dreaming again of their honeymoon. The two days they had in a little hunting lodge in the hills just outside Tulgovichi. There was one of those tourist magazines left in their room. And on the cover was a picture of a yellow school bus picking up a couple of kids, the bus framed in front of nicely clipped lawns, mom and dad waving good bye. It was the suburban America she had dreamed about ever since.

Dreams, though, are only that. They're meant to deceive. Now, after almost forty years of marriage and twenty five years living in America with Mr. Kohmsky, seven of those in New York City, she felt like giving up, felt almost as ground down as she did when they lived not far from Chernobyl in Tulgovichi. She glanced at Mr. Kohmsky whose large frame barely fitted into the small space beside her. He looked gruff and morose. He *was* gruff and morose. He had always been like it. He had only one love, and that was Russian literature. So naturally, he despised America.

Sarah was just five years old when they left the USSR for America soon after the Chernobyl disaster. Mrs. Kohmsky had no family, and Mr. Kohmsky's two brothers up and left right then. The youngest one, Nicholas, was only fourteen. He just disappeared one night and hadn't been heard of since. And the other one, Sergey, came to the bus station to see them off and said, "You'll be hearing from me one day," and winked as though he had some secret plan. And Mrs. Kohmsky could hardly contain her delight when Mr. Kohmsky had been offered an adjunct position at the State University of New York at Albany, teaching Russian literature. The image of the yellow school bus leaped into full view. She was going to heaven and Sarah would grow up there. The disaster was heaven-sent as well because it made it easier to get the necessary visas to get out of the USSR.

The real school bus wasn't like on the magazine. Well, it was, but the picture had lied to her, there wasn't any other way to describe it. Just like

1

in the picture, she stood in front of their little modest suburban house, its lawn, though, unkempt, holding Sarah's hand as the bus pulled up. Sarah pulled back and did not want to get in. The bus driver came down, nice and friendly, and between the two of them they coaxed and prodded Sarah up the steps and into the bus. Mrs. Kohmsky knew right there that the dream had been shattered. Every morning she had to push and cajole Sarah on to the bus. The other kids pointed at them and laughed.

A battle had begun. Sarah did everything to delay getting ready for school. Mrs. Kohmsky cooked her a hot breakfast every morning. And every morning Sarah sat stubbornly and refused to eat it. And as the years of school passed, a terrible thing happened. Sarah gained weight, even though she seemed to eat so very little. And her father one day, in one of his fits of depression, called her a fat little pig, and Mrs. Kohmsky cried as she cooked the breakfast. How could this happen in American heaven?

At first Mrs. Kohmsky blamed America – the fast food and all that. And besides, Sarah wasn't all that much fatter than the others. Yet, every time the school bus stopped, the other kids taunted her, until Mrs. Kohmsky had to admit that her daughter was in fact, a very fat person, so fat that people noticed and looked at her with the disdain that they save for parents they blame for their children's defects. Instead, Mrs. Kohmsky blamed the Chernobyl disaster that was it.

Sarah, for her part, withdrew into herself. She rarely spoke to anyone, including her parents. And she was mercilessly bullied on the bus and at school. She told no one because there was no one to tell. She made up for it all by burying herself in her studies, excelling in everything, thereby incurring further the wrath and derision of the other kids who were "cool." But she got her reward with a place at NYU, which was immediately neutralized by her parents' insistence on moving to New York City to take care of her. And then she won a public service scholarship to Columbia Law School and before they knew it she had graduated from there too. Then, instead of joining a law firm, she received a fellowship to pursue a master's degree at Oxford University, the one in England. These were amazing achievements that the Kohmskys took for granted.

Mrs. Kohmsky remembered well the day Sarah left for Oxford. It was July 4, 2003. They drove her to the airport, and not a word was said, except finally, by Mrs. Kohmsky, "have you got your ticket and passport?" to which Sarah did not answer. A terrible thought shot into her head. Would Sarah disappear like her uncle Nicholas?

They had never told Sarah how they managed to get free of Russia, of the groveling helplessness of their lives in the USSSR. Sarah had never shown any interest, anyway. She had no doubt heard of the Chernobyl disaster, but never seemed to link it to their coming to America. She seemed to remember little of her childhood in the USSR. No wonder, really, because she was kept at home as much as possible confined in their one room, and schooled by both her mom and dad who would not entrust her education to the Russian bureaucrats. Perhaps it was their fault. In those days, life was difficult for Jews anywhere, and it was especially so in the USSR then. And everyone lived in such terrible poverty one could hardly say that Jews fared any worse than others. But they were not really Jews, they didn't really believe in the spiritual stuff.

So in contrast to her scholarly endeavors they had not taught Sarah anything of the spiritual side of life, never gone to temple. They had just gone along with the annual Jewish celebrations, good excuses to enjoy dining with Sarah at home and on rare occasions with a few of their friends. Of course, Sarah had no friends.

"Last call for Albany," called the station attendant. The train pulled away from Penn station. Stragglers walked up and down the aisle looking for any remaining seats. Soon, they would be heading up the Hudson. There had been a freak April snow storm. Everything would look beautiful, though there was something somber about blossoming trees drooping sadly under the weight of snow. It reminded her of the last good-bye. At the airport, Sarah had insisted on saying good-bye from the curb. They never had a chance even to get out of the car. An all-too-quick good-bye. Cruel, really. They had never heard from her again. That was eight or nine years ago. They had sent letters, of course. Even phoned Oxford university officials. She had graduated, they knew that, but since then, no trace.

*

The head office of the FBI in New York was in Albany, the state capital. Mr. and Mrs. Kohmsky had tried contacting the FBI in Manhattan, but it was impossible to get their attention. They had more important things to attend to, trying to protect New Yorkers from terrorism, they said. Investigating the whereabouts of a missing adult daughter was way down their list.

The FBI office in Albany was housed in the old Post Office Building, an imposing 19th century edifice on Broad Street, built of huge chunks of concrete, gray and heavy, seeming to lean forward to pedestrians as they approached the entrance. Why a post office should look so serious was anybody's guess, but it seemed right for an FBI office.

"Mr. and Mrs. Chomsky, just take a seat and the Director will be with you in a minute.

"It's Kohmsky."

The receptionist had already left her desk to notify the Director of their presence. Mrs. Kohmsky rummaged in her handbag and withdrew a crumpled photo of Sarah. She turned it over in her hands, rubbed it hard between her thumb and fingers.

"The Director will see you now."

"Mr. and Mrs. Chomsky. Welcome to Albany," smiled the Director.

"It's Kohmsky, not Chomsky," grumbled Mr. Kohmsky as he and his wife stood stiffly in front of the large mahogany desk, confronted by the big American flag, the golden eagle looking down on them from atop the pole.

"Oh yes, of course, my apologies. A simple mistake — must happen often." The director rummaged around in his desk drawer and withdrew a folder. "Please take a seat."

"We're hoping you can help find our daughter Sarah," said Mrs. Kohmsky as she handed the photograph across the desk.

"But why have you come all the way to Albany? We have a very big office in Manhattan, you know."

Mrs. Kohmsky sighed. "We've been there on many occasions. We've tried the New York Police Department. Tried and tried. They say it's a low priority case."

"Oh, I'm sorry. I assure you I'll do everything I can to help you." The Director pressed an intercom button on a desk unit that probably dated back to the 1960s. "Agent Jones, step in a moment." He looked closely at the photograph.

"When was this photo taken?"

"The day she graduated law school. About eleven years ago," replied Mrs. Kohmsky.

There was a knock at the door and Agent Jones entered. "Ah, Agent Jones. Take this photo and see what you can find in our missing persons database. Her name is Sarah Kohmsky and these are her parents."

"Pleased to meet you, Mr. and Mrs. Chomsky. I'll get right on it."

"Excuse me, it's Kohmsky, and we know she's missing, so why do you want to look her up in your missing-persons database?" Mr. Kohmsky was annoyed, as usual.

"Mr. Kohmsky, please be patient," replied the Director. "Our databases are used extensively by our agents all around the world. We will put out a request. Our agents are very thorough. If she has been sighted, we will quickly hear about it."

"But they did that in the Manhattan office. It seems hit or miss to me. Why can't you send an investigator to where she was last seen, which was Oxford university where she graduated in the summer of 2004?"

The Director ignored the request. "Do you still have family back in Russia?"

"My husband has two brothers, I have no family. They were killed in the war and afterwards."

"Are you sure Sarah has not gone there?"

"We have lost touch with everyone. After the Chernobyl disaster his brother Sergey, who worked at the power plant but thankfully was not on duty at the time of the meltdown, took off to we don't know where. And the youngest, Nicholas, who would have been only about fifteen at the time, still in high school, took off, he was talking about that even before the disaster."

"They didn't migrate like you did?"

"Not as far as we know. Sergey had a pretty good job with the government. But when things broke down, he wasn't paid. He probably left for the mountains, that's where he always said he'd go if things got too difficult. But which mountains, we have no idea."

"We did receive some money once," said Mrs. Kohmsky, trying to be helpful. Mr. Kohmsky pressed his foot against her toe.

"You did? From your brothers-in-law? Is that unusual?"

"Well, we thought they had no money."

"And how long ago was this?"

"A few years, maybe four. Not sure."

"How much was it, if I may ask, and how did it get to you?"

"I don't see what this has to do with our missing daughter," Mr. Kohmsky interjected.

"Maybe if we can find your brothers, there might be a lead to Sarah. That was her name, right? Sarah?"

"She never knew them. Never met them. We hardly spoke of them to her."

"So the money?"

"We bought a car with it. It was one of those Visa gift cards that had a fixed amount of money and you used it like an ordinary credit card.

Didn't need a PIN or anything. Quite a lot of money. Our old car hadn't worked for a couple of years."

"I see. So what bank was it?"

"There didn't seem to be any particular bank. Or if there was I don't remember. The car salesman was suspicious, but when the money came through, he was happy."

"Do you have any receipts or anything like that we could use to trace the money?"

"We never kept anything. We sent a thank you card to the address on the envelope, but it came back address unknown."

There was a light knock and Agent Jones returned.

"I take it you found nothing?" asked the Director.

"She is listed, sir, missing since June of 2004. Nothing else though, just a copy of the photograph you gave me."

"Have another look for cross links to our other databases. There might be something."

"I'll get on it. Shouldn't take a minute."

"Mr. and Mrs. Kohmsky, you understand that there is a rule of thumb that after five years missing, we in law enforcement classify such cases as probably deceased."

"She is not a case. She's our daughter and we love her."

"Yes, yes of course. I'm sorry. I just don't want to give you any false hopes."

"False hope is better than none," said Mr. Kohmsky aggressively, "anyway I thought it was ten years."

The Director ignored him and turned to Mrs. Kohmsky.

"Is there any reason why Sarah would just go missing like this, without a word to you? Was she —"

"Rebellious? A bad girl? Is that what you want to say?"

"Well, I —"

"The answer is no, but I can tell you that she was different from us. Though she wasn't born here—she came to America when she was five—in many ways she's more American than Americans. We tried to explain a couple of times, at least I did, but she never understood our roots in Russia, and was embarrassed by it all, and made fun of our English accents."

Again, Mr. Kohmsky pressed on Mrs. Kohmsky's toe, but she shifted away.

"Remarkable," said the Director.

"She is a very smart girl."

"Too smart," interjected Mr. Kohmsky, unable to stop himself.

"What do you mean?"

"Forget it."

"So there was a disagreement?"

Mr. and Mrs. Kohmsky looked at each other, then at the floor.

"Mr. and Mrs. Kohmsky you must tell me as much as you can. Without detailed information that only you can give, there's little chance that we can find her."

"We did have an argument one time, but it was a while ago," said Mrs. Kohmsky glancing nervously at her husband.

"And?"

"She told us we were stupid Jews and it was people like us that caused 9/11," interjected Mr. Kohmsky.

"She said that? But, if I may say so, you are all Jewish, aren't you?"

"It sounds worse than it was. Sarah and I were just arguing over her not eating her breakfast and she burst into tears and yelled at us then ran out."

"And when exactly was this?"

"It was the day she graduated from Columbia Law School."

Both the Kohmskys looked down, ashamed.

At this point Agent Jones returned, looking concerned. He stood behind the Kohmskys. "I did find one cross link but I think you need to come and verify the link because it requires an extra level of security access that I don't have."

"Excuse me a minute," said the Director as he followed Jones out of the office, closing the door carefully behind him.

"What have you found, Jones?"

"There may be a link to a known terrorist, Shalah Muhammad. He's Iraqi, Shiite, but may be working for the Iranians and could even be Iranian. The record isn't clear. Anyway, he lectured in political science at Oxford on and off up to some years ago, then dropped off the radar screen. That's all I had access to. If you can get us the additional level of security, we can find out more."

"Surely the boys in the Manhattan office know about this. But where's the link with Sarah Kohmsky?"

"I'm hoping it's in the next level of security."

The Director punched in his password. A photograph immediately popped up of a group on the Oxford campus, standing on the lawn of the campus coffee shop, the famous round library in the background. Shalah Muhammad stood proud, supremely confident, amidst a group of happy students, all dressed in graduation regalia. Sarah stood right beside him, her head leaning on his shoulder, he with his arm reaching around her waist. She was much fatter than in the photo her mother gave them. He read the risk profile:

Shalah Muhammad is the suspected master mind of the USS Cole attack and probably consulted extensively for the Nine Eleven attackers. He is considered the brains of Iranian terrorist intelligence. He has cut ties with Al Qaeda considering them to have deteriorated into an amateurish terror group, prone to hasty and poorly planned missions. Before suddenly giving up his position at Oxford, he advocated the overthrow of America and the West and destruction of Israel, all in the name of establishing an Iranian caliphate that would contain all the countries to the immediate south and east of the Mediterranean. He will stop at nothing to get what he wants and is a heartless, violent disciplinarian. Probably the most dangerous terrorist today, who, with his extensive network, has replaced the remnants of Al Qaeda.

"But she's Jewish, isn't she? That would be a mighty leap, and would indicate a huge rift between her and her poor old mom and dad."

Agent Jones nodded in agreement. "But sir, the guys down in New York must know this too."

"That's why they've given them the run around. I'd better give them a call."

*

Shalah Muhammad was a popular fellow at Oxford. He hung out at the local pubs with his students, bought them drinks, got them and himself drunk often. The more boisterous and irreverent students took to calling him Moses, which he pretended to take good-naturedly, but got back at them by constantly demonstrating to them how poorly educated they were. He especially delighted in stopping them in mid-sentence to correct their sloppy grammar. He was a master of the English language, having been educated at Harrow, the school for England's upper crust. There, he had excelled at everything except cricket and refused to play grid iron. For that, he was mercilessly bullied and he still held a grudge against all those who took it out on him. Sarah could see how much he hated being made fun of. She felt very close to him because she thought she saw how vulnerable he was. She knew what it was like to be bullied and made fun of. She never joined the other students in taunting him, though she could not be sure of that because there were times when she got very drunk and couldn't remember much of the night before.

The night of Sarah's graduation was such a night. She woke up the next morning in Muhammad's flat. She was lying on his bed, but he was nowhere to be seen. Had he? Had they? It was some time until she staggered off the bed and made it to the bathroom just in time to throw up. She wondered if he'd said his prayers, being a Muslim and all. He had been at her to convert. But she had refused. Kept saying that she had no faith and saw no need of it. Her parents didn't have any either, so they said, yet they celebrated the special religious holidays with other Jews. And they never had any friends who weren't Jewish. So they were hypocrites, in her eyes. She'd never told them of course. She never told them anything. They were like strangers to her. Strangers from a far off land. Besides, her mother berated her for being fat even when she herself wasn't all that thin. And her father, well, who knows what was hidden behind his gaunt face and bushy beard? He was so deep, her mother always said. Fact is, he just never talked hardly at all. Just grunted and mumbled. One day she had asked him why they came to America. "Don't you remember?" he said scornfully, "you were five when we left. It should be obvious." She pursued the matter no further. He had no time for her, no time for anyone. He was completely stuck inside his 19th century Russian novels. And her Mom waited on him hand and foot. Not that he needed much waiting on. She served him up a Russian stew on Sunday, and they ate it for most of the week, garnished with a different boiled vegetable each night. And he washed it down with vodka, which almost made him happy.

In 1996, Sarah went to college at NYU, where she made the shocking discovery that she was a lot like her dad. She liked to be on her own, to bury herself in her books. It served her well. She began to master Russian literature too. But she also read Arabic which she guessed would have appalled him, so it gave her all the more pleasure to indulge in it. Being fat at college wasn't good either. Though she was not made fun of like she had been at school, the other students mostly ignored her, or behaved as though they were embarrassed to be with her because they didn't know what to say. Sarah could guess what they were thinking. "How could you let yourself get so fat? Why don't you stop eating?" Her books were her answer. And getting A's on everything she did, especially Arabic in which, by the time she graduated and went on to Columbia Law School, she was wonderfully fluent.

It was through her Arabic that she discovered the existence of Shalah Muhammad. She had started to browse through Arabic web sites, reading the classics in literature, following the political diatribes of the mullahs, which she recognized as way over the top very early on. Then she one day caught a reference to Shalah's accomplishments at Oxford; he had given a talk on the political future of Iran, and had challenged the received doctrine that Iran was run by incompetent nincompoops. On a whim, she sent him an email asking if she could come to study with him. To her surprise she received a quick reply, written in perfect English, suggesting that, once she finished her law degree she apply to Oxford's special Masters in Law program in criminology.

The noise of a key in the door shook Sarah back to consciousness. She was sitting on the toilet, mostly clothed. Struggling to stand, she managed to drag herself into the hallway. It was Shalah Muhammad.

"So you're awake! Do you know what time it is? You look like shit!"

Sarah stood, leaning against the wall. "I, I don't really know —"

"OK. OK. Don't worry. Nothing happened. You passed out at the pub and we had to get you to bed. My flat was the closest." Shalah smiled his nicest, superior smile. His face was gray, the creases around his mouth and eyes accentuated. His gray beard was carefully and impeccably groomed, but he still looked every bit of his forty five years.

"You don't look that great yourself."

"Come on. Clean yourself up a bit and I'll buy you a coffee. Or a hair of the dog, if you would prefer."

"But I look like hell. And my clothes, they're a mess."

"Come on. I have a proposition for you."

"Like what?"

"Can't tell you here."

"Woo! Sounds mysterious."

"It is."

*

Mr. and Mrs. Kohmsky grabbed a seat on the Hudson River side of the train. Their visit to Albany had turned up nothing, except to confirm what they had long suspected. The FBI was keeping something from them. They said Sarah was dead. The FBI were such simpletons. The Kohmskys, especially Mr. Kohmsky, were very experienced in dealing with the most corrupt and devious government officials one could imagine — those in Chernobyl. Government officials rarely told the truth. Lying was an occupational necessity.

Mrs. Kohmsky leaned her head against the window and let the cold come through to her forehead. She could read the lying right in their faces; the slight twisting of the mouth, an air of superiority, the deep love of power, imperceptible except to the experienced victims of government officialdom. A small tear snaked down from the corner of her eye and began its journey over her wrinkled, reddened cheek. Sarah wasn't dead. She knew it. They would find her. They would never give up. And going to study for a Master's degree at Oxford wasn't running away, was it? It's true she hardly ever talked to her parents, but that was understandable. Her father hardly ever spoke either. It was left to her, the mother of the house, to do the talking. Maybe if they'd given Sarah more freedom earlier. Maybe they should not have moved to New York when she went to NYU. They did it because it saved a lot of money. She did not have to live in the dorms, which Sarah would have hated anyway, wouldn't she? Mom knew her Sarah. She liked to keep to herself, and how could you do that in one of those awful dorms that reminded her of an orphanage for grown-ups?

Mr. Kohmsky stirred, stretched his long legs into the aisle. The train was well on its way, skirting the river, flying past the last remnants of 19th century factories. There had been a lot of rain over night. The river was high. The trees getting greener the closer they got to New York City. "We have to take it to another level," he said.

"You mean the CIA? But how do you contact them. They're not in the phone book, are they?"

"We'll go to the State Department. They'll help us."

"Perhaps the Russian consulate too?" Mrs. Kohmsky realized how silly that was as soon as she said it. Her husband of course did not answer.

*

"So what's the big mystery?" asked Sarah. She had insisted on dropping by her little flat on the way to the coffee shop so she could put on some fresh clothes, not that she had many, and comb her hair and splash a little water on her face. She put on her long draping dress, one that she had bought at a second hand shop. It was the kind that pregnant women wear, a dark blue, almost black, and made of a material that hung very loosely, rather like a big shawl. It had tiny flecks of silver woven into it and matched her small sequined pocket book that was just like her mother's. Now they sat in a little pub restaurant, looking out over the river. It was a quiet Sunday morning. Shalah had insisted on taking her out for a good solid English breakfast. It was the best thing to overcome a hangover, he said. But she couldn't face it. She just wanted tea and toast.

"I'd like you to come and work for me," Shalah Muhammad said as the waiter arrived and plunked down his large plate of three eggs and several rashers of bacon.

"Really? Are you serious?"

"But first I have to give you a job interview to see if you're qualified," he smiled mischievously.

"Only if I can ask you some questions in return," Sarah countered.

"Fair enough. But tell me first, how come you are so well educated, you know so much English and European literature, your Arabic is impeccable, and you are an amazing lawyer. I thought the American education system was the worst in the Western world."

"You forget my parents are Russian. They made sure I was good at languages, and of course my father lives and dies for Russian literature. It's all his life is, actually. And my mother. Well, let's not go there. But what about you? How come you teach Marx and Engels all the time, and hardly ever mention Islam, except when you're trying to convert me? Are you not a believer?

"And you are not a believer, you are not a Jew?"

"My parents are Jews, or at least they call themselves secular Jews. They say they don't believe, but they made me sit through all the Jewish holiday celebrations, most of which celebrate Jews getting slaughtered, or just escaping slaughter."

"So I ask again. You are not a Jew?"

"I told my parents that I hated Jews."

"So you hate yourself?"

"And you are not a Muslim?"

"Ah, we have reached an impasse. It is important for your job that I know where you stand. Do you really hate Jews, or just your parents?"

"I think Judaism is a narcissistic religion that encourages individuals to set themselves apart, think they're special, better than everyone else. The American version is especially so, because American culture is 'all about me' so Jews are very comfortable in that culture, even though they criticize it as being crass and boorish. And Islam?"

Shalah Muhammad chopped up his fried eggs, mixing the runny yoke into a half cooked (by American standards) rasher of bacon. He gulped it down, chewing noisily, his mouth open. He wiped some yoke from the corner of his mouth and stared carefully into Sarah's eyes. His gray eyes were cold and penetrating. It was a look that would scare any young woman, or man for that matter.

Sarah took a loud bite of her toast and chewed it aggressively. "Well?" she said, her mouth full, "what about Islam and Marx? Aren't they incompatible? Marx was an atheist wasn't he?"

"He was a Jew and an atheist, just like you."

"I am not a Jew. I just happen to have parents who are, although, as I said, they claim they are not real Jews, just secular Jews."

"There is no half way. You are either religious or you are not. I am a devout Muslim, but because of my work, I do not practice it openly, and I must even appear to be an unbeliever."

Sarah stared back at him. "You're lying."

"You are very perceptive, my dear, which is why I want you to work for me."

"Well, I can tell you I don't believe in Judaism or any other religion. They're all self-serving nonsense."

"So this is your American education speaking."

"Prove to me you are a devout Muslim."

"I have three wives."

"Liar. Anyway, that's hardly evidence of devotion."

"I have a wife in Baghdad, one in Teheran, and another in Cairo."

"Your wives must be very happy. How can you afford them?"

"I am paid very well for my work."

"Professors do OK, but they're not paid enough to support three wives in three different countries are they?"

"Teaching at Oxford is not my full time job. I just do it so I can look over bright students and recruit them to my cause."

"Your job is a 'cause'? What kind of job is that?"

"It's political."

"What kind of political?"

"If I tell you, there is no going back."

"Tell me!"

"I work for MEK, a terrorist group with a long history in Iran. I am a follower of Massoud Rajavi."

"You're joking, right?"

"I don't joke about my cause."

"What's MEK?"

"The People's Mojahedin Organization of Iran, Mojahedin-e-Khalq or MEK for short."

"You're a terrorist then?"

"That's not the right word. But yes, my work involves managing much of the organization and planning of missions designed to destabilize the Western world."

"Why pick on the West?"

"Because it is a venal, ruthless, violent, so-called civilization that has oppressed my people for hundreds of years. It is corrupted by greed which eats away at its very soul."

"So why not let it destroy itself, just like Marx predicted?"

"Marx was wrong. He underestimated the power of greed. Not to mention the power of power. The latter, Stalin understood that."

"Then why do you teach Marx? Why not teach how good and superior Islam is?"

"Islam is a complicated religion that cannot be taught easily to Westerners like you. They do not understand it because its logic and thinking are not Western. Marxism, on the other hand, is very Western in its logic, and the emotional appeal to young people of Marx's ideal of 'equality for all,' never fails to entice them into a revolutionary ideology."

"And after the revolution?"

"As you know, that was Marx's weakness. He had really no idea. It's where the dictatorship of the Caliphate comes in. That's what we are aiming for."

"The destruction of Western Civilization?"

"Much of it. Actually, only the democratic part of it, which has clearly become an absolute failure. Look at America. It's collapsing. Its political and economic structure are in turmoil."

"But that's because of capitalism, not democracy."

"Capitalism and democracy are not compatible."

"And the U.K.?"

"It is already finished. Look at it. All that's left is a nation of drunkards. But we will hasten the fall."

"So you want me to become a terrorist too? It's ridiculous. I don't hate anyone or anything that much. Not even my parents. I'm just not political."

"As I said, this is no joking matter."

"But I know nothing about bombs."

"You don't need to. I need you because you are a non-believer. It means that you will think in an objective way, see things that I may not. Make sure my logic does not stray. Humans are weak. They stray from the course very easily. And, most important, I know I can trust you," he paused for effect, "and, just as important — maybe the most important reason — you're a lovely sweet person with whom I know I'll be spending a lot of time."

Sarah looked down at her now half cold cup of tea. She lifted it for a sip, staring into the cup. She placed it on the saucer and reached for the hot water. No one had ever expressed the slightest interest in her in any way, least of all acknowledged how smart she was. People always simply assumed that fat people were happy, silly people who should go on a diet. She was overcome. "I, I don't know."

"I can pay you a lot of money. Our organization is supported by some of the richest people in the world. My main job, in fact, is to manage that money and to spend it wisely."

"It's not the money. I mean, you can't expect me to decide, right here and now, to become a terrorist. It's crazy."

"I'm sorry, I know. But there's no other safe way to ask you."

"And terrorist attacks, how do you do them?"

"We have an extensive network, including links with organized crime. So we can get anything or do anything we want. Doing stuff is not the hard part. Figuring out what to do is the biggest challenge."

"I need to think about it."

"You understand that, now I have told you all this, you are already recruited. And once hired, in the European socialist tradition, you can never be fired."

Shalah Muhammad grinned, almost sneered, giving her his piercing look, "I'd have to kill you if you quit."

Sarah was not quite sure if he was joking or not. He had always seemed a very gentle person. It was one thing she liked about Muslims. All those she had met had a very gentle nonviolent disposition. It was hard to think of them as terrorists.

"I, I, don't want to go back to America. I don't have any real plans. Just drifting along you know. And there's my parents. They will wonder what happened to me. I haven't corresponded with them since coming to Oxford. I should let them know."

"So your answer is yes?" It was as if he were asking her to marry him.

Sarah looked at Shalah's gray handsome eyes. They beckoned her. He smiled kindly, stroked his graying beard, then reached across and held her hand softly. He thought so highly of her, he had been honest with her. She could love this man, maybe she already did. She smiled back, her eyes watering.

"I, I want to, I really do. But it's so quick. It's not fair to make me decide so quickly. I need a cooling down period."

"Do you have a mobile phone?"

"Yes, of course."

"Give it to me." He extended his hand. She reached into her pocket book and gave it to him, all without thinking.

"I am going for a walk along the river," he said. "Stay here and I'll be back in half an hour. You can then give me your decision. Don't speak to anyone while I'm gone." He walked out.

Sarah watched him stroll along the riverbank. He was smoking a cigarette, looked so calm. She ordered another pot of tea and went to the bathroom while she waited for it to come. She already knew what she wanted. She wanted *him*. But getting what one wants isn't always a good thing.

The tea came and she set about the ritual of pouring herself a cup. She had ordered a slice of chocolate hedgehog as well. Without realizing it, she had turned her time to ruminate on her situation into a modest celebration.

She thought of her mom and dad. First time she had called them 'mom and dad' for a long time. It was always 'my parents.' She didn't quite know why it had been so hard for her to communicate with them all these years. They didn't make it easy. They obviously disapproved of her looks and took her academic accomplishments for granted. It wasn't enough, though, for her to hate them. And she didn't hate them. She just didn't care much about them. Wasn't really interested in their lives, because they didn't really have lives. And living with them was like living in a freezer that had no food in it, just ice cubes. Her mom babbled on about the good times in Chernobyl, even though everything she said about life there sounded awful. And her dad, well, he simply lived in his books and never communicated anything personal at all. So one talked, and the other didn't. It made them both into distant, unreal persons. Not 'family' if that is supposed to mean that the members of the family loved and talked and understood each other. There just wasn't any feeling there at all. But in Shali (her secret name for Shalah, which she dared not use in front of him) there was feeling, lots of it. Complicated she acknowledged. But it was *life*. In him there was the promise of a full life, brimming with excitement. How could she refuse?

Sarah finished off her hedgehog slice and sipped her tea. She did not have her watch, but she guessed it must be near half an hour since he left. There were some postcards by the restaurant checkout. She quickly retrieved one and the cashier kindly loaned her a pen. She returned to her table and was about to write a note to her parents when Shalah

Muhammad appeared beside her. He smiled kindly down at her, his upper lip, though, wanting to curl, as it does when one sucks a lemon.

"Well?" he asked, taking his place across the table.

"Will I have to kill anyone?"

"It is terrorism, after all, so people will die most likely, but not directly by your hand."

"Well, look at me. I couldn't hurt a fly!"

"That's another reason I want you to work for me."

"And there's another?"

"Yes. Your Russian heritage. I have a deal brewing with the Russians and need someone like you to see it through. There's a lot of money involved."

Sarah sipped her tea. She looked around the room and saw the many old ladies sipping their tea also. She looked directly at Shalah.

"OK. I'm in!" She wanted to leap up and kiss him. But he saved her the embarrassment. He leaned across the table, his jacket almost tipping over the little milk jug, and kissed her on the forehead.

"There's my girl! I knew you'd do it. We will do great things together!"

"But I will need to contact my parents."

"I see you are ahead of me. But now I'm afraid you cannot. It will help the CIA or FBI or whoever starts trying to track me, if they are not already doing it. As a matter of fact, I am concerned about that photo one of our little group took in front of the library on graduation day. It is probably already in the hands of the CIA, and we are in it, rather close to each other."

"You mean one of our group is a spy? Don't be silly! You're paranoid."

"Sarah. You must be careful. The CIA is everywhere. They probably already know who I am. Paranoia is a benign affliction in my — our — business."

"You're making me scared."

"Scared is good."

"And speaking of business. I never even asked how much my salary will be and how many days off I get for holidays!"

Shalah Muhammad reached inside his jacket and withdrew a wad of tightly bound notes. "This will get you started." He counted out a few thousand pounds.

Sarah had never seen so much money all in one place. She took it without counting and stuffed it into her pocket book. "And my holidays?"

"That's the bad news. Like cops, terrorists are always on duty."

They both laughed. Shalah reached over and retrieved the postcard on which she had written only three words:

Hi Mom and Dad.

She barely noticed.

"In two days we leave for Cairo. I will introduce you to one of my wives so she will see that our relationship is strictly professional. You should buy some new clothes, pay off anything owing on your flat. If you need more money, let me know."

Sarah looked at him, unable to control her inner passion. A strictly professional relationship? It didn't seem possible. She knew she loved him, but now it was infused with the glamour of his profession.

"So what will be my first mission?" she asked, half joking.

Shalah Muhammad surveyed the entire restaurant with a hawk's eye. He leaned across the table, whispered in her ear, his nose rubbing her lobe, "to kill Yasser Arafat."

2. Alexandria

Sarah did not get to meet Shalah's wife in Cairo. He dropped her off at a small, safe house, in the middle of what looked like a slum to Sarah, the long, depressing section on the way to the airport on the outskirts of Cairo, streets lined with half-finished houses, the second floors composed only of protruding rusting steel rods that one day would be covered with concrete.

Although her Arabic was fluent, it was clear to her that there was no way she could begin to communicate with anyone in this slum. She stood out as a westerner, an American at that, and she had already deduced that Americans were not popular in these parts. She sensed, especially from the men, a seething envy loaded with a lustful disgust. They would love to rape me, and do it with pride, she thought. She looked to Shalah trying to convey her fear.

"Stay inside, keep off the streets, and you will be OK," he instructed as a teacher would to a student, "Tomorrow we will go to Alexandria to begin your first mission."

"But the target is in Palestine, isn't he?"

"Preparation, my dear. Preparation and planning. These are the hallmarks of professionalism."

"But I was going to meet your wife," she complained.

"It cannot work this trip. Besides, it's too soon. You are on probation until you have served your apprenticeship," he smiled.

"So you don't trust me?"

"I trust you yourself implicitly. But I cannot trust you completely until you are experienced. The inexperienced make blunders they cannot help, if you understand me."

Shalah grasped her hand firmly in both his hands, all the time looking around, always on the defensive. The alley was teaming with the busy lives of people who ignored them. He led her up the few steps into one of the concrete and stone houses, the color of the desert. The door was not locked. He pushed it open and nudged her in. She turned to say good-bye, but he had already pulled the door closed and left. Faint rays of light slipped through the gaps of old boards that shuttered the two small windows facing the rear. A kerosene lantern burned in the corner, where embroidered cushions lay on the floor and a woman sat, sewing. She wore an old cloak, probably adapted from of an abaya, her gray hair wound tightly into a bun and held down with a net. She motioned Sarah to sit beside her. Sarah looked around the room. There was a small fireplace in the opposite corner where a young girl sat kneading doe, baking pita bread.

"Sit," said the woman, smiling kindly, "I am told you speak Arabic."

"I try," said Sarah as she sat down beside her host.

"Shalah told me all about you."

"Then you probably don't know much." Sarah tried to get a good look at her face.

"You need not look so hard. I am Shalah's mother. Is it not obvious?"

"I, I, guess so. My apologies. It's a bit dark for me to see. But yes, I guess it's the light gray eyes, no?"

"It is enough for me to know that you are American and also Russian, a worthy contradiction, if I may say."

"You may. But what of Shalah? How is he so well-schooled, such a man of the world?"

"Shalah is an only child for which he has never forgiven me, but I could not help it. I almost died when I had him, and could have no more."

"But, how could you afford to send him to Oxford?"

"Would you like some tea?"

"I'm sorry, I did not mean to pry."

"Yes you did, and it's all right. Shalah was a very bright child and the Mullahs at the madrassa where he first went to school insisted on sending him to England for his education. They paid for it all. Unfortunately, it meant that I lost my only child first to the Mullahs, then to the English."

Sarah searched for the hint of a tear that might accompany such a plaintive remark, but could find none. Hers was a stern face, one that had seen much hardship. And the father? She wondered, but had not the temerity to ask.

*

Early the next morning Shalah Muhammad walked through the unlocked door. Sarah and his mother had slept on the cushions and were now sitting up sipping more tea. Sarah stood unsteadily, struggling to raise her weight from such a low soft cushion. His mother looked across at him, expressionless.

"We go to Alexandria," he said, "hurry so we can beat the hot sun. We're in a Land Rover with no air conditioning."

"And what's in Alexandria?" asked Sarah.

"The notorious Locusta."

"Who?"

"You'll see."

Sarah turned to say good-bye to her host who had resumed her sewing and did not look up. Shalah pulled at her hand. They left, Sarah muttering something like "thanks for the tea."

They climbed into the Land Rover and the driver navigated slowly through the crowded alleys, trying to avoid deep holes filled with mud and sludge, slowly weaving though clumps of people talking, bartering, gesturing, grudgingly giving way to the vehicle. When at last the jeep entered the freeway to Alexandria, Shalah Muhammad spoke.

"Locusta was a notorious poisoner enlisted by the Emperor Nero to kill his step brother Britannicus who was just 14 at the time, but was a popular boy and enough of a threat to Nero that he wanted him dead — along with the many others whom he saw as a threat to his reign. But, since Nero thought it may not sit well with the Senate if he started killing off his relatives, he wanted the death to mimic a regular illness, to happen over a period of time."

"But that was nearly two thousand years ago."

"Right. But there is a woman, Locusta, who deals in poisons and recipes for poison who lives in Alexandria."

"And?"

"We will ask Locusta for a poison that mimics regular illness, just like Nero did to get rid of Britannicus."

"But why? Who?"

"I told you who, didn't I? We will hasten Yasser Arafat's demise. He's already supposed to be sick. You'll help him out of his misery."

"But why?"

"Don't you follow current affairs? Arafat is a tool of the Americans. He lives off their money. And—"

"And what?"

"He has a Western wife."

"So?"

"You will befriend her. You speak French, right?"

They fell silent. Sarah was at a loss for words. The whole thing seemed utterly ridiculous. She reached carefully for Shalah's hand and clasped it lightly, seeking, perhaps, some reassurance that she had not gone completely mad. Here she was, in a cab with the world's most lethal terrorist, going to visit some witch who claimed to be a descendant of a notorious poisoner of 2,000 years ago. Yet it had all happened rather easily, without drama or conflict. Could she kill someone? "Can I do better than Raskolnikov and kill without guilt?" she asked herself. What was Shalah thinking? She tried to steal a sideways glance at his face. He sat expressionless, gazing out at the desert.

But then he turned to her, a faint smile, his gray eyes sparkling a little.

"You are a very brave person," he said, clasping her hand firmly, "all you need to be sure of is that Arafat deserves to die, and surely he does."

Sarah stared out the discolored window on her side. She was frightened. Not of Shalah or anyone else. But of herself.

"But this one is even easier," Shalah continued, "he is going to die anyway. You will just help him on his way. He is an evil man, killed many innocent people unnecessarily. And now it is time for him to get out of the way and let history move forward."

"How sick is he? What's wrong with him?"

"They say he is suffering from heart failure. But you can see those bulbous lips he has. I favor the rumors going around that he has AIDS."

"What do his lips have to do with that?" In fact Sarah thought he was the ugliest disgusting looking man she had ever seen.

"They say he has an entourage of teenage boys constantly in his attendance."

"Then his wife is probably not with him much at all."

"We will see when you meet her."

"You know her?"

"I know everyone."

*

They reached the outskirts of Alexandria where the driver left the freeway and navigated up to the shore front in the north then took the sometimes bumpy road south to the city. They turned a sharp corner and suddenly the famous lighthouse and harbor of Alexandria came into view. As they drew closer to the harbor, the houses became more like villas, interspersed with small shops catering for tourists seeking luxury and a good time. It was more like a Mediterranean resort than a Middle Eastern city. The jeep eventually pulled up in front of a small shop with a narrow storefront adorned with all kinds of sea shells, dried seaweed and coral, shark's teeth, sea urchins, and numerous snorkeling and beach paraphernalia. The sidewalk was littered with ancient urns, statues, and other trinkets that had presumably been retrieved from the several sunken cities and ships in and around the harbor. Shalah, obviously excited, stepped out, pulling Sarah with him.

"This is it! Now you will meet Locusta, the 2,000 year old witch!" he said joyfully.

Shalah brushed aside the hanging strings of shells that covered the doorway, their chime announcing his entrance. There were narrow rows of shelves containing knick-knacks, beach souvenirs, cheesy sculptures one would find in any beach shop, clams biting off a toe, starfish made into ballerinas, periwinkles poised on oyster shells; there was no end to the ugliness. Sarah began to giggle. Shalah was amused and led the way further into the shop. In contrast to the brightness of the desert sun outside, inside there were no windows. The shop was one long deep cavern, like the insides of an old London tube station.

Suddenly from over their shoulders, there came a refined, high pitched voice.

"Do you seek amusement?"

Startled, Sarah and Shalah turned quickly. Sarah let out a gasp, quickly putting her hand to her mouth.

"You could call it that," said Shalah Muhammad, "we are especially interested in your beach recipes."

"Ah, a customer who knows what he wants, I see."

"As always," he said, turning to Sarah, "I am most honored to introduce you to Locusta, the greatest and certainly oldest witch on earth."

"My goodness, Dr. Muhammad, you are much too kind! And such flattery too! And who is this, this ah, woman you introduce me to? A fan? A lover?"

"Pleased to meet you," Sarah put out her hand, "I'm Sarah."

Locusta took her hand in hers with a graceful sweeping motion, raised it to her lips and kissed it lightly. Her gown of light, translucent silk, floated through the air. Her hair was unexpectedly, for a witch, closely cropped, thick and blonde, with tinges of sea blue. "Beauty is not what it looks," she whispered, looking quizzically into Sarah's eyes.

"I, I —" stammered Sarah.

"What Sarah's trying to say is that she expected to see a wizened old witch, stringy hair, only a couple of black teeth, and a nasty pimple on the end of her nose with a huge hair growing out of it," laughed Shalah.

"So sorry to disappoint, Sarah. Witches must keep up with the times just like everyone else, if they want to be successful. Ask Shalah here, and he'll tell you."

"She has a Master's Degree in biochemistry from Oxford. That's where we met. She's not just up to date. She's ahead of her time."

Sarah could think of nothing to say. Locusta's slender body seemed so light, as though she stood inches off the ground. Her silk gown floated around her, seeming to make her body bend and quiver as if under water.

"So the recipe?" asked Locusta as she closed the door of the shop and put up a sign BACK SOON.

"Sarah needs a poison that mimics a recognizable illness."

"Who for?"

"You know better than to ask that."

"Oh course," Locusta smiled, "I can make just the potion you need, though it will take a little time to generate the right amounts of ingredients. I call it 'Coral Blue'."

"Is that just a name, or is it coral?" asked Sarah, trying to assert herself.

"Coral is all around us here on the rich and beautiful Mediterranean, although more plentiful in the Red Sea. However, there is a rare coral found in protected areas just outside the Alexandria harbor that contains an amazing amount of the ingredient I need for this potion. Using a secret process that I discovered in the annals of Tacitus, I can extract what we scientists call "palytoxin" from ground-up coral. I'm convinced that this is what the ancient Locusta used on the unfortunate Britannicus."

"How long?" asked Sarah.

"How much?" asked Shalah Muhammad.

"Since you have not told me the identity of the deserving person I will have to quote you the highest price, which is $100,000, half now, the other half after treatment whether or not successful. Do you desire death or disability?"

"Ultimately death," answered Sarah, at last asserting her responsibility for the mission.

"Male or female?"

"Male."

"Age?"

"Middle age."

"Height and weight?"

Sarah looked to Shalah. "Average I'd say."

"Physical condition?"

"Sickly, weak heart, we think."

"Excellent! It will take me two days. Find yourselves an excellent hotel, I recommend the Four Seasons, knowing how Shalah enjoys luxury and having all his special needs catered for. Dive the ancient ruins and anything else that will bring you pleasure. You could play at being Antony and Cleopatra," she said mischievously, her head held high, her eyes looking mockingly down her Alexandrian nose. "Shalah will no doubt want to visit Alexander's tomb, thoroughly despoiled by the Christians, but nevertheless it will satisfy his messianic delusions." She turned to Shalah, "isn't that right, oh great one?"

"Nothing could ever satisfy me, as you know. But I begin to think that you have been sipping some of your own potions."

"And my $50,000?"

"You have an Hawala?"

"Of course. Doesn't everyone who does business in the Middle East?"

"Tell him to call this number." He handed her a small piece of paper, "code word Nero and state the amount. The rest is up to your Hawala."

*

Sarah's fantasy of a blissful stay with Shalah in an exotic hotel played out except for one essential ingredient: it was without Shalah. He deposited her at the Four Seasons hotel and she did do some snorkeling. But Shalah did not stay there. He had distant relatives, he said, who had insisted he stay with them. He was lying of course. She knew that. But it didn't change anything. She couldn't help loving him. Perhaps it was not love; more a kind of infection, probably incurable.

*

Arafat made his final appearance of twenty seconds in a TV news interview some three months later. His condition had obviously deteriorated. He barely had enough breath to talk, forming his words with those bulbous lips, but speaking only in an inaudible whisper, his hands shaking uncontrollably. The new albuterol inhaler his wife had given him had not improved his breathing. In fact he had seemed to get worse. His heart frequently slipped into fibrillation and he could not stand without assistance. He died on November 11, 2004, according to the *New York Times,* "from a stroke that resulted from a bleeding disorder caused by an unidentified infection." In that same article, Sarah read, with smug satisfaction, the *New York Times* had ruled out poisoning as the cause of death.

Soon, democracy came to Palestine and Hamas became the official governing body of the region. Much to Shalah's disgust, however, Hamas did not live up to his expectations. It dithered around, did little to force Israel to its knees, in fact, it basically continued Arafat's policies even though making it look like they were glad to be rid of him. They simply weren't accustomed to thinking of themselves as free. They could think only of how to extract more money out of the West to support the slums and camps with just enough money to maintain them as camps in perpetuity. Because they had forsaken Islam — Shalah repeated this to Sarah many times — they had lost their way, were unable to think of themselves as an independent body, to think of how to build themselves into a nation. Until they broke out of these shackles, they would remain a rich charity supported by the West at its discretion: no Caliphate can be built on charity, especially charity of the West.

3. Fences

Seven years after the death of Arafat, Larry MacIver leaned back while the makeup artist put on the final touches.

"Not too much. I've got a faculty meeting to attend right after this. I don't want them making fun of me."

"Dr. MacIver, let me do my job. Mr. O'Reilly is a stickler for everything being done right. He likes his guests to look as great as he does."

"That would be impossible," he grinned.

"If there's time, stop by after and I'll remove it for you"

"How long till I'm on, anyway?"

"That's not my department. I'll be done with you in a few minutes, though. Then you go back to the Green Room."

MacIver looked at himself in the mirror. "She has done her job well. I look younger than my 55 years," he said to himself as he stroked his close cropped, slightly silvered sandy beard and admired his full head of golden hair, combed with an old fashioned part on the left. He had to admit that it was thinning a little at the front, but it was still a full head of hair that he imagined other men of his age would envy.

"OK. We're done."

He climbed down from the make-up chair and straightened his suit. Tried to stand tall, all six feet of him, and buttoned his suit jacket. He disliked suits and especially the ties that had to be worn with them. But his agent had insisted that he should not look like a musty old academic in a corduroy jacket with leather elbows. It would just give more ammunition to O'Reilly to make fun of him. But the real reason he did not like suits was that they all looked loose on him because he was so thin, the consequence of his compulsive running. He ran five miles a day, every day, rain, snow or shine. If he missed a day, he could not sleep at night and when he finally got to sleep, he'd then wake up feeling depressed and would remain so until he could run again. He'd been doing this since the day his divorce became official. On reflection, maybe he should have taken it up

27

earlier; might have saved his marriage. Not really. It wasn't as simple as that. He wondered right then whether either of his kids ever saw him on television, whether she'd tell them who he was. Not her fault, though. Fact was, he chose work over family. But she did force him to make that choice. And once he had made it, he cut it all off, put it all away completely. The child support went to her bank account automatically. She invited him to their birthdays. He never went.

They were calling him.

"Professor MacIver?"

He headed for the Green Room and met O'Reilly's assistant on the way. She didn't look anywhere nearly as beautiful as the women who bantered with O'Reilly on camera.

"So there you are," she said, "let's just run through a few questions on our way to the set. We have just a couple of minutes."

MacIver handed her an index card. "Here's a list of some questions O'Reilly might like to ask me. Makes it easier and quicker for us both."

"He won't be needing that. Mr. O'Reilly writes his own questions. This isn't the lame stream media, you know."

"Ouch! I stand corrected!"

"So your book is titled 'Good Fences, Good Neighbors Make: How Fences Save Lives and Keep Order' right?"

"That's right."

"And you wrote this book after visiting Israel to study the fences they built to stop suicide bombers from getting to their targets?"

"Partly. I also studied the uses of fences and walls throughout history. The Romans really perfected them, and used them both as offensive and defensive weapons. Not to mention the many walled cities that still stand throughout Europe."

"And what about the Berlin wall, then?"

"Its role was to keep people in, as well as to keep people out."

"You also argue that we should build a fence along our entire southern border to keep terrorists out and to stop illegal migration?"

"Yes, it's crucial to making our country safe. We should start with the southern border and then do the north."

"You mean Canada is a threat too?"

"Neither Canada nor Mexico are threats in themselves. But both countries have lax immigration control which makes it easy for terrorists to get into their country and then make their way to the United States.

"You're convinced that these fences work?"

"My scientific research in Israel shows they do, without any doubt."

"OK. I think we're good here. Remember, Dr. MacIver this segment has just one minute. So you have to say what you want to say as concisely and clearly as possible. I'll be back for you in a few minutes."

MacIver walked back and forth. He was nervous. He had watched the O'Reilly Factor before. It would be hard for him not to make a fool of himself. His agent had tried to talk him out of appearing and to just stick with the regular networks. But MacIver was not one to shrink from a challenge. And his agent had admitted that this was the perfect venue to promote his book. O'Reilly's views on illegal immigration were very compatible with MacIver's findings.

"O.K. We're on!"

She led MacIver on to the set. O'Reilly, staying seated at his table, leaned over to shake hands.

"Welcome to the Factor, Professor MacIver. We have one minute. Short and pithy is what we need!" He immediately turned to the camera.

"In our Back-of-the-Book segment tonight, we have Professor Larry MacIver, an eminent forensic scientist at Rutgers University School of Criminal Justice, who is convinced that fences prevent terrorism, and has written a book to prove it. The title of the book is 'Good Fences, Good Neighbors Make: How Fences Save Lives and Keep Order.' Quite a title professor. So tell me professor, what do you think about putting a fence between us and Mexico? As my viewers know, I am a big advocate of controlling our borders as the first step to immigration reform."

"My research on the fences in Israel shows conclusively that they have reduced suicide bombing by ninety per cent over the past decade."

"But we haven't had any suicide bombings here in America. Are you saying that unless we control our border with Mexico by building a fence all along it, suicide bombings are inevitable?"

"Maybe not suicide bombings as we see in Palestine and Iraq, since they are weapons especially suited to the local context. But the nine eleven attacks were also suicide bombings that made use of local vulnerability and access. Any terrorists, Al Qaeda or any other, can easily cross our Mexican border, which makes planning, organizing and managing a terrorist attack much easier."

"What exactly do you mean? Give us an example."

"Terrorists always attack the targets they can reach most easily, which usually means targets that are unprotected and close to their base of operations. So once across the border, they are free to choose any target they want, and set up their base close to it. That's why the nine eleven terrorists settled in Newark."

"But a fence would not have stopped them."

"No, they used false documents to cross our borders. So we need both an effective fence and careful control of access points."

*

It was the last faculty meeting for the year, so MacIver thought he'd better attend. He had rushed out of the studio, hailed a cab, and tried to wipe off the makeup as he sat in the back seat. He was annoyed. He always was after a media interview. There was so little time and the questions came so fast that he hardly knew what he was saying. It seemed to go well, but there were things he left out, wanted to emphasize, wanted to put up a stronger show against O'Reilly.

He was late for the faculty meeting. Not that it mattered. Nothing of importance ever happened. He had only missed the Dean's announcements, all of which he already knew, or could have known, had he not automatically deleted all the emails the Dean sent around. Anyway, the Dean never announced anything of importance. If it were important, he would not announce it. That was his principle. And, quite frankly, MacIver agreed with it. He would do the same.

He tried to enter the room quietly, but the Dean stopped talking as soon as he came in. The faculty, all sixteen of them, stared at him with disfavor. Not because he was late, but because they all knew he had just taped an interview with O'Reilly. This was a compounded sin. Not only had he appeared on a television show, *verboten* for serious scientific researchers, but it was on the O'Reilly Factor, the show academics loved to hate, considered it to be infantile nonsense, not a fitting venue for a serious academic. It smacked of crass self-promotion, an attribute derided by his colleagues, even though, MacIver had often pointed out, they all, every last one of them, thought only of their own promotion and would, given every chance, do anything they could to set back the careers of their colleagues. And the vehicle they used to do it was the epitome of the science establishment, peer review.

The Dean, grinning broadly, turned to MacIver as he found his seat. "Glad you could make it Larry. Congratulations on your appearance on the O'Reilly Factor. I hope you managed to get in a plug for our school?"

"I certainly did. The Rutgers School of Criminal Justice is now on the radar screen of millions of conservatives across the country, even the world."

"Let's hope it results in lots of applications for admission!"

There were titters among the faculty, all trying to hide their jealousy. What a pity that the scientific quality of his work was so highly regarded! It made it so hard for them to express their derision openly!

MacIver sat quietly through the rest of the faculty meeting, which lasted for another two hours. There were committee reports, students discussed, arguments over curriculum revision, arguments over the hiring of new faculty. He had heard it all before. His thoughts were elsewhere. He had a plane to catch.

*

MacIver had met Captain Rahav at a conference of the American Society of criminology in Philadelphia some years ago. He had just finished a presentation on target hardening, emphasizing the importance of barriers and security fences and in passing, mentioned the wall built in Israel to protect its population centers from suicide bombers crossing over from the Palestinian territories. When it came time for questions, Captain Rahav asked the first one, or rather offered the first criticism on MacIver's talk.

"I am Captain Shlomo Rahav. I have worked on the security fences in Israel. I wish to correct the mistaken impression created by the American media and reflected in your presentation that we are building a wall — which conjures up the picture of something like the Berlin Wall. In fact, it is a series of fences, mostly hi-tech wire fences, with a ditch and road running along each side, and rolled barbed wire at the edge of the road."

"I stand corrected Captain. But do you have any data that demonstrate the effectiveness of the fences in stopping suicide bombing?"

"No study has been done officially. But I can tell you, I have worked patrolling the fences and helped plan parts of them. I have no doubt that they have saved many people's lives."

"But you need a scientific study in order to convince the skeptics. You have data you say?"

"We do, but it is guarded closely for security reasons. But you should come to Israel and see for yourself."

"I would like to do that very much."

The session ended. Rahav and MacIver had lunch together and became instant friends. They designed a study to test the effectiveness of the fences right there on a paper napkin.

*

Captain Rahav extended his hand, a roughhewn hand that had seen a lot of hard work.

"Welcome, Larry. The flight was fine, I hope?"

"As good as it could be. I enjoy watching the El Al security procedures in action. They're so much better than ours. I always feel very safe."

Rahav beckoned to a young officer who took MacIver's bag and placed it in a rather beaten up Dodge Caravan.

"Do you need to rest, or can we go straight to our operations center? I have a special treat for you, if you are up to it."

"What's the deal?"

"We are monitoring a suicide bombing operation which we think may be under way very soon. Thought you'd like to see our high tech operations in action. We do more than just build fences."

"Such as?"

"We move them where we want them."

"Barriers you mean?"

"That and other things."

"Let's go straight to it!"

A young officer, probably a conscript, opened the door and they climb into the back seat. It would be an hour or more until they arrived at the Israel Defense Forces suicide bombing operations center in Jerusalem.

"How is the family?" asked MacIver.

"We are all well. Although Frieda is a little down this week. It's the anniversary of Simon's passing."

"Oh yes, I forgot. You lost your son in a suicide bombing of the coffee shop near the King David hotel a few years ago. I don't know how anyone could get over such a tragedy."

"They don't."

Silence seemed the only way to cope with such sadness. The van had left Tel Aviv and headed along the freeway to Jerusalem. They passed olive and orange groves, rich and prosperous. They passed high rise apartment buildings, a lot of new construction, and soon the road wound through the low hills that led to Jerusalem, bare hills lacking vegetation, wind gusts here and there whipping up clouds of dust. What a desolate wasteland thought MacIver as he closed his eyes and drifted off to sleep.

*

They arrived on the West Bank via Jordan. Kommie held tightly to Shalah's waist. She had never liked motor bikes, and this one had to be the worst. But it was worth it to be able to hug Shali from behind, turning her head so she could rub her cheek into his back. This form of transportation was not typical of Shalah Muhammad who liked the trappings of money and style when he traveled. So did Sarah. It was the best part of her job, contrasting so incredibly with the Spartan lifestyle in which her parents had raised her. She pulled her head back to talk.

"How much longer?" she yelled.

"Half an hour. Depends if there's a checkpoint. Shouldn't be."

Sarah pushed her head between his shoulder blades. The years had slipped by. And to end up here, in this God forsaken desert? Shali had treated her well, though. She wanted for nothing. Almost. She wanted Shali, but he would not give himself to her. Claimed it would not be fair to his wives. And, as he had promised, over the years she had met all three of them, and countless numbers of his children. They were lovely, softly spoken women who were clearly devoted to him. Any women who spent any time with Shali seemed to be devoted to him, she concluded. He had a mysterious attraction to them. But he kept his distance. Maybe that was why they were attracted to him. Who knows?

They had only one quarrel in all this time. It was over him spying on her. Literally spying! He revealed it to her only a few weeks ago, even though she had known it for years, but did not want to believe it. They were having breakfast in the Cairo Hilton, the one on the Nile. And out of the blue he said, "So how is your uncle these days?"

She had never ever spoken of her uncle or any of her relatives that she was rumored to have in Russia. Her mom had occasionally prattled on about them over the years, but Sarah had taken little notice. It seemed that her mom and dad had fallen out of touch with them anyway.

"I have an uncle?"

"Of course you do. Two of them, I think, your father's brothers, no?"

"Supposedly. I don't even know their names. I never listened to mom's prattle, and dad never spoke of them or anyone else for that matter. Why do you ask? How do you know?"

"You forget I am a terrorist and a spy. It is my business to know everything about you."

"You don't trust me?" Tears flooded into her eyes. "You don't trust me? And we've worked together all these years?" Sarah stood up in anger, knocked over her tea cup, and the chair flew backwards.

"Kommie, it's not what you think."

"What else could I think? You've been spying on me all this time, me your most trusted friend and servant!"

Shalah Muhammad rose slowly and walked around to pick up her chair. He moved it slowly into the back of her legs, and gently placed a small kiss behind her ear. "Let's sit quietly and I'll tell you all about it," he whispered,

"I did not expect you would be angry. When you hear what I have to tell you, you will be very excited, I should think, happy."

Sarah, who had lost quite a lot of weight since she had graduated from Oxford, but was still quite plump, steadied herself at the table and, still crying, slowly allowed Shalah to slide the chair under her. The tea had spilled on her shirt and trousers. Since losing weight, she had taken to wearing military-like khakis. She dabbed at the spots with a napkin she had wet from the hot water pot and continued to sob.

Shalah moved back to his place, then reached over to pour Sarah another cup of tea. "Are you ready for this?"

"What, what is it?"

"Your uncle Sergey, you have heard of him? Your dad's younger brother, who these days considers himself to be a Chechen, fled to Kyrgyzstan in 1991 soon after the collapse of the USSR. Why he had to flee so quickly to escape the Russian or former Soviet authorities doesn't matter, though he clearly upset someone."

"So?" Sarah responded belligerently.

"So, he's a big wig in the Russian mafia."

"And this should make me happy?"

"I hope so. Because I have a mission for you to go meet with him and broker a deal."

Sarah wiped the tears from her eyes with a table napkin. Her cheeks were flushed, eyes red. She was taken aback. The trouble was she didn't know how to feel. She didn't think of herself as having relatives. It seemed like a kind of fairy tale.

*

The motorbike slowed down and slid to a stop. Sarah kept hugging Shalah's waist, her face buried between his shoulder blades.

"There's a problem," she heard him say.

"What?" she looked up. Unlike Shalah she wore no helmet.

"There's a checkpoint up ahead."

"So we've been through lots of checkpoints before. What's the problem with this one?"

"It's new, very new. I think they are tracking us."

"You mean the IDF?"

"Who else?"

"How can they do that?"

"They have their spies too, and very good ones. There could be a tracking device on the bike."

"But you got it from a trusted source, you said."

"Sometimes the trusted make mistakes or aren't careful enough. Or just plain can't be trusted."

"What are you going to do?"

"I'm going to get another bike."

He turned the bike around and they drove back to the small village they had just passed. Shalah had noticed a small garage on the edge of the village, a dull concrete structure, an open door, car and bike junk strewn all over, an old petrol pump, and a vintage Coke cooler. They pulled up to the cooler and dismounted. There seemed to be no one around, so Shalah helped himself to a Coke from the cooler, which he noticed was unplugged, though it was filled with a little ice. A small figure emerged from the doorway, wearing old overalls, heavily greased up.

"I need another bike. This one is broken," said Shalah.

"Looks pretty new to me,' said the mechanic.

Shalah pulled out a wad of bills. I'll trade you this one for another.

"We don't do trades and anyway we don't have any bikes."

"What do you have then?"

"Got the old truck over there." The mechanic pointed to an old 1960s Ford Explorer.

"Looks kind of old."

"Maybe. But it's a beauty. It's a 1969 Ford F100 Explorer, 360 ci, V8, 4bbl carb, and C6 transition."

"Wow, you really know your cars," smiled Sarah. The mechanic ignored her.

"In America it would be worth thousands."

"Not in that condition," Sarah pointed out.

"It's a bit heavier than I would like, but on second thoughts, it might just be the thing I need," said Muhammad.

"You give me the bike and $2,000 and it's yours," offered the mechanic.

"Deal!"

Shalah Muhammad counted out the money and gave the mechanic the keys to the bike. They shook hands and Shalah, gripping him fiercely, warned, "this truck better run good, or you're dead meat. Understand?"

The mechanic tried to pull his hand away and eventually Shalah let it go. The threat had been effectively communicated.

"You could drive that thing through a stone wall, that's how tough it is," boasted the mechanic.

"That's just what I had in mind." Muhammad threw his helmet to the mechanic who was forced to catch it. "The keys?"

"In the truck."

"Petrol in the tank?"

"Only a liter. Can't leave any in it 'cos someone will steal it."

Shalah climbed into the truck and after a little practice, drove it to the old pump.

"I can only let you have 20 liters. Have to keep some for my regular customers." The mechanic began pumping gas, the old fashioned way and stopped at 20 liters.

"All right. That will do. We don't have time to fill it any more anyway."

"That's 120 Shekels."

"Yeh, right. Take it out of what I gave you. Come on Kommie, climb in. We have to hurry." Sarah struggled to climb up to the cabin. She had hardly slammed the door shut when Shalah sped away and drove directly towards the checkpoint.

"There are no seat belts," complained Sarah.

"That's the least of our problems. We have to get to the check point before the IDF figures out that we have switched vehicles."

"Why don't we just take the freeway?"

"Because we might run out of petrol and we don't want to create a spectacle on the freeway. Do you know how much petrol these trucks consume?"

They peered ahead through the dirty and cracked windshield. There were two officers standing out on the road, in front of the portable boom gate, guns at the ready. "Probably conscripts," thought Muhammad. "What are they doing both standing out in the open like that?" He had to fight really hard against the urge to slam his foot on the accelerator and drive right through them. They'd get in a shot or two, but they'd probably miss.

"What are you going to do?" Sarah asked.

"Stay calm and show them our IDs."

He let the truck roll to a stop a few yards from the boom gate. The young officers approached them, one on each side of the truck. Sarah had trouble winding down the window on her side, Shalah was already talking to the officer on his side. Each of them presented their Teudat Zehut, Israeli ID cards.

"Where are you going," asked the female officer on Sarah's side.

"My friend is taking me to visit Bethlehem, the place where Christ was born," answered Sarah in her strongest American accent.

"Do you own this truck?" the other officer asked Muhammad in Arabic, "you don't look like the kind of person who would own this kind of truck."

"Rented it from the garage in the village. My other car broke down."

The officer stepped back and opened his phone. He was suspicious.

"He should command me to step out of the truck," thought Muhammad. He began to wind the truck door window up.

The officer put his hand on the rising window and said, "Just a minute sir, I still have your ID."

At that moment, Shalah Muhammad grabbed the conscript's hand and pulled it inside the truck with all his might and at the same time slammed the truck into reverse and zoomed backwards, dragging the officer with it. He pulled the steering wheel round with his free hand so that the truck slid into a fast arc, knocking down the officer who had been in the process of handing Sarah back her ID. Sarah reflexively wound up her window and pushed her feet against the dash board.

"Hang on!" yelled Muhammad. He let go of the officer who fell to the road. Quickly, he shoved the truck into ONE, the rear wheels spun and the truck lurched forward. He ran over the officer who was scrambling to stand. The female officer had already raised her Uzi and was in the act of pulling the trigger when the big mudguard of the Explorer truck rammed her against the checkpoint box, knocking over the box completely. Not satisfied, Muhammad backed up and ran over the other officer who was writhing on the ground already severely injured. When he was convinced that they were both dead, he took a deep breath and looked over to Sarah who sat petrified, still pushing her feet against the dashboard.

"Are you OK?" he asked.

Sarah hugged her legs, then let them fall to the floor.

"I'm OK," she said. It was the first time she had seen Shalah's violent side, though he had hinted of it every now and again. So far, all their so called terrorist action had involved planning, management, and deal making. All except, of course, her own first assignment to kill Arafat. But that wasn't violent, was it?

"You better get out and collect our IDs," said Shalah, always testing her. She was on the verge of vomiting and did so as soon as she stepped down from the truck. She forced herself to approach each of the lifeless conscripts and retrieved the IDs. When she returned to the truck and climbed in beside Shalah, he said, "There's my girl."

*

Sarah's body responded to trauma by closing down. She fell into a deep sleep and did not wake until the truck ran out of petrol just as they reached Bethlehem.

"You can wake up now, we're here," Muhammad laughed as he opened the door to her side of the truck. Sarah struggled to wake up. Shalah extended his hand to help her step down from the truck. She looked around her. They walked across the street and picked up one of the many local vans to Jerusalem and soon they were in the midst of a Palestinian slum, close to Jerusalem. It teemed with people, buying, selling, eating, shouting. Shalah led the way and Sarah followed him through a maze of alleys until they finally reached the steps of a dilapidated building, pock-marked with bullet holes and shrapnel. Shalah withdrew a key from his pocket, and opened the door.

"This is your house?" Sarah asked.

"Not exactly. It's one of our safe houses that we use for preparing suicide bombers. And as you know, that's why we're here."

There were no windows. Inside it was dark and gloomy, except there was a bright light focused on a handsome boy standing against a bare wall, his arms outstretched. A woman, robed in an abaya, circled around taking a video of the boy. There was only one chair, and Shalah Muhammad took it. Sarah sat on the floor at his feet, a place she was used to, hugging her small backpack to her knees. She was happy to be there.

Halid the handler barely acknowledged their presence. He was putting the finishing touches to the bomb vest. Shalah Muhammad broke the ice.

"You're wasting your time, Halid. They're on to you."

"Doesn't matter. He wants to die."

"It's an unnecessary risk and —"

"Do not insult the honor of his murdered father!" The boy's mother broke in, annoyed, but not shifting her eyes from the iPhone that she held with outstretched hands, taking a video of her son.

Shalah ignored her, "— a waste of money," he continued.

The mother raised her voice to a screech. "He dies for freedom!"

"And $10,000," muttered Shalah, sarcastically.

Halid the handler spoke softly to the boy. "You're sure you want to do this?"

The boy, who turned fifteen just the day before, cocked his head high, his deep black tousled hair the envy of everyone present. "Yes," he said, a proud smile on his fresh adolescent lips.

"You will detonate the vest yourself? If you can't, I can do it with my phone, or your mother could if you prefer."

"No, I can do it. In the name of my father, Inshallah!"

"Speak, my son! Show the world your beautiful mind," announced his mother, holding the iPhone high, circling around him.

Halid looked across to Sarah. She smiled a little and nodded slightly. Shalah Muhammad nudged her with his foot. "Kommie, the money," he said.

Sarah pulled out two tightly bound wads of bills and handed them up to Shalah.

"The Jews have captured or killed all but two of our bombers this year. None of them made their targets," scorned Shalah, as he handed Halid the money.

"So?"

"So this is the last one. We're terminating the program."

Halid the Handler was not pleased. "You're a bunch of fucking assholes —"

"Watch your language in front of the boy —"

"How will I feed my family? You and your smart-ass friends sit in Teheran, think you know everything. Our suicide bombings have changed the face of terrorism. Without them, you'll lose the support of the camps —"

The boy continued with his speech, egged on by his mother. "— for the love of my father and my family and for our freedom —"

"This kid will make it," said Halid, "besides we've got a very experienced driver and he has a real-time GPS phone."

"A what?"

"It automatically updates when they close roads and move checkpoints."

"Bull shit! I tell you, they're on to you. We're done with suicide bombing. Get a new job."

Shalah Muhammad abruptly rose and pulled at Sarah's shirt. "Kommie," he commanded, "we're out of here."

Halid scowled and walked back to the boy.

Sarah struggled up, reached for Shalah's hand, but he walked past her. She followed, slipping her arm through his as he turned to Halid and spoke to him in a formal way, as though conducting a job interview, "We need missile operators. Or maybe we could use you in Iraq, but I don't think you'd fit. The handlers there are much younger, mostly Iraqi."

"When will you be back?" asked Halid.

"If all goes well, in three months, the anniversary of nine eleven."

"I heard something big was coming —"

"And make sure there's a big screen TV when I come back."

"Oh, and would the general like anything else?"

"You could put a bed in the bedroom."

"Sure, anything you say."

Shalah Muhammad and Sarah stepped out to the street. Shalah stopped to put on his sunglasses. A taxi pulled up, the door flung open, the driver bounded up the steps, pushing right past them. Sarah looked to Shalah but he did not return the look.

"These people are insane," he said. "They've been killing Jews for decades, and where has it got them? Still no Palestinian state. Still no freedom! It's time for a radical change."

An old Toyota Corolla pulled up and they climbed in the back seat.

*

MacIver felt a light nudge to his ribs.

"Larry, we're here. Hope you had a good nap, you poor old thing," joked Rahav.

"I think best with my eyes closed," smiled MacIver.

The old van pulled into a small parking lot next to an ancient but well renovated building.

"We're in the Christian sector of old Jerusalem. We like to be right in the middle of things."

"So this is what kind of operations center?"

"You'll see." Let's go right in. Our young officer here will take your things and drop them off at the Ma'ale Hachamisha Kibbutz Hotel where I know you like to stay."

"Great," MacIver yawned, "let's go to it."

They walked to the back of the building where Rahav nodded to a guard standing at the door. MacIver had to remind himself that this was Israel, and get used to the preponderance of armed personnel, especially in old Jerusalem. Once inside, he was surprised to see that there were no more locked doors. They walked straight in to the Operations Room where several civilians, or officers not in uniform, sat at consoles arrayed around the room. A large screen displayed a map of the West Bank and locations of fences, walls, street barriers and checkpoints. It was an electronic map that could be drawn and redrawn at will. MacIver picked up a laser pointer and immediately felt right at home.

"This is our bomber?" he asked as he pointed at a pulsing blue car image.

"It will be. The driver has stopped to pick up the bomber," Rahav replied.

"How do you know that?"

"He has one of our cell phones."

"He's one of yours?"

"Not exactly. He doesn't know he has one of our phones."

"Brilliant! So you've infiltrated them?"

"Not exactly. We supply almost all the available cell phones in the West Bank. One other thing, before you get wrapped up in this pursuit."

"What?"

"Have you ever heard of Shalah Muhammad?"

"Don't think so."

"He's probably the smartest terrorist operating around the Middle East these days."

"So what does he have to do with our suicide bomber?"

"We think he is the brains behind all suicide bombings on the West Bank at present, and certainly is supplying the cash."

"So?"

"So we nearly caught him at a check point this morning. Unfortunately, he was too smart for us and outwitted the two young officers who were manning the check point. We were tracking his motor bike. He was probably on his way to direct the suicide bombing that we are now watching in action."

The blue image of the car began to move. MacIver was having trouble paying attention to Rahav. "It's moving!" exclaimed MacIver excitedly.

"The damned terrorist killed both the officers. Drove over and over them with a truck and destroyed the entire checkpoint."

"Gee, that's too bad. Why don't you pick him up at the safe house, then, since you must know where it is if you can track this bomber from start to finish?"

Unfortunately, he already slipped through our fingers. He was at the safe house for only a brief moment, then left. But we'll get him at the right time."

"No doubt you will. So let's play Pac-Man with this bomber!"

"I'm a bit young to have played that game," Rahav responded, "but I suppose you mean getting around barriers and closures."

"You're not that young! But yes, you're right."

"The street pattern was changed as soon as we saw our taxi driver on the move to pick up his rider," said Rahav.

"You knew that too?"

"A calculated guess. But we've arranged the barriers and closures to give him little choice but to follow the route we want, regardless of where his target lies.

"So the old checkpoint was here," MacIver moved the pointer, "and the new checkpoint is here?"

"That's right. So long as we have not messed up the traffic too much, he should come into our checkpoint in about twenty to thirty minutes."

MacIver put down the pointer. "I want to be there!"

"Larry, you're not trained. It's too dangerous."

"But I must interview the bomber. Find out how he came to do this."

"You can do that once we bring him in."

"But he may blow himself up."

"And if you're there, you too!"

"It's a risk I'm prepared to take. I'm a trained psychologist, you know."

"But you're not a trained bomb specialist. You're not going."

"I have to. In the name of science."

"We have plenty of failed suicide bombers in custody. You can interview them."

MacIver was not listening and was already at the door. Captain Rahav, not altogether an agile person, was too slow to catch hold of him. Throwing up his hands in dismay, he nodded to an officer to follow. He knew Larry too well to think he could stop him now. For a scientist, he was really much too headstrong. There was no stopping him. He supposed that tenacity was an important attribute for a scientist too.

MacIver was no sooner outside than he realized that he had no idea where he was going.

The officer called out. "Wait up sir. I'll take you. Follow me, this way. The bike is around the corner."

"Bike? We're going on a bike?"

The officer led him around the corner and into a small courtyard. "Hope this is OK sir?" He hurried over to a gleaming motor bike, which sported a rear seat almost as wide as a horse's saddle.

"I have to spread my legs over this?" laughed MacIver.

"It's the only way we can get there in time. Your helmet, sir." They climbed on the motor bike. "Hang on, and lean with me when I lean!"

The officer revved the bike, kicked it into gear and they took off so abruptly, MacIver clung to his driver in panic. For MacIver, this was a most unpleasant experience. Hanging on to someone for dear life went against his deepest, innermost idea of himself. *He* was the one who others should hang on to. *He* was the driver in life, not the follower. He clung to the officer, but hated every minute of it. Took little notice of the crowded streets of old Jerusalem as they twisted and turned to get through the traffic and avoid hitting pedestrians. He hardly noticed it when they at last sped through the Jaffa gate and entered the broader streets of modern Jerusalem and finally ended up on a sandy road, speeding headlong into an endless desert. He was greatly relieved when he felt the bike slowing and eventually stop.

*

The checkpoint was a solitary steel box at the apex of a series of heavy concrete street barriers that formed a narrowing funnel along the sandy road. There were blast deflecting steel shields placed at various points around the checkpoint. Two young conscripts manned the post. There was a simple boom gate that operated to stop traffic.

MacIver stepped off the bike and immediately regained his composure. In fact, he felt exhilarated. One of the officers who looked not much older than a teenager, maybe *was* a teenager, addressed the officer.

"Expecting a zero sir?"

"In about five minutes. Seen much traffic?"

"Not much sir. Only been here an hour after all." The young man looked across at MacIver who stepped towards him.

"Oh, this is Professor Larry MacIver from America. He's doing research," said the officer.

MacIver nodded, smiled and offered his hand, to which the young conscript did not respond. The officer noticed.

"Sorry professor. They're trained not to shake hands or to get too close to anyone they don't know."

"Of course. I should have known better. You guys are doing an incredible job, and my research is going to prove it," said MacIver, addressing his remarks to the conscripts.

"Oh thank you."

The officer broke in. "Here they come!"

The taxi, a beaten up old Ford Focus, approached slowly, dust billowing out behind it.

The officer stepped in front of MacIver and the conscripts. "I'll take care of this. I've done scores of them. Keep your eyes open though, and all of you, stay behind the shields and barriers."

The taxi pulled up to the boom gate. The driver poked his head out the non-existent window.

"Hello officer."

The officer saluted. "Where are you going and who is your passenger?" he asked as he peered into the back seat.

"He visits his uncle who has found him a job washing dishes in the King David Hotel," replied the driver.

The officer grabbed the handle of the back door. It was locked. "This car actually locks?" he asked, trying to lighten the tension.

"Hey it's a beautiful car!" laughed the driver. He twisted around to unlock the door by hand.

The officer signaled to the conscript. "Keep the driver in the car, but get his cell phone." He then opened the back door and put out his hand to the teenage boy who sat nervously inside. "OK son," he said quietly, "this is normal procedure. I just want you to take both my hands and get slowly out of the car."

The boy complied, but he was no sooner out of the car than MacIver was standing beside him.

The officer first raised his voice to MacIver, but then controlled himself. "For God's sake, get back behind the shield!"

MacIver ignored him. Instead, he spoke directly to the boy. "Do you speak English?"

The boy looked down. No answer. Not unlike any teenager, thought MacIver.

The officer interjected, getting upset. "Professor! Get behind the shields! You're screwing things up!"

The boy lifted his head and said defiantly, "of course I speak English. You think I'm an idiot?"

"Officer, let go his hands, slowly," ordered MacIver.

"Are you kidding? He'll blow us all up!"

The boy struggled to release his hands, but in response the officer reflexively tightened his grip.

"Release him, damn it!" yelled MacIver.

The conscripts raised their weapons nervously, one pointed at MacIver.

"Step away, Professor," ordered a conscript calmly.

Instead, MacIver moved closer to the bomber and slowly reached inside his jacket.

The officer looked panic-stricken. "You crazy son of a bitch!" He let go of one hand and grabbed MacIver. The bomber twisted free and ran forward, past the boom gate.

MacIver turned quickly to the conscripts. "Leave him! Don't shoot him!" MacIver strode briskly towards the boy who eventually slowed, then stopped. He had realized that he didn't know where he was running to. MacIver moved closer. "Take it easy son. What's your name?"

The boy glared back and held his arms out to the side.

"So let's get you out of this harness," said MacIver, confident he was in charge.

The boy bomber reached inside his jacket. The conscripts yelled warnings, the officer yelled, "Hit the ground! Down! Down!" All weapons were pointed at the bomber but MacIver was in the way. He stood back, hands on hips.

"You're not going to do it, are you?" he said solicitously.

"My name is Ali." The boy ripped his jacket off, revealing the bomb vest. He grabbed the detonator cord. "I want to die for Allah and my family."

"But now is not the time, is it? You haven't reached your target." MacIver stretched out his hand.

There was heavy breathing all around, otherwise silence. The wait seemed forever. Sweat poured down everyone's face, except for the boy bomber, who looked serene and incredibly handsome right at that moment.

MacIver extended his hand a little forward. "I'll make up the $10,000," he said.

The boy, insulted, jerked at the detonator cord. "You Americans. All you think about is money."

"So how did you become a suicide bomber so young?" asked MacIver.

"My father was Hezbollah." He raised his arms to the sky, looked up, thumb extended over the detonator button at the end of the cord.

"Ali, it's not the time. Tell me of your father."

"He was murdered by Jews when I was three years old."

"Your mother told you that?"

"Everyone told me that."

Silence. The officer and the conscripts shifted anxiously on their feet. Their arms sagged under the weight of their weapons. The rustling of clothing as they moved broke the silence.

MacIver stepped a little closer. The boy stared defiantly into his eyes.

"Stop! Come no closer! Allah has sent me a sign," cried Ali.

MacIver stopped and stretched out his hand. Suddenly, he heard behind him the noise of the taxi starting up. He snatched a quick look over his shoulder. The driver slammed the car into reverse, backed crazily away from the boom gate, skidded and swiveled a hundred and eighty degrees and sped off. One of the conscripts fired, half-heartedly, but missed.

Ali remained still. "It is not the time," he said.

"Where was your driver taking you?" asked MacIver as he took a very small step forward.

Ali slowly lowered his arms and allowed the detonator cord to dangle. MacIver forced a grim smile and took another step.

Ali raised his hand, palm facing MacIver. "No! Stop! A bomb expert has to defuse me."

"So what was your target?" MacIver persisted.

The officer slowly inched forward and muttered an expletive as he moved past MacIver. "You are an asshole," he whispered.

"I would like to speak to my mother," said the boy, slightly embarrassed.

"Of course we can arrange that, can't we officer?" replied MacIver.

The officer did not answer. He was now standing close to the boy, one hand gripping Ali's right hand, the detonator hand, the other feeling carefully for the wires and the transponder that would detonate the explosives unless disarmed. There was still the danger that it could be activated by his handler's cell phone.

"How much time do we have?" asked the officer. "Where was the target?"

Ali looked down, licking his lips nervously. "I can't tell you that."

"I need to know how much time we have. If your handler does not hear of the explosion, he will detonate it himself. You know that, I'm sure."

"We'll contact your mom. What's her phone number and I'll call her and you can talk," offered MacIver.

"Professor, that's not a good idea. She will very likely urge him to complete the mission by blowing himself and the rest of us to smithereens. I'm losing patience with you, Professor."

MacIver persisted. "Can't you disarm the transponder?"

"Yes, but I have to find the right wire. I think I know where it is, but can't risk a mistake, can I?" The officer lowered his head to look closely into Ali's face. "Ali, who was your handler? What was his name?"

"Why should I tell you that? I am not a traitor!"

"Because if I know who it was, then I will know how he arranged the bomb vest. Each handler has his own favorite way of doing it. Now what's his name?"

Ali hesitated, licked his lips again.

"Come on! What's his name?"

"My target was King David Hotel lobby."

"O.K. so we probably have only a few minutes, at the most. And the handler's name?"

"Halid."

"Now that's better. I know his work. Turn around slowly. The transponder will be right between your shoulder blades."

"Ali. You can use my phone to call your Mom." Here…"

"Professor, I'm losing patience. Please shut up. I'm trying to save us from being blown up, and you're offering this little brat your cell phone so he can talk to his mother."

"You won't get anywhere with these people by talking like that. You have to win him over. Then you get information."

The officer carefully worked his hand down behind the boy's neck, under the bomb vest. With a short, sharp flick of his fingers, he dislodged the connector to the transponder. He breathed a sigh of relief. "OK. Turn around son, I got it. We can now slip off the bomb vest, very, very carefully." He slipped the bomb vest off, and immediately placed it behind one of the deflective shields. He turned to a conscript. "There could be a timer, so it could still go off. Call HQ and have them send a team out to dispose of it and to pick up the brat. You'll need to restrain him with handcuffs or something so he can't run away. That is, unless you have the guts to shoot him if he tries to escape. Keep the boy with you at all times, and keep as far away from the bomb vest as you can. It could go off any minute."

"Right, sir."

The officer turned to MacIver who was handing his cell phone to Ali. He slapped MacIver's hand angrily and the cell phone went flying to the ground. He walked over and ground it into the desert sand under the heel of his boot.

"It's going to be a wild motorbike ride back," muttered MacIver to himself.

The officer got on the motor bike and beckoned to MacIver who reluctantly complied. He had just settled down into the seat and grasped the officer's waist, when the bomb exploded. The bike rose in the air, and then fell to the ground taking MacIver and his fellow rider with it. A huge cloud of dust and sand enveloped them. MacIver heard shouts from the direction of the conscripts. His leg was pinned under the back wheel of the bike. The dust cleared and he strained to look over to the boy.

The officer was already there. The boy lay still. A piece of shrapnel, the smallest piece, had penetrated his skull. He was dead. The conscripts were frightened. "Better call a clean-up squad," ordered the officer.

4. Family

"Passports and tickets. You're leaving out of Cairo." The driver of the old Toyota, with one hand on the steering wheel, turned to hand Sarah a Ziploc bag containing their travel documents. She rustled around in her backpack while Shalah lit a cigarette and turned to look at her. She smiled coyly. She was excited, he could see.

"Are you looking forward to seeing your uncle Sergey? I bet he'll be surprised when he sees you."

"I feel like I already know him, especially if he's anything like my father."

"From what you've told me of your dad, I doubt it. He's Russian mafia, after all."

"I know, I know. But dad's detachment, his, his lack of feeling, at least towards me anyway. I could see how it would be a positive attribute for a mafia boss."

"And he really is a boss, a big boss. My people tell me he is probably the number 1 or 2 in the Russian mafia. That's quite an accomplishment — a scary accomplishment."

"Yes, it's scary. But I'm his long lost niece. I'm sure it will be alright."

"You won't let him bully you?"

"Hey, I don't let you bully me, now do I?"

Shalah smiled, his curly lip smile. "Ah, that's different, though. I don't bully you, do I?"

"You would if I let you. Look how you bullied Halid. He hates you."

"Not hate. Fear. He fears me. And so he should. Seriously, are you sure you can strike a deal with your cunning uncle?"

Sarah lightly kissed Shalah on the cheek. "He's mafia. If there's enough money, no problem."

"I'll go to fifteen million dollars, no more. And that includes missile reassembly, and adding nuclear tips."

"So there're two missiles?"

49

"That was my deal with the Pakistanis. I'll know in a couple of days after I meet with them."

"And they'll be shipped from Mumbai, right? Disassembled?"

"That's the plan."

The Toyota stopped in front of a café next to the Egged central bus station. The driver turned to them once again.

"This is as far as I go. You'll find your guide through the back of the café. Safe trip!"

"Where's our luggage?" asked Sarah.

"Your guide should have it. That right Dr. Muhammad?"

"Should be. Thanks for the ride."

As they stepped out of the car, Shalah grabbed Sarah's arm so tightly that she winced. He guided her towards a pedestrian walkway instead of the café.

"Now I'm telling you," he said in Arabic, his voice in a low grumbling monotone, "you must get clear assurances that they can add the nuclear tips. Offer half up front, the rest only after the missiles have reached their target." He stopped and pulled her towards him and looked almost angrily into her pale blue eyes, their noses almost touching. "You understand?"

"Don't worry. I can do it. He's my uncle after all."

"That's what I'm worried about. I tell you, never trust a Russian, especially Russian mafia."

"Shalah, you're hurting me."

Surprised, Shalah let go. "Oops, sorry. Let's get a coffee and find our guide."

They turned towards the café, linked arms and walked together, the picture of an old married couple.

"By the way," Sarah said with a mischievous look, "you seem to have forgotten that I am Russian."

"No you're not. You're American. Haven't you figured that out yet? You Americans, you have such identity problems."

*

Their guide was seated across the café along with their luggage. They had a half hour to kill until they left. For "various reasons" their guide had informed them, they should not set out for Cairo just yet. Sarah was becoming used to these mysterious logistical arrangements. She still had not quite come to the realization of just how famous a terrorist Shalah was, if not among his enemies in the west, most certainly among the loose and fragmented terror networks throughout the Middle East. All his contacts were obviously respectful, even in awe of him; through fear or simply because of his many accomplishments? She didn't know.

Sarah ordered English tea as usual, Shalah, just mineral water. Now she watched him go through his ritual. He emptied all his pockets, jacket, pants, everything and placed them in neat rows in front of him. You can tell a lot about a person by what he keeps in his pockets, she thought. Systematically he rearranged the rows. On the left were his wallet and money clip. He opened his wallet and leafed through its contents, not all that much. The money clip was bulging to the max. She was used to him carrying around mountains of cash, always in large bills. It caused a lot of trouble. He did use a credit card, always a different one, but rarely. Then on the right were his cell phones, three of them at the moment. Sometimes he had four on the go. Yet he kept them mostly switched off. Then in the middle were his lighter and cigarettes, a small, flat metal container containing his favorite cigarillos that he occasionally smoked on a special occasion, and of course a box cutter. Even his handkerchief, an old fashioned one because he was allergic to tissues, he carefully folded into a small square and placed to the right briefly, before returning it to his breast pocket. Finally, he carefully sifted through the package of travel documents the driver had given them. He handed Sarah hers and laid his out to make sure everything was there.

"All done now?" she joked.

"At least I will not lose or forget something vital. You would be well advised to do the same."

"I do, but I do it all in my head. I'm not senile yet," she jibed.

"Hah, Hah," Shalah responded, not all that amused, as he carefully and methodically returned all the items to his pockets. "Don't make fun of my OCD of which I am proud. It's how I have survived for so long doing what I do."

Their guide approached their table and drew up a chair. "It's not safe for Dr. Muhammad to fly out of Israel right now, so we are going to drive to Cairo."

"How long?" asked Shalah.

"It will take about eight hours, depending on the border, but we should be able to smooth that out. I have people on the other side. It's the Israeli checkpoints that pose the risk, but they are not as thorough as at the airport. I've arranged a limousine, stretch Mercedes. So you should be nice and comfortable crossing the desert. And the café has put together a lunch basket for you."

"When do we leave?"

"The limo should be here any minute. You may want to visit the bathroom before we leave."

*

Rent control. It reminded them of home. Mr. and Mrs. Kohmsky rented their apartment in Washington heights back in 1996 so they could be near Sarah when she went to college and later to law school at Columbia. It seemed a bit expensive then, but now it was amazingly cheap, thanks to rent control. It was just a small tenement, basically two rooms, typical of many in New York City. Mrs. Kohmsky remembered the day they moved in. It was stinking hot, and the elevator did not work. They had to lug everything up five floors. And inside, everything was lovely and clean, that's what the agent said. And New Yorkers seemed to think so too. What they meant was that everything had been painted over with cheap white paint, so everything did look clean. Trouble was that it made everything look so ugly. The many coatings of paint laid like an elephant skin over the walls, ceilings, window sills, doors and moldings. Mrs. Kohmsky disliked especially the moldings that showed bumps and dints that had been covered over with countless layers of paint. There wasn't a smooth surface in the entire tenement. But she had to admit, it was way better than what they had in Tulgovichi where there was no attempt to cover up the dirt and decay at all, and besides, there they had just one room, no toilet, no kitchen both of which they shared with the other five families in the communal building.

It was a beautiful day and Mrs. Kohmsky suggested to her husband that they go for a walk in Fort Tryon Park. There were beautiful trails there and a favorite seat where they both liked to sit and enjoy the view over the Hudson River. It was rare, though, that Mr. Kohmsky ventured out for such pleasure. But this time he joined her.

Their tenement building was at the top of the hill right close to Fort Tryon Park, so it was an easy walk. Mrs. Kohmsky considered asking her husband whether they might perhaps drop by the Cloisters Art Museum as well, but decided against it. Why give him unnecessary opportunities to say "No?" They passed by the gardens, full of bright summer flowers, then walked down one of the western paths. Mrs. Kohmsky marveled at the existence of such a big park, by no means the biggest, in New York City, surrounded as it was by large, densely populated apartment buildings. The parks in New York. The New Yorkers of old had got something right.

They reached the seat and there was, thankfully, no one else there. They sat right in the middle of it, and Mr. Kohmsky pulled out his book and began his reading. Mrs. Kohmsky chewed her lip and tried not to think of Sarah with whom she had taken a few quiet walks along these trails. It was early morning, the breeze was still cool, but the sun was already bathing the trees with warm light, every now and again filtering through to their seat. Mrs. Kohmsky pulled her old woolen cardigan around her and shivered a little.

Down the path a tall young woman jogged towards them. Her light blue track suit fitted her curvaceous body snuggly and as she came closer, Mrs. Kohmsky could see that her long blonde hair was tied at the back with a bright red ribbon. The young lady wore too much makeup for a jogger, thought Mrs. Kohmsky, especially the bright red lipstick. The jogger stopped right by their seat, hands on hips, and turned to look at the view. She then turned to Mrs. Kohmsky and said, "May I?"

Mrs. Kohmsky smiled and nodded. Mr. Kohmsky lifted his eyes from his book ever so briefly.

"Beautiful morning, isn't it?"

"Oh yes, beautiful," answered Mrs. Kohmsky.

"Do you come here often?"

"Yes, but not as often as we'd like."

"You're Mr. and Mrs. Kohmsky, right?"

Mr. Kohmsky, startled, shifted in his seat and looked up. It was as if he had been hit by a bolt of lightning from the past. Back home in Russia, you knew that you were being watched. But here, he never thought it possible. "What business is it of yours?" he growled.

"Allow me to introduce myself. I'm Agent Silenzio. I work for the CIA. I understand you wanted to contact us about your daughter Sarah?" She handed her badge to Mrs. Kohmsky who examined it then passed it to Mr. Kohmsky.

"But, how did you know we were here? We left only a phone number." The question of course answered itself. Mrs. Kohmsky felt a little silly.

"I'm CIA. We're spies. We are supposed to know these things," Silenzio answered, smiling, "now how can I help you?"

Mrs. Kohmsky told her their story, how they had not heard from Sarah for more than eight years, how she went away to Oxford university and never came back. How they received mysterious packages of money. How they had told all this to the NYPD and the FBI who claimed she was dead. But neither she nor her husband believed them.

"We will try to help you find her, Mr. and Mrs. Kohmsky. But I need a little information about her first."

"Oh thank you Agent Silenzio. What do you want to know?" asked Mrs. Kohmsky.

"Did she have any associates, people she hung out with?"

"We don't know. She never told us anything."

"She never sent you a postcard or anything?"

"Nothing."

"Are you sure?"

"Yes."

"Have you seen this photograph before? Silenzio opened a large envelope and produced a rough photocopy of a photograph of the group the day Sarah graduated from Oxford.

Mrs. Kohmsky's eyes widened. She took the photo and passed it to Mr. Kohmsky. He too was startled.

"Where did you get this?" they both asked, almost in unison.

"That doesn't matter right now. As I said, we are spies, it's our job to collect intelligence. Do you know any of the people in that photo? The one that Sarah is standing close to, perhaps?"

They both stared closely at the photo. But both shook their heads.

"We recognize none of them," said Mr. Kohmsky, "when was it taken?"

"We think the day she graduated from Oxford, and of course, the place is Oxford. You can see the famous library in the background."

"Then if you are spies, you must be able to track her. Where is she now?" asked Mr. Kohmsky.

"Unfortunately, that's the bad news. She has not been sighted since."

"But you will keep looking for her?"

"We will. We are trying to track down the person who is closest to her in the photo there. The older one with the nicely groomed beard. Hopefully, we will find him soon, and when we do, perhaps he will be able to help us locate Sarah."

"How long will it take you?"

"Spying is a messy and unpredictable business, Mr. Kohmsky. I just don't know."

"But we have waited so long," complained Mrs. Kohmsky.

Silenzio stood up, began to jog on the spot. "I know, I know, and I'm sorry. I will do the best I can. In the meantime you may keep that photo."

And with that, she jogged away.

5. Sir

Manish Das was very proud of his office. His Professor and Guru, Dr. Larry MacIver had fought very hard to get it for him, so he said. At Rutgers University, like all universities, space was at a premium, as his professor was always saying, so it was over space that the most acrimonious battles were fought. He had heard from student chatter that Dr. MacIver had even threatened to quit if he did not get the office space for him, but he didn't really believe that. His Guru was too smart to make direct threats to anyone. He manipulated things behind the scenes. Anyway, he was so famous, any Dean in his right mind would do anything to keep him happy.

The strange thing was that Dr. MacIver hardly used his own office at all, yet it was arguably the nicest office in the whole building. He had fought a big battle to get it when they were moving into the new building, built for the Law School. He wanted it, he said, because it was the only office that had a view of the World Trade Center. Little was he to know that in the following year, the World Trade center would be no more. The contrast between the Guru's office and his own was huge. Of course his own had no windows, but that was usual for student offices. Dr. MacIver's office had a resplendent polished cherry wood desk that took up half the space of the room. A massive computer with two displays, a keyboard and mouse, were carefully placed on it and nothing else. There was one nicely crafted oak bookshelf, with a total of two books on its second shelf, and the top of the bookshelf was covered with various manuscripts and papers.

Das's office was of course much smaller than his Guru's, but it was crammed full of an incredible amount of stuff. There were four small student desks for a start, lined up against two sides of the room, the other walls lined with book cases. There were three laptops, all running, sitting on the desks, and several displays on the shelves, also running. He was most proud of the bookshelf that went from floor to ceiling because he had salvaged it from a dumpster down near the parking lot. He had fixed it up and managed to attach it to the wall so it would not fall forward, and in it he had placed all his techno knick-knacks. USB drives and cables, transponders of different kinds, bar code readers, a thumb print reader, cameras of various kinds, five different cases for DVDs and CDs that contained an enormous collection of software, some of it of questionable origin, and six two-terabyte hard drives linked in a chain. The drives' LED lights blinked continuously as they kept a close eye on all his files, doing automatic backups. Most important they contained all the video he had collected for his dissertation. Last but not least, there were various printers, all of them constantly running, LED lights continuously blinking as well. Cables ran under the desks and across the floor, covered roughly with tape so that he or his visitors — he tried not to have any — would not trip over them. The most important units in his office though, considered Das, were the two wireless modems sitting high up on one of the book shelves. They were the nerve center of his whole operation. They were his link to the world's databases. Through them, he could find anything he needed, retrieve anything he wanted. The things he could get through them were incredible, so incredible that he was careful not to mention to anyone what he was able to do. Not even his Guru knew what he could do.

Manish glanced at the time on one of his computer screens. His professor would be coming to him soon to make sure he had prepared all the PowerPoint slides. He rarely went to his Guru's office. He always felt uncomfortable there, always felt that his professor not only did not want him in there, but that the professor himself did not like being there. So he always waited for his professor to come to his office, making sure that he had everything, and he meant everything, at the ready. Besides, it was obvious that Dr. MacIver liked coming to his office, or at least standing at the doorway looking in and barking orders. He had been very lucky the professor had chosen him as his own research assistant out of many others. Why he was chosen he was not sure. No, actually he knew why. It was because he was Indian. Not in a negative or racial sense, though if one wanted to dig deeply into the history of western civilization, one might find a racial component. It was simply that he had been trained by his father, a consummate and high achieving bureaucrat in the Indian public service (he never quite understood which department, but in India that didn't especially matter), how to behave as a subordinate. His father had been schooled in the English public schools, learning most correct English grammar and most correct English manners. Most of all he had learned to always remain five steps behind his master, always attentive, but never obtrusive. These were the lessons his father drummed into him when he was a boy, and still reminded him every time they spoke over Skype.

Now, Manish had a well-practiced very slight bow, a nod really, or slight tilt forward of his slender frame when his Guru appeared at the door. He stood quickly, smiled profusely, and always said something like, "At your service, sir!"

His father always told him, "You cannot say 'sir' often enough. Supervisors never tire of being treated as superior."

And Manish implemented his father's instructions to the letter. He was always surprised, and got great pleasure out of it, that Dr. MacIver appreciated him, no, more than that, he really liked being treated in this way, even though he himself joked with Manish and told him to stop behaving like a Rudyard Kipling character (if so, was Dr. MacIver the Sahib?). Never mind that Das's Indian friends kidded him, called him the "colonial boy." He truly did look up to Dr. MacIver, a famous man after all. His friends — actually, he did not have any real friends, they were just fellow students — were simply jealous and would have jumped at the chance to work for Professor MacIver.

Manish went through the PowerPoint presentation one last time to make sure everything was there and worked, just as Dr. MacIver had directed. What an exotic research project, how exciting it must have been for his Guru to visit Israel and collect data in the Palestinian territories. He so wished he could have been there, though the description of disarming the young suicide bomber was pretty scary. So maybe it was lucky he wasn't there. He was not the Rambo his professor was, he thought. He heard the door close down the hallway. "Here he comes," he said to himself. Unlike his professor, Manish's door was always open. His Guru would appear at the doorway any minute.

"All right Das. Everything set?"

Das jumped out of his seat and stepped backwards to the extent that there was room. "Sir, here's the PowerPoint, sir. Very exciting project, sir." Das leaned forward and handed MacIver a tiny USB drive. "It's all on this sir. I tried it out down in the lecture center. Everything's good."

"Yes, it was an exciting time. But more important, I now have the data to demonstrate beyond a doubt that hardening targets reduces terrorist attacks."

"That's great, sir. Would you like me to come and install the slide show, sir?"

"Excellent, Das. I'd like you there anyway, just in case something goes wrong. This high tech stuff, it's great, but there's always the worry that it will not work properly."

"Yes-sir, that's right sir. That's why there are people like me, sir!"

"Indeed, thank goodness, Das. I don't know what I, or the world for that matter, would do without you. Let's go, don't want to be late. There will be a lot of people there, I think. Unfortunately, many for the wrong reasons, the ideologues who demonstrate against the wall thinking that it's the product of Zionism and all sorts of political nonsense."

"Yes sir. Unfortunate sir."

The Professor walked ahead to the elevators, Das following five steps behind.

*

MacIver entered the lecture center and looked up at the rapidly filling rows of seats. There would be at least a couple of hundred people. He saw a few signs "Stop Zionist land grab" and others, but so far no rowdy demonstrators. He looked to Manish who was busily installing the slide show, the opening slide now filling the screen behind the lectern. MacIver's dark business suit and tie made him look like a conservative administrator, which maybe was not a good image to project to a critical audience. But he had dressed this way because he anticipated that there would be media people there and he would be doing a TV interview or two. He waited for a few more stragglers to enter, then indicated to Das to close the door. He felt under the lectern for the laser pointer, thinking that it had been removed, and was relieved when Das appeared at his elbow and handed it to him. Das found a seat at the door. MacIver stood ready at the lectern, then seemed to change his mind, and walked across to Das.

"The Dean was supposed to come and introduce me. Did you hear anything?"

Das jumped to his feet. "I am a poor student sir. Deans do not speak to me," he grinned.

"OK. I know, you poor thing. I just thought you might have heard some student gossip or something."

"Gossip? Oh no sir! I don't listen to gossip!"

At that moment the Dean entered. He shook hands with MacIver and they both went over to the lectern.

"Fellow students, faculty and visitors, I am pleased to introduce to you our eminent forensic scientist Dr. Larry MacIver who has just come back from an exciting trip to Israel —"

"Palestine, you mean," interjected a student, who was ignored.

"—where he has been collecting data concerning the effectiveness of the fences built in Israel with the purpose of stopping suicide bombing."

There was a rustling at the back of the lecture center as demonstrators held up signs and chanted "Land grab! Land grab!"

The Dean continued, unruffled. "This is a scientific study with no political purpose. I encourage you to quietly hear him out. Dr. MacIver is a world expert on crime prevention and is now, quite simply and brilliantly, applying his considerable knowledge and expertise to solving the problem of terrorism. This is surely a worthy endeavor and I congratulate him on his courageous scientific effort. I present to you, Dr. Larry MacIver."

Students chanted, "Tear down the wall! Tear down the wall!"

The Dean quickly moved away from the lectern and departed, Das opening the door for him.

MacIver stood tall at the lectern. "About the wall," he said, "I hope you will hear me out. My interests are only in science. Not politics. Please fight your battles outside and let us get on with our scientific work."

The door at the back of the lecture center opened and security guards entered. There was a scuffle and soon the students sat quietly holding their signs aloft. MacIver resumed his lecture.

"First of all, it is mistaken to think that there is one monolithic wall. In fact, there is only one small section about two hundred yards long where there is a wall, and that is so because it is an area overlooking a busy freeway that would be vulnerable to snipers if the wall were not there. For the rest, there are a series of fences, electronic fences, a deep ditch on each side, an access road running beside them and at its edge twelve foot high rolls of barbed wire. All of this is quite evident in the slide now before you. The history of the first fence is very interesting. It was not, as is often portrayed in the American media, an idea dreamed up by Netanyahu or other so-called Zionists."

"The origin of the fence depends on how far back in history one goes, which is a problem typical of that part of the world. Let's say that the history of the modern fences is comparatively recent, and began with the actions of a small district in South Jerusalem bordering on Bethlehem. The local community leaders got fed up with suicide bombers coming across from the West bank and killing their citizens. They thought, 'Let's build a fence to stop them from getting to our village.' They had few resources and built just a temporary fence at first. And it worked. Only later did politicians pick up on it so that it became what it is today, a well-funded, very controversial national enterprise."

"My research is designed to establish whether or to what extent the fences reduced or prevented terrorist attacks, but it also investigates whether there were any side benefits such as reducing or preventing international car theft, smuggling and other crimes that involve crossing borders. So my interest is purely scientific, though I would say that, should my research show that the fences do not significantly reduce terrorist attacks, then the political trouble surrounding them would be justified. If they are shown to be effective, then it is up to the politicians and policy makers to decide whether the political cost of erecting them is worth the lives saved. That is an issue that I, as a scientist, am not qualified to assess, since I am decidedly not a politician and do not want to be. Now, let's get to the study and most important, the data."

A student raised her hand. "Dr. MacIver?" she called and continued without waiting for a response, "I saw you on Al Jazeera. Is it true that you disarmed a suicide bomber who was only fourteen years old?"

"Well, I'd really like to get on with presenting my project. But to answer your question, while in Israel this last trip, I visited a movable checkpoint operated by the IDF, and it happened that a suicide bomber approached a checkpoint in a taxi while I was there. I did help them disarm the boy, since my early training as a psychologist was useful in getting him to understand the implications of his actions and making it possible for him to avoid feelings of humiliation if he did not complete his mission. But I did not disarm him. That I left to the experts. There's no doubt that I would have blown us all up if I had tried to remove the boy's bomb vest. Now, the data."

*

Manish looked down at his phone. He figured there were probably just ten minutes of the talk left, then questions. Thank goodness! He had heard all this before over and over again. He found it hugely difficult to sit still for any length of time, so he fought it by fidgeting with his fingers, picking his nails, and trying to think of something else — daydreaming, to be precise. Lately, his thoughts kept going off to Delhi, imagining his wedding, an incredible match arranged by his father and mother, anticipating a lavish three day affair. Garlands of flowers around their necks. Ravi Shankar music playing quietly in the background, hopefully played by a group distantly related to him on his mother's side, the sitar player, his mother claimed, the daughter of the second cousin of Ravi Shankar himself. He longed to be with her, having met her only on one very brief and heavily controlled occasion, when she was brought to say hello to him just as he was leaving for America at the Delhi airport last summer. He looked down at his iPhone again, surreptitiously thumbing through his photos till hers came up. "Beautiful, beautiful Niki," he said to himself. "I love you and soon we will be together forever." But he was jolted from his reverie by a little ding informing him that a text had arrived. He had thought he had the phone on silent, but must have checked the wrong box. He noticed his Guru quickly glance across. But he was wound up and really into his presentation. The text was, could you believe it, purportedly from the New York City mayor's office, from her assistant, someone called Foster. It was marked URGENT and read:

"Dr. MacIver is requested to join the Mayor and a TOP SECRET group of counter terrorist professionals at the Skyline Drive restaurant at 1.00 pm. today for an URGENT meeting to plan a response to a credible terrorist threat to New York City. Please respond immediately. For Madam Mayor Newberg, Foster."

Manish quickly pounded his iPhone with lightning fast fingers. "Dr. MacIver pleased to attend. For Dr. MacIver, Manish Das, top research assistant." He looked across to the lectern. MacIver was winding up, had turned to face the screen and, pointer in hand, highlighted the line graph that clearly sloped downward.

"So in sum, using my target hardening approach of street closures, barrier arrangements and movable checkpoints, last year we reduced suicide bombings on Israel's West Bank by 95%. And I guess that's it. I have time for a few questions."

A student immediately raised her hand. "You said there was no need for infiltration of the terrorist cells?"

"Assuming there are any. But that's right. Electronic surveillance is safer and provides more accurate data than do spies."

"But surely spies understand the context better?"

"They might. But their problem is they rarely know what information is important and what is not."

"But surely context is the key to understanding," interjected a professor.

"Spies collect everything and end up with enormous amounts of information that is impossible to analyze. I bet you that the CIA has warehouses full of information that they have never looked at."

MacIver was about to say thank you for attending and move away from the lectern, when his eye was caught by the most beautiful woman he had seen in many years. She raised her hand, smiling broadly, her voluptuous mouth accentuated by bright red lipstick. "So spies are obsolete?" she said, provocatively.

"Let's just say that spies are not scientists and don't know how to form hypotheses or how to collect data to test them." MacIver was bedazzled and could hardly think straight.

She grinned some more. "But —"

Das was at his elbow. "Sir, sorry to interrupt, sir." He held up his iPhone for MacIver to read the text he had received from the Mayor. "Sir, the mayor of NYC wants to meet with you, sir."

"Now?"

"Sir, seems very hush-hush and urgent, sir."

"Good time to stop anyway." MacIver looked out to the audience. "My apologies, but I've been called away. Something urgent it seems. Thank you all very much for coming."

The audience applauded lightly. MacIver's eye was still on the gorgeous blonde beauty who asked that pesky question. She made her way down to the podium, but he had already begun to move to the door, having noticed a TV reporter just outside. Das had also noticed his professor's admirer and waited up for her. She smiled and brushed past him, intent on catching her quarry.

Manish called to his professor. "Sir, I think this young lady wants to speak with you."

MacIver turned just as she was upon him.

"I think we're going to the same meeting," she said, "allow me to introduce myself. I'm Monica Silenzio, Director, New York-New Jersey Counter Terrorism Fusion Center. We're going to the same meeting, with the Mayor of NYC?"

MacIver's eyes were on her lips. "I believe so. It's very urgent and super-secret, at the mayor's request, I'm told."

The reporter came towards MacIver who looked briefly in his direction.

"Excuse me a moment," said MacIver, "I promised this reporter an interview." He stepped briskly away and Silenzio was left standing with Das.

"Is your boss always that rude?" she asked.

"My apologies, er, Madam, Miss, er Doctor Silenzio. I think he's a bit flustered. I think maybe you caused it, if it's OK for me to say so, my apologies."

"What did I do?"

"Not what you did, doctor, what you are, if you will excuse my saying so, doctor."

Silenzio looked at Das with great amusement. "You know your boss pretty well, huh?"

"It is my job," answered Das, relishing this opportunity to speak not only to a beautiful woman, but to a chief of the Terrorism Fusion Center. She must be a high up mucky-muck, he thought to himself. "He won't be that long. He always likes to speak to the media. Considers it part of his duty as a responsible scientist. It will only take five minutes or so. Maybe we can wait, and possibly go to the meeting together."

"That does sound like a good idea," she smiled. Das ushered her back into the lecture center and seated her in the front row while he busied himself at the lectern, removing MacIver's presentation from the system, switching off the projector.

*

MacIver, with one eye on Silenzio, tried to direct his attention to the reporter. "If you look at my list of questions here, you can ask me any one of those. Should make it easier for you, saves you having to come up with the questions yourself, which I know must be hard, since this is not your field, so how would you know what to ask?"

"Frank Brown, Nine News," said the reporter as he took the list of questions and looked at them briefly. "The wall the Israelis built has all but stopped suicide bombing?"

"If you were at my talk, you would know that it is not a monolithic wall, but a series of wire fences —"

"OK. Fences, then. So they really do work?"

"Indeed they do, along with a lot of other things that the Israeli Defense Forces do, especially moving their checkpoints around, monitoring suicide bombers' movements."

"They can actually do that, they know who the bombers are?"

"Well I can't go into that in detail of course. They have a very hi-tech operation."

"I heard that you yourself disarmed a suicide bomber?"

"I don't know how this story got about. I was one of a team that intercepted the bomber, a young teenager. We managed to talk him out of it."

"The anti-Zionists who came to your talk say that the wall, er excuse me, fences, have been built right along the Green Line, splitting communities in half, separating Jews from Arabs, an apartheid line, the protestors called it."

"There are places where this has happened, but I have to say, the Israelis have been very responsive to local communities and have actually shifted the fences where it was obvious that they damaged communities. I do not believe that the construction of the fences is essentially for political reasons, that is, to define a *de facto* border on the West Bank. I am convinced that, because my research has shown that they save lives, the true justification is for security of local communities. They were politicized after they were built, not before. But as I said in my talk. I am not a politician. I bow to the political decisions that are made. All I ask of politicians is that the decisions they make are informed by data, that they be evidence driven. And in that case, they have to factor in the numbers of lives saved by the fences against whatever the political gains would be from taking them down."

"So do you think suicide bombing is likely to happen in the USA, just like in Israel? Is that why you are doing research there, because you think it might come over here?"

"Well, strictly speaking, it already has come here, hasn't it? The Nine Eleven attack was a suicide bombing, wasn't it? It's just that the bombers used a different means of getting to their targets and didn't have to wear bomb vests."

"What I meant was, do you think we should be building a fence like the Israelis, along our open borders to Mexico and Canada?"

"I do. I know it's politically toxic to say so, but it's the only way we can make sure that terrorists cannot first of all get themselves into our country, and second, transport the equipment and materials they need to use in their attacks."

"But a fence would not have stopped the nine eleven terrorists."

"Quite right. But carefully controlled border entry, including careful screening and document verification which I have been advocating for many years, long before the nine eleven attack, would have. It's a whole package. We do many things, a fence is just one part of it."

"One last question, Professor. You seem much more practical than your academic colleagues. What do they think of your work?"

"I have excellent colleagues whom I respect greatly."

The reporter looked at MacIver quizzically, but decided to leave it go. MacIver knew that the question and the answer would be edited out of the interview.

"Thank you for your time professor. It will be on the local evening news. That's Nine-Prime at 6.00."

*

They were heady days for Ruth Newberg, daughter of the media tycoon Rupert Newberg, when she won election as New York's very first female mayor. But now, it had to be acknowledged, she was an embattled Mayor, mercilessly attacked for several months — some of her supporters would argue ever since she got into office — by the mainstream media and the huge cohort of bloggers who relentlessly reported on and criticized her every move and every statement. The New York Post called her a walking-politically-correct-senior-Barbie Doll. The *New York Times* called her just plain incompetent. There was garbage on the streets, citizens were constantly harassed by freeloaders, beggars and muggers. The murder rate had never been so high and hate crime was endemic. There were demonstrations almost daily about one cause or another. Traffic was at a standstill. The subways were snarled by demonstrators and even small-time fire bombers. Her police department had become a kind of renegade operation under police commissioner John Ryan who had given up on her long ago. She had even increased the size of his force by some 25%, but he still just went ahead and did what he wanted. She threatened to fire him and he openly challenged her to do so. He was immensely popular and to fire him would bring down her mayoralty. Their yelling matches in her office and his were the talk of the town. He wanted her job, it was pretty clear. It reminded her of when Rizzo was the police chief of Philadelphia where she grew up in the 1960s and through his cunning antics and policies, "a policeman on every corner," became Philadelphia's most popular mayor ever. There was still a huge mural of him in South Philadelphia.

The supposed imminent threat of a terrorist attack was an opportunity. The intelligence had not come from NYPD but the CIA. Her own police commissioner Ryan had insisted that there was no impending threat because if there was, his counter terrorism force, now with agents in many parts of the world as well as Brooklyn, would have heard about it. That was another thing that annoyed her. He was trying to be the FBI or CIA, claiming that he could do the job much better than could they. So her administration was pretty much cut off from all the significant players in counter terrorism, except for one avenue: the New York-New Jersey counter terrorism fusion center, headed by her good friend Monica Silenzio. It was thanks to her that she felt confident enough to go ahead with this press conference and make public the threat.

"It's time," said Foster, her tireless young assistant, "surprisingly, there are hardly any protestors, and just the usual gang of reporters." He led the way down the small flight of worn marble steps of City Hall and out the door where he had arranged for a podium and the usual audio paraphernalia. It was set to the side of the main door, just at the head of the steps so she could look down on the rabble, as she called them. She stood at the podium and took a deep breath, Foster at her side.

"People of the Great City of New York," she announced, "this will be a very brief statement. You have probably heard that the threat level of terrorism has been raised for this city. I can affirm that a credible threat from the CIA that a group, unknown as yet, plans to attack Ground Zero — now known of course as the Freedom Tower — on the anniversary of the nine eleven attack. I should add that the exact day and time is supposition on our part, since the chatter only indicated an imminent attack, not mentioning the day. My advisers tell me that it's pretty much a sure thing that the terrorists will choose the anniversary date in order to garner the publicity that they crave. While some have pressed me to keep silent and not divulge this information to the people of New York, I consider it your right to know what is going on so that you may take the necessary precautions. I urge the citizens of New York to be vigilant in the coming months prior to the anniversary of nine eleven, and to report anything suspicious to the terrorism hotline of the New York State Police. I also ask you to be patient with the preventive actions we will be taking, in fact have already begun to take, as we harden targets, close various streets and alleys and increase surveillance at certain venues and on public transport. Now, I will take a few quick questions."

"Madam Mayor, Tyler Simkin, New York Times."

"Yes Mr. Simkin. I think I remember you," Newberg responded with a faint hint of sarcasm.

"Is this really a credible threat? Your own police commissioner just yesterday in an interview with the New Yorker stated that there were no current threats, because his undercover counter terrorism task force would hear about it if there were."

"When it comes to counter terrorism intelligence, we in the mayor's office prefer to listen to the experts, and the experts are the CIA and FBI. The FBI, by the way, concurs with the CIA assessment."

"But the commissioner insists that he has already thwarted several potential terrorist attacks, because his own counter terrorism task force has infiltrated local Islamic communities in New York City and Brooklyn."

"I have not heard him say that. To my knowledge we are not doing it and never will do it." She pointed to another reporter with raised hand.

"Todd Sloan, New York Post. If I could pick up on that. The FBI has also charged that NYPD has interfered with their outreach to Islamic communities in Newark."

"My office never has and never will condone police infiltration, spying or surveillance of Islamic communities whether in New York, Newark or anywhere else."

"So you will demand that the police commissioner cease his spying on innocent Muslim communities?"

"To repeat. We do not spy on the good citizens of New York. I do not condone it anywhere, least of all in Newark where our police have no right being there anyway."

"Abdul-al-Kahmar, Newark Times. Madam Mayor, will you ask the Police Commissioner to resign?"

"This conference is over. Thank you for your attention." Foster guided his boss into City Hall and out the back door to a waiting helicopter.

*

Manish Das felt a little awkward and embarrassed to be alone with Monica Silenzio, such a beautiful woman, as they sat in the lecture center. In the interest of his boss, he decided to retrieve him from the media interview, so he turned to Silenzio and said, "Excuse me, I think I'd better find out where he is," and was about to open the door when it opened, and in walked MacIver.

"Sorry about that," he said, "you know how it is. The media are like a pack of dogs. They won't let you go once they get a hold of you. Shall we depart? He smiled at Silenzio. "Where are you parked?"

"Just a few blocks away," she answered.

Das held the door open and led the way out to the old parking lot across Washington Street. Newark was full of such lots that looked like what they were, places where old houses had been bulldozed away, leaving crumbling rubble, and in the better lots, crumbling black top. He led them past the old bar that had been left on the corner of the lot, to MacIver's gleaming, deep black Nissan Maxima. MacIver and Silenzio followed, walking in awkward silence.

"May I offer you a lift?" asked MacIver

"That's OK. My car's just a block away."

"Sir, throw me the keys, sir," grinned Das. He unlocked the car and stood grinning at Silenzio. She scrutinized the car and couldn't help noticing the two stickers attached to the back passenger window, a position suggesting that the car's owner did not really want anyone to see them.

One read, LOVE LIMBAUGH and the other, now old and peeling, OBAMA 2008.

"We'll drop you at your car then," said MacIver, "Do you know the best way to the Skyline Restaurant?

"Never been there. But I've heard of it."

"It will take us a good thirty minutes."

Das joyfully played chauffeur and opened the back door. Silenzio climbed in as he half saluted her.

MacIver walked to the other side. "You better not salute me!" he said to Das, half joking. He winked at Das who held the door open and carefully closed it shut after his boss slid into the back seat next to this most beautiful woman. "To the parking lot," he ordered, and, turning to Silenzio, asked, "are you sure you won't go all the way with me?"

"Not even to the restaurant," she quipped. "I have things I have to do after the meeting. It's just easier to have my own car there."

Das loved driving this car. He gave a quick look in the rear view mirror and saw that his couple was well placed.

*

Buck Buick, *Captain* Buck Buick since last week, sat in his patrol car, parked behind the Newark Performing Arts Center. His iPad glowed in the shadow of the building, so ugly from the rear, not unlike the lady mayor he was watching on the local TV news. The mayor had just finished her news conference, and parts of it that related to Newark were being played over and over again by the local Newark TV news and various web sites. He wasn't sure what to make of it. Didn't want to run afoul of her police commissioner, a nasty piece of work if ever there was one. If his own chief knew what he was about to do, he'd be dead meat. But the fact was, life in the Newark PD was pretty boring, even heading up the new counter terrorism task force, which amounted to zilch, his eager beaver new recruits clamoring to dress up like Muslims and infiltrate the mosque. Really idiotic. Besides, there were enough people doing that what with the NYPD and the FBI as well! What a bunch of jokers they all were. He yearned to be back in the bomb disposal unit in Iraq. At least there, everyone knew what each had to do. You knew that your life was on the line as was your buddy's. One misstep, and you or your comrades were blown into a thousand pieces, or worse, reduced to a couple of smaller pieces that couldn't walk or talk. But the juice ran high! It was living to the max! He had tried lots of other ways to sample life to the full. "Get married and have kids," that's how to live life to the fullest, people said, especially those who had kids. He had watched his fellow marines who were married with little kids. They suffered, oh how they suffered. None of them would do it over, he was sure, and some had said so. And what happened when they came back from active duty? Life sucked. Sitting around wiping the kids' runny noses, the wives, maybe without meaning to, belittling their military lives by making them change dirty diapers, play mindless kiddie games with one or two year olds. What sort of life was that? True, he'd tried marriage a couple of times. It was great for a few months. But then he yearned to be back in action, back where there was adventure and the high possibility of being blown to hell. The best solution would be to have a new wife waiting for him each time he rotated back from the front. Now there's an idea! But no wife, no kid, better to have a really well trained and experienced prostitute waiting for him. Now there's an even better idea!

The text had come from Foster, the mayor's trusty assistant. "Meeting set for 1.00 pm. Today, Skyline Drive restaurant. Please confirm attendance." He began to text an answer, but then stopped. Better they're left worrying. Anyway, he was not at all sure whether to get mixed up in this crazy venture. When Foster had called him yesterday and asked him to join the secret task force he had said, without a moment's hesitation, "No way!" He did not want the NYPD to become his enemy, and he was sure that was what would happen if the mayor's police commissioner found out about it. And the police commissioner was an ex-marine himself. So no way. Foster did not let up, though. Next thing the mayor herself came on the line. "Look," she said, "I know I'm asking a lot. And I know I'm putting you in a difficult position asking you to do this without Okaying it with either your own chief or mayor. But I really need a forceful, practical man like you who is used to pressure. It will be a very diverse team, CIA, FBI and a forensic scientist. I know with the right blend of action and expertise, we can do this. I have chosen the members of this task force very carefully. Each one of you is essential for its success. That means that without you, Buck, I have no task force. Simple as that."

"You said, forensic scientist?" he asked. "You don't mean Larry MacIver, do you?"

"You guessed it!"

"Then count me out. He's a pointy headed pompous SOB. No way can I work with him. Besides, he thinks I'm an idiot." He tapped END and the call ended. Immediately, the phone rang again. "Foster, I said no!" he said yelling into the small device.

"Look. Just give it some thought. I'm in the process of setting up the first meeting and inviting members of the task force to join. Anyway, there's a very good reason for you to join us."

"That's impossible. There is no reason that it would make sense for me to join you."

"If I told you that Monica Silenzio was going to chair the task force, would that make a difference?"

"You're kidding."

"No. I'm not."

"You win the argument, at least for now. I'll think about it."

"Terrific. I'll text you tomorrow to confirm the time and day. It will be tomorrow if we can manage it."

And with that, Buick had put his career on the line, for it would be on the line if any of this got out. And knowing New York, it surely would eventually leak out, especially if there was any serious action involved.

Buick was about to drive off when a car drove through a light that had just changed to red. Reflexively, he switched on his siren and gave chase. It was a new white Audi A6, the sort he really enjoyed pulling over. The driver quickly stopped. Buick pulled up behind him, lights still flashing. He ran the number through the Newark PD database of stolen cars. It was not stolen. Too bad! He climbed out of his car and slowly swaggered to the vehicle. The driver sat inside, petrified. Buick cast a large shadow on the car as he approached, hand resting lightly on his holster.

"License and registration please driver," he asked officiously.

6. Skyline

Das insisted on taking the long way to the restaurant, the scenic route along the six mile long Skyline Drive that for the most part hugs the side of the steep hilly terrain of the Ramapo mountains, crossing the Ringwood State Park. It was the end of summer and the narrow windy road was enclosed intermittently by the leafy foliage of oaks and maples and occasionally opened out to residential or commercial complexes. Das pushed the car, taking the curves as fast as he thought he could without his boss yelling at him, switching on the hi-tech GPS system, though it was not as hi-tech as the one he had installed in his old Dodge Caravan. He glanced quickly at the rear vision mirror to make sure Silenzio was still following. She was, with difficulty.

"If you slow down a bit, Das, not only will Monica be able to keep up with us, but we could also discuss the progress you're making with your dissertation," said MacIver who enjoyed needling Das just enough to keep him focused on his work.

"A good idea, sir. I will slow down, though it's not as much fun driving your fantastic car, sir. She is doing all right in any case sir. She's a pretty good driver."

"OK. Then what about your dissertation. Have you completed collecting data yet?"

"Sir, I'm sorry sir, but my borderline Asperger condition does not permit me to do two complex things at once. I can't drive the car and talk about my dissertation at the same time. I'm sorry, sir. I'll try sir."

"Asperger's? You've got that?"

"I'm afraid so, sir. That's what they said at the student health center. Don't you remember? You made me go there."

"Well I have to confess I don't know what it is, but frankly, I doubt very much whether it's a real illness. These psychiatrists, they keep inventing new diseases. It's how they make their money."

"I hope you're right, sir, because they say there's no cure for it sir. Anyway, sir, my data collection will never be complete. Maybe that's a sign of my Asperger's. I just can't stop collecting the data, sir."

"You can't stop?"

"That's right sir. There's just no end to it, sir. It's like I collected bottle tops."

"How big is the database now? How many cars are in it?"

"I don't know exactly. Several hundred thousand, I'd guess."

"Then maybe you should stop now? How many of them are stolen?"

"Depends what you mean by 'stolen' sir, doesn't it? Sir please, sir, I must concentrate on my driving. Don't want to smash up your beautiful car, sir."

"OK. Then we'll meet later this week in your office and you can show me all you've done. Is Monica still with us?"

"Yes, sir. Still with us. Around the next curve and up the steep hill and we come to the restaurant. Shall I drop you off and then park, sir?"

"You think I'm too old to walk, Das? Go straight to the parking lot."

"There it is, sir!" The Maxima emerged from the woods into a wide open expanse and in the distance, some twenty miles away, was the most stunning view of the New York City skyline. "Wow! Sir! Isn't that amazing?"

"It certainly is. It's not often that cities can be said to be beautiful in themselves. But I guess they are, at a distance."

"A very nice view for a terrorist, sir," mused Das, having just stopped the car in the parking lot, facing the view.

"A very nice view for anyone, Das. What are you suggesting?"

"Oh, nothing sir. I was just wondering if seeing such a view, a terrorist might get some ideas. Looking at a bomb drop on it from this distance would be pretty spectacular."

"A mushroom cloud, you're thinking?"

"Yes, sir. Scary."

"A totally silly, idea. I can't imagine how a terrorist organization could pull off such a caper. Far too complex."

Silenzio pulled in beside them, and they walked together to the restaurant entrance, silent, overwhelmed by the glowing beauty of New York City. Mindful of his father's advice, Das kept five steps behind.

*

Foster was waiting for them at the entrance. "Professor MacIver, Doctor Silenzio. This way please."

"You're a doctor?" MacIver turned to Silenzio.

"P-H-D, John Jay College of Criminal Justice, and Agent 33, CIA."

"And CIA?"

"At your service!"

Foster ushered them upstairs to a small secluded conference room from which they admired once again the famous view of the New York City Skyline. "The mayor will be here shortly. She's just wound up a news conference back at City Hall."

"Who else is coming?" asked MacIver.

"FBI Agent Lee, director of the Newark branch office and, I think, Captain Buck Buick, head of the Newark PD counter terrorism task force."

"Buick? But he's an idiot! He's out of control! Why did your boss choose him?"

"The mayor, she likes to have everything balanced, Professor."

"Balanced? You can't balance him, he's an outlier! And Lee is useless too, just like the rest of the FBI!"

"I'm sure the mayor has her reasons, Professor."

MacIver gazed out the window, then tried to make eye contact with Silenzio, who instead was carefully leafing through the materials Foster had deposited at each place on the table. It would be hard concentrating with Silenzio in the room, thought MacIver. Maybe when Madam Mayor arrived the ecosphere in the room would truly be balanced.

"If you will excuse me a moment. I will get the mayor," said Foster. "She is hiding out in another room. We arrived some time ago. She doesn't want to be seen. This is a top secret meeting. We don't want the media to get wind of it."

Just as Foster departed, a waiter entered and placed a water pitcher and glasses on the table as well as writing pads and pencils. He bowed obsequiously to no one in particular. "I bring anything else?" he asked in a thick Russian accent.

"No thank you. That's fine. More glasses perhaps," answered Silenzio.

The waiter left, and as he did so Fred Lee entered. Silenzio rose to shake hands.

"Fred Lee, FBI, Newark Office. Hi nice to see you again Agent Silenzio."

"Likewise. And you know Professor MacIver?"

"We've met."

MacIver remained seated. "And this is Manish Das, my research assistant," he said.

"Very pleased to meet you sir," said Das as he jumped up from his place in the corner of the room and extended his hand, half bowing at the same time. Lee nodded and shook Das's hand, squeezing it so hard Das struggled to hold back a grimace.

"So what's the big secret?" asked Lee.

"I thought the FBI owned all the secrets," responded MacIver.

"An attack on Ground Zero perhaps?"

"Where did you hear that?" asked Silenzio, fully engaged.

"Like the professor said, we own all the secrets — those worth knowing, anyway."

"You spies are pathetic. Secrecy is just a cover against accountability. That's the only reason you put such store in secret information," lectured MacIver.

The door opened and Mayor Newberg entered, closely followed by the Russian waiter, then Foster. All rose in unison, muttering "good afternoon Madam Mayor" and such like. Ruth Newberg, looking every bit her age of 62, projected a warlike image, as though she was about to preside over the war room planning the invasion of North Korea. Her face had a lined, battered look, though well covered by copious makeup. She walked directly to the head of the table and plopped down. She was not that much over weight, but enough for people to make unkind comments. She was currently on a diet of salad and boiled eggs, the latter only because her dietician had told her she must eat protein if she insisted on being a vegetarian and didn't like cooked vegetables. Her dark grey business suit fitted snuggly accentuating what her figure used to be. She wore her usual blue silk scarf tied loosely around her neck.

MacIver looked from the mayor to Silenzio who had seated herself across from him and realized that he had not taken the slightest notice of what Silenzio was wearing. The room was well balanced all right, he mused. Then he noticed that Fred Lee had taken up the position across the table from the mayor.

"OK. Let's get down to business," said Madam Mayor as she signaled to Foster to send the waiter from the room. "Wait," she said, "where's Buick?"

"Should be here any time soon," Foster answered, "I'm sure he received our message."

Mayor Newberg began. "Agent Silenzio, could you bring us up to date please?"

"Sure, Madam Mayor. Fact is, we have picked up quite a bit of chatter that Al Qaeda is planning an attack on Ground Zero."

"When?" interjected Lee.

"We're guessing it will be next month, the forthcoming anniversary of nine eleven."

MacIver shifted in his seat. "So you actually have no idea."

"That's a bit strong. There is some indication."

"What is the statistical probability?" asked MacIver.

"We don't have that kind of data."

"Then without hard evidence we should assume that there may be an attack some day in the future and plan carefully, without getting into a panic."

"There's going to be an attack, and it's going to be soon." Silenzio was annoyed but remained calm.

"We will know very soon, in fact in a few days. And it will be certain," Lee said with an air of confidence.

"What do you know that we do not?" asked Silenzio.

"I'm not at liberty to share that information just yet. But I can tell you for sure that it's Al Qaeda. I will be able to tell you more in a few days."

MacIver laughed. "You guys. It's all you know what to do, sting operations. All they achieve is the entrapment of otherwise innocent Islamic immigrants."

"I did not mention a sting operation. And you liberal progressive professors have no idea how the real world works."

Mayor Newberg coughed gently to regain attention. "OK. OK. Now let's keep an open mind."

At this point, the door flew open so hard it banged the wall, and Buck Buick entered, uniformed, hand on revolver holster. He was yelling over his shoulder to the waiter to bring him a pizza. He quickly surveyed the occupants and sat himself beside Silenzio.

"You all know Captain Buick?" said Madam Mayor, "he has graciously agreed to join our little group — and I want to emphasize that his boss does not know it. So please let's keep it that way."

"Why the secrecy?" asked MacIver impatiently.

"I have my reasons, but they mainly concern the press. I want to thank Buck for agreeing to join us at considerable risk to his position at Newark PD."

"What a hero."

"Professor MacIver, please!" scorned Newberg. "You all understand I can't ignore Silenzio report. However low the probability, I must take action."

"To cover your ass." muttered Buick.

"At least we agree on one point," quipped MacIver.

Mayor Newberg continued. "Call it what you like. But Professor MacIver, isn't prevention your thing?"

"It certainly is. I'd be very happy to help you. The solution is simple."

"Really?" said Buick.

"Yes, really. We harden all likely targets. Make them inaccessible. Make them impenetrable."

"That's it?" Buick was fed up already.

"Well, it's quite a lot."

"You mean we sit around and wait to be attacked? It's pathetic."

"I wouldn't put it like that."

"I would! We need to infiltrate them, and take the animals out."

"That's really stupid. You don't know who or what to infiltrate," argued MacIver, he too annoyed and losing patience.

"Al Qaeda of course, who else?"

Fred Lee grabbed the opportunity to enlighten the group. "The FBI knows who they are. And we are about to bring them in. And of course it's Al Qaeda."

MacIver sighed. "Madam Mayor, I don't think I can work with these fools."

"You could start by not calling them fools!" Mayor Newberg straightened up as if to begin a formal speech. "I'd like to thank you all for agreeing to meet with me. Our city, our country, is in danger. I must take every step I can to prevent another attack occurring, whatever the target. I understand what you say, Professor, and we have already gone quite some way in identifying those targets most attractive to terrorists. But we also must at least make all effort to find out who may attack us, and, to use Buck's words, take them out if we can. I know this is the traditional, not very innovative approach, but it's the most common approach of law enforcement and I can't ignore it for that reason. Otherwise, if another attack occurs, I'll be accused of inaction, or worse dereliction of my duty to protect the city."

MacIver stared at the table while Buick smirked and winked at Silenzio. Foster looked to the Mayor; there was an awkward silence. He took the opportunity to say something neutral. "If I may, Madam Mayor, just make a quick bureaucratic announcement to our participants. The city will be paying you at the maximum rate allowed, for your time, plus reasonable expenses. Please take the forms I have left in front of you at the end of our meeting, fill them out and get them back to me as soon as possible."

Mayor Newberg continued. "Now let's move on. Do you have anything more to add, Agent Silenzio?"

"Only that we are reasonably certain that the target will be Ground Zero, and we think it's fair to assume that the attack will occur on the anniversary of nine eleven."

MacIver quickly responded. "But you don't know at all, and it's an unwarranted assumption given the very poor quality of your data. We must act based on hard evidence, facts, not speculation based on some vague report of 'chatter'."

Das half-raised his hand several times, waiting to be recognized.

At last, MacIver noticed and said to the mayor, "My apologies Madam Mayor, I failed to introduce my much trusted research assistant, Manish Das. I think he wants to say something."

"Pleased to meet you Mr. Das. Welcome to America. And where are you from originally?"

"Mumbai, Madam Mayor," Das replied as he half stood, then sat again, raising his hand in a series of nervous twitches.

"What is it you wanted to say, Mr. Das?"

"Just that, if sir allows, if it's Al Qaeda, surely they will pick Ground Zero because it's their style, sir, sorry sir."

MacIver frowned and shot Das a piercing look. "We know nothing of the sort. It's mere speculation. We are scientists, not soothsayers!"

Das sank into his seat, for the moment, crushed. "Yes, sir, of course sir. I was getting carried away, sir."

Buick couldn't resist entering the fray. "You see professor. Even your own student disagrees with you. This sitting back and waiting to be hit. It's...it's... un-American!" He jumped up from his chair as if to emphasize how right he was. At this moment the waiter arrived with his pizza. "Anyone want any? Silenzio?" Buick asked, smiling broadly.

Silenzio smiled and shook her head. The others aggressively ignored him. Fred Lee leaned forward in his seat and took a deep breath.

"I think I can put this to rest," he said smugly, "I can reveal, on the understanding that we are all in this together and that you can all keep a secret — and that especially applies to the Professor — we do have a sting operation in progress, and we'll be bringing in the terrorists any day now."

"I knew it," said MacIver, also smug.

Mayor Newberg responded, clearly pleased. "That's an excellent first step. Perhaps you could include Captain Buick in the questioning once you bring them in? We all need to share information here. You remember the report of the nine eleven commission. This was their biggest criticism of law enforcement."

MacIver was unimpressed. "It's a waste of time, money and worse, fritters away much needed trust we might be able to get from the Islamic community. If they think they're potential FBI suspects, why would they share information?"

Mayor Newberg, exuding an air of tolerance responded, "Professor MacIver, we will multiply our efforts, with your assistance, to identify targets at risk and make them harder for terrorists to reach. Anything more? Oh, and one more thing, we will assume that the attack will occur on nine eleven. So we have just one month to get all this done." She rose, indicating that the meeting was over, and left without another word. Foster followed her quickly, calling out over his shoulder to remind them all to fill in the forms. Buck Buick and Fred Lee departed also in silence.

MacIver remained seated, as did Silenzio who turned to him and said, "do you have time to come for a short ride? I'd like to show you something you'll find interesting."

"Depends what and where." MacIver eyed Das wriggling around in his corner.

"I can drive your car back, sir. Why don't you go back with Dr. Silenzio?

"I don't really have the time. But if it's on the way back."

"Besides, sir, if it's OK, sir, I'd like to take the time to survey the streets around here for my car theft project."

"Good idea Das. OK, Monica, if I may call you that, let's go."

"If I can call you Larry," she said with a grin.

7. Dental Work

It was incredibly hot and incredibly humid. Shalah Muhammad's shirt was already soaked in sweat and the day had only just begun. Yet he still wore his jacket. He felt undressed without it. Hyderabad was his favorite city, especially Old City. He called to the auto rickshaw driver to let him off at Charminar, and he strolled down to the Laad bazaar, then turned off into a side street which was crammed full of pedestrians rushing to and fro, as people do only in India's crowded downtown streets and alleys. He resisted visiting the Gulzar House where the famous Hyderbadi pearls were brokered and sold. He might go there on the way back and buy some loose pearls for his wives who enjoyed stringing them or working them into their garments. He knew a place where he could buy them at bargain prices. But, business came before pleasure, he said to himself, smiling as he remembered his old teacher at the Harrow boarding school in England. It was his favorite saying. "Business before pleasure, young man," he would say. And it had stuck. He never deviated from that rule.

The street narrowed into an alley, where the shops were more like stalls at an open market. It was hard to find one's way through the crush of busy people. To make it worse, young men, mostly bearded, strained on their bicycles carrying enormous loads of cloth, cotton, and other wares. They were totally bent on going forward. Too bad for you if you got in the way.

Dentists' row came up suddenly. He had visited here often when he had a tooth ache, and enjoyed watching the dentists sitting in their own chairs, calling out, offering the best painless services, special deals on two for one extractions. At last he found the booth he was looking for, decorated in gaudy colors, a sign in bright red saying, SMILEY HOUSE and beneath it the slogan, HEALTHY TEETH, HEALTHY MIND. And on a brass plate at the entrance, tacked on to the wobbly pole that held up a canvas awning to shield the dentist chair from the sun, was written in a careful but amateurish hand, DR. KUMAR JAMAL. DDS. OXFORD.

Shalah approached the dentist who was dressed carefully in a bright white open neck shirt, slim tight fitting gabardine pants, and of course, had a sparkling white smile to match his shirt. His beard was almost non-existent. It had been carefully cropped and groomed to be as short as possible but clearly visible.

"Do you have a cleaning special today?" asked Shalah Muhammad.

"I'm sorry sir, but the special ended yesterday. But I do have a special on extractions if you have a coupon," replied the dentist in almost perfect Farsi.

"You speak Farsi?" asked Shalah, surprised.

"Of course. I am from Western Punjab, the best and most beautiful part of Pakistan," the dentist said proudly, "but of course, I have my DDS from Oxford."

"I have a coupon for two extractions."

"I'm sorry sir, the coupon to which I am referring allows only for one extraction. Are you sure you need two extractions?"

"I'm sure."

"Perhaps you had better step in and I'll take a look." Dr. Jamal slid out of the chair and beckoned for Shalah to take his place, and he did so. "Open wide, now. Ah, yes, I think you're right. It's two. You're sure you want to do two extractions? It will of course cost much more than one."

"I will pay for two."

"Very good, sir. But by the look of it, it will be too much for you if I do both today. Besides my assistant is not here, and he speaks only Urdu."

"Then when? I can go to someone else, you know, and probably get a better price."

"Price is important, but when it comes to extractions, quality is much more important, wouldn't you say sir? Besides I have the best equipment and I guarantee the extractions will be totally painless."

"And how expensive?"

"You understand that doing two costs a lot more than one."

"I thought two was always cheaper than one."

"No, much more, but guaranteed for a lifetime."

"That's not very long."

"Very funny, sir! Would you like to make an appointment for the extractions? I have a very special comfortable chair in the back. And you can watch TV as well."

Dr. Jamal slid a curtain back exposing an empty space surrounded by more curtains. Shalah followed him and Jamal closed the curtain behind him. They stood close to each other, almost touching.

"We can do it whenever you want," whispered Jamal in Farsi. "I have it all set up. It will be easy."

"So, they will be disassembled, or will we have to do that?" asked Shalah Muhammad.

"We will do it. I take it they don't have to be completely disassembled?"

"Just enough to allow packing into a crate that doesn't look like a missile."

"And the money?"

"Ten million U.S. dollars now, ten million on receipt of shipment."

"Thirty million, half now. I meant it when I said two is a lot more than one."

"Twelve and twelve."

"Deal. And where do we ship to?"

"The Port of Newark, USA. I will send you details later. Actually, I will not. My Russian colleagues will be receiving the shipment. They will contact you."

"Excellent! And the down payment?"

"We need to find an Hawala."

"No problem. There's one in the next street, behind Gulzar House."

"OK. So let's be clear. These are two short range mini Nag missiles, right?"

"Right. Fifty miles max range. We have already located them in Bangalore. The security is minimal. Shipment from there through Mumbai port a breeze."

Dr. Jamal opened the curtain and led Shalah Muhammad out, placing a "back in 5 minutes" sign on the dentist chair. As they wound their way through the crowd of shoppers and vendors, Shalah sought additional assurance.

"Your boys can do this, right?"

"Of course. No problem. This is easy. No violence. We have people inside."

"You understand the consequences of failure?"

"Really. This attitude is insulting. We never fail. Never!"

"OK! OK! Just so we both understand."

They made their way through the Gulzar house, through a back door and into a small alleyway which was nevertheless crowded with seemingly too many people trying to get through too small a space. Dr. Jamal waved to an old wizened man, dirty turban on his head, sitting in a doorway on a low stool, cell phone in hand. "I have a customer for you!" he announced in Telugu, as he and Shalah Muhammad squatted down beside him.

Shalah had to guess what he had said. "I don't like this. What language is that? I thought it would be Urdu," he said with a hint of suspicion.

"Oh, Sorry. It's Telugu. The Hawala does not speak Urdu. He's from Vizag which is about 360 miles south of here where Telugu is mainly spoken. My cousin lives there, that's how I know him."

"How much? Where to?" grunted the Hawala.

"It's from Dubai and it's twelve million U.S. Dollars."

"Ah! My friends in Dubai. They have so much money there! Your contact should call this number." The Hawala indicated a name and number on a grubby hand written list. Shalah Muhammad opened his cell phone and made a call.

"This is nine-one-one. Yes, the amount is twelve million U.S. Dollars. Call Hawala Felix, in Dubai. I am texting you the number now."

"Have him send the money to this number," said Jamal as he handed the Hawala a piece of paper.

"To Bengaluru?" asked the Hawala.

"Right, Bangalore," he said.

"It will be a few moments, depending on how efficient your man is in Dubai. May I offer you some chai?" He signaled a boy who immediately ran off and returned quickly with three small cups, passing them out carefully. The Hawala raised a cup as if proposing a toast. "To money, praise be to God!" They all raised their cups just as the Hawala's cell phone rang. He answered, "Yeh, good. OK." He tapped END, then dialed another number. "Hello? Yeh. Good. Twelve million," and closed his phone.

"It is done. My fee is one thousand U.S. Dollars. The boy will take it."

Shalah Muhammad pulled out a wad of bills from the inside pocket of his jacket and counted out ten $100 bills.

*

Monica Silenzio guided her pure dark green 2012 Volvo wagon with tinted windows into the parking lot. They were somewhere in Hoboken, New Jersey, a run-down industrial park, so typical of the back streets of New Jersey. The lot was covered with old decaying bitumen. New Jersey weeds, far more powerful here than in any other state, thrust their way through the bitumen making cracks and holes, and even where parts of the lot were concreted over, it was no match for New Jersey's weeds. They just forced their way right through it. At the far corner of the large lot which contained few cars for its size, was an old warehouse, a long low steel structure, covered with unpainted corrugated iron, a glass and brick front stuck on to the warehouse, as though it were an afterthought, and probably was.

The Volvo rolled to a halt. Silenzio jumped out and darted around to the passenger side just in time to open the door for MacIver.

"Gees, you're an accomplished chauffeur too!" he joked. "Where are we?" He had bantered and joked with her all the way, but she would not tell him where they were going. "You spies," he joked, "you just can't help holding everything back."

Silenzio took a small bow, smiling vivaciously, her wavy blonde hair blowing in the Hudson River breeze. Her smile was a complicated smile that kept MacIver guessing. It was not a seductive smile. It was more a smile that told him she was just playing around with him. It conveyed an air of superiority and confidence. "I shouldn't be doing this," she said, "but you're so well-known and respected, this time I think it's OK."

"You mean, it's OK to open the car door for me?"

"No, silly! Letting you into this place."

"And what exactly is this place? It doesn't look all that secret. Not even any barbed wire around the property. Very bad security, I might say as an expert in the field."

Silenzio walked up to a blank wall beside the glass lobby door and spoke to it. The wall slid open. "Come on," she said.

MacIver, amused at the security antics, followed. They entered the lobby and were faced with another plain wall, this time with a mirrored glass panel, a hole in the middle, chest high. Silenzio inserted her bare ring finger with difficulty. A light blinked. She straightened up and spoke in a deep monotone, "Agent 33 Monica Silenzio with one guest, Larry MacIver."

"That's it? We're in?" asked MacIver

"Not quite. Put your finger in."

"I could say something."

"Don't."

"Which one?"

"Your favorite."

MacIver inserted the middle finger of his right hand. He couldn't help running his tongue against his upper lip. The action was reflected in the mirror. A sliding door opened and Silenzio grabbed his arm to guide him in. MacIver found himself in a cavernous warehouse with rows and rows of filing cabinets. Behind a large glass panel there were workers, some wearing headphones, seated by computer consoles, tape recorders, mountains of books and papers. MacIver stared at the sight in amazement.

"The cabinets?" he asked.

"Data from wiretaps, and whatever, collected since nine eleven."

"The CIA collected all this?"

"And the National Intelligence Agency. We share information just like the Nine Eleven Commission said we should."

"Admirable. And the workers over there?" MacIver pointed to the people behind the glass partition.

"Translators."

"But how could they ever do all this?"

"They can't. They're only up to 2003."

"Ridiculous!"

Silenzio raised her eyebrows.

"Sorry, it's terrific you have shown me this, but —"

"But what?"

"Well it's just a terrible waste of scarce resources."

"Who says they're scarce?"

"The current chatter you quoted at the meeting."

"There's a rating system. Some chatter can be put on fast track. Has to be approved by someone with gold security clearance. There's a protocol."

"Say no more. I understand. So it's basically useless, and probably not timely either, even the 'fast track' chatter." MacIver stepped towards the work room.

Silenzio grabbed his arm. "You can't talk to them. You don't have clearance," she said.

"But what could they possibly know that would risk national security?"

"That's not the point. It's protocol. Come on, let's get you back to the university where you belong."

MacIver shook his head in despair, derision, or both. But he looked sideways at Silenzio. He liked the feel of her touch on his arm. He tried to get a whiff of her gorgeous hair. She guided him out through the security rigmarole, then to the car. She opened the door for him and MacIver gently touched her hand as she gripped the door handle.

"Why did you bring me here?" he asked, "it obviously supports what I said at the meeting."

"It's my way of saying what I can't say in public. Besides, I trust you."

Taken aback MacIver released her hand. In truth, he wanted to hug her really hard.

*

Mr. Kohmsky sat still, staring at the wall. Mrs. Kohmsky sat beside him, fidgeting in her handbag. It was the one that Sarah had refused when offered to her. She said she had no use for it.

Mrs. Kohmsky had nagged her husband until he gave in. She knew he would. He didn't believe the FBI nonsense about Sarah being dead. They were lying. They both knew that. They had a lot of experience listening to government officials lie. The rule of thumb was to assume everything was a lie until proved otherwise. So she had convinced Mr. Kohmsky that they should try going to the New York State Police. They were supposed to be better trained than the NYPD. Maybe they could help track her down, or at least give them some lead they could follow up themselves. Now here they sat in the Manhattan Office of the New York State Police, hoping someone could give them some answers. The small waiting room was comfortable and the chairs soft. The entire office was quiet, very different from the NYPD offices that always bustled with activity. It gave the impression that this branch of the New York State Police was not at all busy.

Deputy commissioner Sylvia Celer emerged from her office. The Kohmskys stood immediately to greet her. She cut an imposing figure, a very tall slender woman in her fifties, her dark grey uniform perfectly pressed, the creases accentuating her angled features. Instead of ushering them into her office, she sat with them in the anteroom right where they were.

"Please remain seated, Mr. and Mrs. Kohmsky. Now what can I do to help you?"

"Our daughter Sarah," Mrs. Kohmsky stuttered as she sat back in the soft chair, "we don't know where she is, haven't seen her for more than eight years. We've tried everywhere, NYPD, FBI, but they say we should assume she is dead."

"And why do they say that?"

"They won't say. But we know in our hearts that she is alive somewhere."

"They are lying to us," muttered Mr. Kohmsky gruffly, still staring at the wall. "They are keeping information from us. They know something."

"I can't imagine that they would keep information about your daughter away from you. What evidence do they report that suggests to them that she is dead?"

"They checked their missing-persons data base and found her there, but we don't think that means anything. The photo they have is the one we gave NYPD years ago. Besides, we have given them evidence that she is still alive, but they just ignore it."

"Evidence? What evidence, Mrs. Kohmsky?"

"The money we received from Chernobyl."

"From where?"

"Chernobyl, Russia."

"And you think it comes from your daughter?"

"Not exactly. In fact we received some just last week. We decided this time to come to you because we have heard that the New York State police are the most professional police and that you specialize in finding missing persons. We saw it on your web site."

"I have to agree with you on that, Mrs. Kohmsky. Do you still have the money?"

"It's here." Mr. Kohmsky shifted slightly, dug his hand into his old denim pants and produced a small brown envelope that was covered with stamps and certainly looked like it had traveled all the way from Russia.

"May I open it?" asked Commissioner Celer.

"Of course," said Mrs. Kohmsky, "the money is all there. We haven't touched it yet. There was no note at all. Nothing."

Commissioner Celer opened the packet and retrieved a thick wad of 100 Euro notes. "And you think this money is coming from your daughter?"

"Who else?"

"But why would she send you money? You're not poor are you?"

"Well, we're comfortable. We've always done our best to make sure Sarah was not wanting for anything. So we don't really know why she's sending us money."

"She's guilty, that's why," growled Mr. Kohmsky.

"Guilty?" asked the Commissioner.

"Guilty that she hasn't got in touch with us for so many years. What did we do to her to deserve this? We gave her a good home and good education. And then she just runs away."

"So you think she ran away? That nothing foul has happened?"

"As we've told all the others. We haven't seen her since she went to do her Master's Degree in Oxford. Not one word from her ever again."

"Was there a disagreement between you before she left? Bad words?"

"No, nothing in particular. We never argued, actually," said Mrs. Kohmsky.

"She never said anything?" asked the Commissioner.

"Well, we are – were - a pretty quiet family. We didn't ever say much to each other," offered Mrs. Kohmsky.

"This money. Do you mind if I keep it for a little while? I'll have our people at the State Crime Lab examine it. There may be some clues there. May also be a clue as to where the envelope came from?"

"Well it's from Chernobyl, of course."

"You came from there, right?" asked the Commissioner.

"Yes, but we have lost contact with everyone who lived there. Mr. Kohmsky had two brothers, but they left there years ago, at the same time we came to America."

"And do you know where they are now?"

"We never heard from them again," said Mr. Kohmsky, "never."

"Have you ever tried to contact them?"

"No," answered Mr. Kohmsky abruptly.

"I see." The commissioner carefully replaced the money into the envelope.

"Please help us," pleaded Mrs. Kohmsky.

"I will put my people on to it right away. I can't promise you anything, of course. But we will give it a try."

"Thank you, commissioner," said Mrs. Kohmsky, dabbing at a little tear at the corner of her eye, "you are most kind."

The Commissioner stood as if to end the conversation, and Mr. and Mrs. Kohmsky stood with her. "One thing puzzles me," said the Commissioner, "how come these envelopes come from Chernobyl? I thought no one lived there since it was destroyed in the nuclear disaster way back when."

"We thought so too. We don't know exactly, except that we think that some people have moved back into the general area. But that's only very recent. We've been getting these packages for years."

"Before Sarah disappeared?"

"At least since she was a teenager."

"So why then would you conclude that the money was coming from her?"

"We know it doesn't make sense. But it's our only hope. Maybe she has gone back to Russia and met up with her uncles or something."

"And the money you've received before. Always from Chernobyl, always Euros?"

"Yes. Although of course it was not Euros before there were Euros."

"What was it?"

"U.S. dollars."

"Did you tell the FBI and NYPD about the money?

"Of course," said Mr. Kohmsky, "they said it had nothing to do with the case. They're lying."

"I see. Mr. and Mrs. Chomsky, I mean Kohmsky, I'll be in touch. But don't get your hopes up. The NYPD and FBI are very good at their work. They have a worldwide network of operatives. If she were alive, they would have found her by now."

Mr. Kohmsky, unusual for him offered his hand, which the Commissioner received, and they said their good-byes.

8. Family Visit

Sarah was full of apprehension as she slid into the back seat of the well-polished black Mercedes C240. The driver closed the door softly behind her and gave a slight nod of his head. He spoke no English.

"How long till we get there?" she asked in her excellent Russian, even if with a quaint Ukrainian accent.

"Ah, you are from Ukraine?"

"Sort of. I was born there but my parents migrated to America when I was five. How long till we get there?"

"It will be about two hours."

"That long?"

"The last hour is through mountains. Very beautiful though. Best in the world."

Sarah Kohmsky had never met her uncle Sergey, even though when she spoke with him on the phone, he behaved as though he saw her every day and had watched her grow up. "And what of my other uncle?" she had asked. Uncle Sergey had simply replied, "Oh, he's gone. Been gone a long time." She had not followed up. She wasn't sure what "gone" meant.

The car glided through the dull streets of Bishtek. These former Soviet towns — that's all this was, really, hardly a city — seemed to embody her father's personality, depressed, dull and gray, never quite coming alive, people looking vacantly in front of them as though there was nothing to look for, or look at. It was a terrible atmosphere of emptiness, or maybe better described as loneliness. Her father was always alone. That's what had made her so alone herself. No, detached, maybe that was a better way to put it. He was disconnected from people and didn't seem to know why, didn't seem to even realize the extent of his loneliness. She could not remember feeling close to him; in fact she could not remember ever being hugged by him, or even touched by him. He must have surely. But she couldn't remember one instance. He never spoke, he never touched. He just thought. Or at least, that's what she assumed he was doing in all that silence.

Her uncle Sergey didn't sound that way at all on the phone. In fact, just the opposite. He talked and talked like it was just yesterday. How he and her dad had played soccer and ice hockey together. How they had explored the streams and hills of the Ukraine. It sounded like just one happy childhood. Was he really her uncle? But Shalah had assured her that he was indeed her uncle, and Shalah would know. His network of spies discovered this fact by accident when they were searching for a reliable Russian mafia group with whom they could contract to do the new nine eleven attack. Shalah was convinced that the Americans would not be looking for Russians, but for Islamic militants. In fact, he knew that was their mindset from his spies in New Jersey. It was a nice surprise when an old photograph of Sarah turned up in uncle Sergey's dossier put together by one of his operatives. He had recognized her immediately, even though she must have been just a teenager when it was taken. And Sarah had later confirmed it when he showed it to her. She couldn't understand how her uncle could have got the photograph because she thought that her father never communicated with him, never heard from him again, once they left Chernobyl. Her mom had told her that uncle Sergey had worked at the power plant, but was not there at the time of the disaster. In fact she did not know where he was. She never mentioned the other brother. Her mom must have secretly sent the photo, though how she knew where to send it was a mystery. Unless, unless it had to do with those strange envelopes stuffed with money that would come from the Soviet, with the Chernobyl postmark. Sarah wondered, now, how the money could have gotten through the corrupt and penniless postal workers of the USSR, and even later under the Ukraine when after the collapse of the Soviet Union, nobody had any money, food, or anything. Was it uncle Sergey who sent the money?

*

Her driver had switched on the radio which, Sarah was pleasantly surprised, was playing Tchaikovsky's violin concerto. Trouble was the driver hummed along with it, out of tune. Classical music was never meant to be hummed to, she thought, even if the hummer were in tune.

They were in the mountains now. It was high summer and they were just beginning to leave behind the rich greens of the oaks and maples and elms, climbing higher into the firs and pines. The snow covered peaks could be glimpsed if she pushed her face against the window, or looked up through the moon roof. The narrow but well-made road curved graciously through the mountains and valleys. She saw waterfalls, whitewater, precipices and deer. Her driver was right. This was a beautiful place, perhaps the most beautiful and unspoiled scenery she had seen.

"Are we getting close?" she asked.

"In a few minutes. You will be happy to see your uncle again, eh?"

"Quite," she answered.

Sarah saw the road rise steeply ahead, and the driver shifted down a cog. The Mercedes responded and gave a throaty hum as it surged forward. At the very top of the steep rise, the forest cleared and a large wrought iron gate slowly opened ahead of them. The car slowed, rolled into an immense cobblestone courtyard and pulled up in front of a huge stone villa, where uncle Sergey stood waiting at the bottom of a large flight of heavy stone steps. Her driver jumped out and hurried round to her door.

Uncle Sergey put out his hand. "Welcome to my humble abode," he smiled.

"Hello uncle Sergey."

"My dear, how beautiful you have grown!"

"But we've never met. How do you know that?" quipped Sarah.

"Ah, just like your dad. No time for formalities! Of course I have seen your photographs."

"How? My dad never communicated with anyone, least of all you."

"Men, Russian men. What can I say? Of course your mom kept in touch from time to time."

"She never said anything to me."

"Probably, she did not want your dad to know."

"Well, whatever. Nice place you have here."

"Wait till you see the view!"

Sergey leaned forward and tried to complete his welcome by gently kissing Sarah on each cheek. She allowed him, but did not really respond. He stood back and said, looking into her round and almost smiling face, "My dear, welcome, welcome. It's a terrible thing that our families have been broken up for so long. Family. When you come right down to it, that's all we have, you know."

Now Sarah did smile, not happily, but at her uncle's lame attempt at wisdom. "Yes, uncle Sergey, at last we are together," she said, almost mocking him.

"Ah, your father all over again. It's amazing, but very reassuring," said Sergey, grasping her hands affectionately. "Come, let's get you settled."

Three men dressed in black suits descended the stairs to retrieve her luggage. Uncle Sergey took Sarah's arm and guided her up the steps. They spoke Russian.

"I didn't know you lived so well, uncle Sergey."

"And would you believe, on no income!"

"You Chechens always were resourceful."

"When you have a government that can't pay you, you must look for other means."

"You are Chechen, right?"

"If you say so, my dear."

Sarah laughed and went as if to kiss uncle Sergey on the cheek, but did not quite do so. She had to resist getting too close to him. It could interfere with business. She turned to look out across the valley."

"Yes, Sarah, that is all mine, or more or less mine. It's the government's of course, but I take care of it for them. The great waterfall you see down there," he pointed across to the right of the villa, "runs a hydroelectric station that produces enough power to supply most of Bishtek."

"Amazing!"

"Come inside my dear, I hear we have big business to discuss."

They entered the huge lobby, large enough for a hotel, which it actually was, since uncle Sergey employed "many men doing many things," as he described them, and he liked to keep them close to him. The lobby was over furnished with very large items hewn from natural logs. There were stuffed animals and animal heads on the walls, giving the impression of a well-used hunting lodge. Sarah looked down and saw that she was standing on a thick rug of a black bear, complete with head.

"I'd like to freshen up a little before we get started, if that's OK."

"Yes of course. How inconsiderate of me. Petrovka will show you to your room." He signaled to a maid standing in a far off corner of the lobby.

*

Uncle Sergey stepped out of the lobby on to the top of the landing overlooking the steps and the view of the waterfall. He opened his phone and began to text, but then changed his mind and made a call instead.

"Turgo?"

"What is it?"

"I just want to be sure you're on board with this."

"She's here?"

"Yes. Now this is what I'm going to do. No, wait a minute. I don't want to do this on the phone. Meet me down at the observation tower. I'm going there now."

"Down gravel path?"

"Yes."

"I come."

The observation tower jutted out from the villa and was entered from the outside. It literally hung out over a precipice, giving an unnerving view of the waterfall and the hydroelectric generating plant. Sergey entered the glass enclosed deck and looked back up the path to see Turgo shuffling along. He cut a pathetic figure, hunched over in his disheveled grey suit, too big for him, looking like he had slept in it, and probably he had. Poor Turgo, thought Sergey, he's fallen on hard times, but soon all that will change.

*

Turgo had been his boss at the Chernobyl power station. But neither of them was there for the disaster. In fact, they were far away in Bishtek selling nuclear waste to one of Khadafy's henchmen. Turgo had reluctantly joined Sergey on his first adventure. And it was an adventure, since they had done the deal, and got half the money, when news of the Chernobyl disaster reached them and the Libyan had demanded his money back because, he said, obviously they could not produce the goods. It was then that Sergey decided that he was a Chechen, and disposed of the Libyan right there in front of Turgo.

"These Libyans are no good anyway," he said as he pocketed his revolver.

Turgo was mortified. He was such a worrier. He stood there shivering and shaking and whining. "I'm going back to the plant in Chernobyl. I can't do this kind of work," he whimpered.

"It's not work. It's adventure! Besides you can't go back to Chernobyl. It's radioactive."

"I've got to. What about my family?"

"Forget about your family. Worry about yourself." Sergey realized he said the wrong thing. That's all he does is worry, he mused. He fiddled with his revolver in his pocket. Turgo watched him and became frightened. "Don't worry. I won't do anything to you. Go on. Go off wherever you want. But my advice is to stay away from Chernobyl," said Sergey.

Of course, Turgo went back to Chernobyl, or at least he tried to. He could not get within fifty miles of the place and ended up on the streets of little towns begging for money or a bit of food. It was a few years later when Sergey encountered Turgo working at the counter of the Tulgovichi post office. He couldn't believe it. Turgo at first pretended not to recognize him, but soon, weak as he was, he gave in.

"How did you end up here?" Sergey asked.

"It's a long story. My wife and daughter. They are both dead. Radioactive poisoning they said. I got a pension, or used to until the Union collapsed. Then I managed to find a job here when the worker and his family also died."

"Your good fortune, huh?" observed Sergey, insensitive as usual. Turgo did not answer. "I need you to do me a favor," continued Sergey. Turgo looked apprehensive and said nothing. "Can you mail this small package and make it look like it came from Chernobyl?"

"What's in it?"

"Money. And I know how much is there. So don't try swiping it. I'll give you $100 to take care of it."

Turgo looked at him puzzled, but too timid to ask him why he was doing this. He looked at the address and recognized the name. "Oh, I see. I'd be very pleased to do it. And the return address?"

"Make it this post office, and to you or any name you want to make up. But not mine."

*

Turgo, lost in thought, entered the observation tower, leaving the door open behind him.

"Turgo!" yelled Sergey. "Close the door. The noise of the waterfall is deafening. We need to talk."

Turgo pushed the door shut. He looked at Sergey, a mixture of apprehension and longing in his eyes.

"OK. Now, are you sure you're up to this?"

"Of course," said Turgo, "I am nuclear scientist, I was top of class in my heyday."

"It looks like this is all going to happen. I'll provide you with four assistants, two of them bodyguards and the other two technical assistants. Some of them are already in the USA."

"What must I do?"

"When you get there, take delivery of two disassembled Nag missiles and assemble them."

"Ah yes, those are the new Indian short range ones. Very good! And the payloads?"

"Here's the challenge. Our clients want nuclear tips. But frankly, I think they're crazy, or at least don't fully comprehend the technical challenge of installing nuclear tips and further, we don't have anything nuclear that we could adapt to these missiles, do we?"

"You are right. Nuclear tips have never been installed or tested on these short range missiles. The stuff we have either here or stashed away in the USA will not work. Or at least would take a year or more to adapt."

"Here's my strategy. I'll try to talk my niece into doing a bio toxin payload. Ricin. That hasn't been tried either, but at least it's easier to do, isn't it?

"And the ricin?"

"You will have to manufacture it over there. It's easy to do. My young brother Nicholas, an American, will get the castor oil from which you can make it and he'll set up a manufacturing lab in the kitchen of the safe house which he has acquired already."

"I have never made ricin before, but I hear it's not difficult. However, it's the delivery that is the challenge."

"So innovate. I suggest some common explosive payload laced with ricin.

"I can do that. This is for both missiles?"

"We do one with ricin and the other we do with high explosive to make as big a bang as possible. Has to look good, you know. That's what our clients like most of all."

"And the explosives? Where are they?"

"They are already in the safe house. Nicholas acquired it. He can get anything."

"What type of explosive?"

"That I don't know. I just told Nicholas we wanted high explosives that can be packed into a small space. Now we come to the most important part. We cannot, repeat, cannot, tell our clients any of this. And this applies especially to my niece. She's very sharp I can see, and she also works for one of Iran's most ruthless terrorists, or maybe it's Al Qaeda. Who knows? I don't really care. So you say nothing. You push your role as the nuclear scientist. Got it?"

"I do understand."

"I will tell her that we already have the nuclear materials stashed away in our safe house in New Jersey."

"New where?"

"New Jersey, idiot! America! It's a state that is right next to New York. You don't know that and you even have a Green Card?"

"Whatever you say, Sergey. I can do whatever you want. But —"

"But what?"

"What about the money?"

"It's going to be a lot of money, more than you will be able to spend in your lifetime. Sarah's outfit has money coming out of its eyeballs. I don't know where they get it, although I have my suspicions. Anyway, I don't care, so long as we get our share of it."

"And how much is that?"

"We'll know after we have talked with my beautiful and smart long lost niece. You just be sure you make no slip-ups. She'll catch on if you do. Then she'll report to her boss, and we'll be done for. And I mean done for."

*

Uncle Sergey walked across the lobby to meet Sarah as she followed the maid into the room. Turgo followed, haltingly, not sure whether he should follow or not. Uncle Sergey grasped Sarah's hand with great joy and turned to Turgo.

"Turgo! Come meet my beautiful niece!"

Sara strutted forward and vigorously shook Turgo's limp hand.

"I am the nuclear scientist," blurted Turgo, "pleased to meet you, miss?""

"I'm Sarah, Sarah Kohmsky. Call me Sarah. Pleased to meet you."

"Ah yes, Kohmsky. Pleased I meet you. Think I knew your father years ago, even before you born," replied Turgo, trying hard to be enthusiastic but not to make any slips.

Uncle Sergey led them to the large coffee table that sat not far from the lobby entrance, surrounded by deep overstuffed couches and chairs, upholstered in rich off-black leather. They sat towards one corner of the table, Sarah sitting separate on a chair, the other two on a couch.

"Now, my dear, tell us what you want. My best wishes by the way to your mom and dad," Uncle Sergey added.

"I come from my colleague Shalah Muhammad, who I think you know, uncle Sergey."

"A shit-head, that much we know. But he is a very good operator." He immediately noted that his remark upset Sarah. Was there a spark there? He wondered.

"We are planning," Sarah looked around the room.

"It's OK. You are among loyal friends. Nothing will go beyond these walls."

At this moment Petrovka appeared with a tray of Russian tea and placed it on the table. Sarah waited for her to leave. "We need a scientist who can reassemble two mini Nag missiles and attach nuclear tips."

"Of course, I am scientist," said Turgo, "but missiles, they very new, no?"

"Yes, the very latest model. And they should be on the way to the port of Mumbai as we speak."

"That Muhammad, he's good all right," mused Sergey.

"It's who you know, and he knows everyone."

"I bet he does," said uncle Sergey, convinced that he saw a very slight reddening of Sarah's cheeks. "And what do you want from us? More importantly, how much will you pay?"

"We'd like you to arrange shipment of the missiles out of Mumbai through the Port of Newark. Then provide technicians to reassemble them and add nuclear tips. Shalah tells me that you already have safe houses in the New Jersey area."

"And then?"

"Fire them of course, and hit the target."

"This Newark, it's close to New York City, right?" asked Turgo

"Right. About sixteen kilometers, but the launch will be North of Newark, more like thirty kilometers away from Manhattan."

"So what is the target?"

"The target is Ground Zero. Or, as they are starting to call it, now that the tower is near completion, Freedom Tower."

"Ground What? What is that?" asked Turgo.

"What was left after Bin Laden destroyed the twin towers on nine eleven." Sarah turned to Sergey. "Can you do it?" she asked.

"For how much?"

"Ten million dollars now, another five million when you hit the target," she paused, "with both missiles of course."

Uncle Sergey looked over at Turgo who smiled nervously. Sergey could almost see the dollar signs in his retinas.

"How much time?" asked Turgo.

"It must be right on the anniversary of the Bin Laden attack. September 11, 8.34 AM. U.S. eastern standard time."

"That gives us roughly two months," observed Uncle Sergey.

"Can you do it?"

"It is too little time, unless we get the missiles there within two weeks," complained Turgo with his characteristic negativity that attracted a disapproving glance from Sergey.

"For that amount of money, we can do it," said Sergey.

"Excellent!"

"And now the down payment?"

"Do you have an Hawala?"

"Of course. He is my nephew."

"Tell him to call this number in Dubai, code word zero." Sarah handed over a cell phone, but then pulled it back. She had forgotten Shalah's exhortation:

We must, absolutely must, have the nuclear tips. The operation is nothing without them.

Holding on to the phone, she looked hard into uncle Sergey's face, examining every line on it, watching his eyelids flutter, nostrils pulled down, his bottom teeth, stained with nicotine, pressing on his upper lip. "You understand," she warned, "that we must have the nuclear tips. Without them the operation is nothing."

"No problem my dear. We already have a store of nuclear materials tucked away in the USA. We saved them for just this purpose. My brother in America has it all set up."

"That's very good to know," said Sarah, then, suddenly realizing what Sergey had said, looking very puzzled, she asked, "wait a minute, you said your brother in America? My father is part of your operation? Surely not!"

Uncle Sergey coughed a little to clear his throat. He had made a slip. "Did I say that?" he asked with feigned surprise, "no, of course, not your dad. Good heavens, could you imagine that? The poor old man is stuck in the 19th century and will never get out of it, you know that."

"I do," said Sarah suspiciously, "so who do you mean?"

"It was no one. Just an operative. I don't know how I could have said that. Naturally, I think of all my operatives as family," he said unconvincingly.

Sarah leaned across to her uncle sticking her chin out just like her mother did when she was upset and determined to get her way, which wasn't often. "Uncle Sergey, or whoever you are, you need to come clean with me. I can't do business with someone who is holding back on me, who I can't trust."

There was a long silence, broken only by Sergey clearing his throat, and Turgo strangely beginning to hum, almost under his breath. Sergey had to reveal the truth. "All right. But I tell you it's not a good idea to know too many names of those who you are dealing with in such a big operation as this one. Anyway, your boss probably already knows who it is."

"Well?"

"It is my little brother Nicholas, your uncle. He is fourteen years younger than me, sixteen younger than your dad."

"But why is he in America? Is he actually American?"

"He left Russia when he was just fifteen years old, just around the Chernobyl disaster and never came back. Then some years later I heard through my other contacts that he was involved in exporting cars out of Newark, and we have done business ever since."

"I don't believe you. I'll ask my dad."

"There's no point. Your mom and dad know nothing of him, least of all that he has been in Newark all the time you have been in New York."

"I want his phone number."

"That's not a good idea, Sarah. It puts him at risk; you and me as well."

"Give it to me, or our deal stops right now."

Uncle Sergey got up and paced up and down the bear rug, looking at the bear's face staring up at him. Then he sat down again. "You promise not to call him until after the successful completion of our operation?"

"Fair enough. Give it to me."

Uncle Sergey opened his phone and scrolled down his contact list. He tapped the contact and showed the phone to Sarah, who copied it into her own phone.

"Thank you uncle Sergey," she said with a sweet smile, "now where were we?"

"I said we had nuclear materials all ready at our safe house in Newark."

"Oh, yes. I was about to say again that Shalah will be really pissed off if the attack is not nuclear. He has heard that you were pushing for a bio toxin attack with ricin."

"Ricin? No, not at all. We can do it of course, and it would be very spectacular if I may say so. A real first in terrorism!"

"Yes, very good. And I could do it too!" added Turgo, trying to be helpful.

"Uncle, no! There will be hell to pay if you do ricin. No bio toxins of any kind, understand? We want nuclear tips."

"Of course, of course. We are well prepared for nuclear. All that is required is for Turgo to meet up with the nuclear components. "

Turgo smiled and wriggled in his seat, crossing and uncrossing his legs. Sarah handed over a phone showing the text of the Hawala number which uncle Sergey began to copy. But Sarah stopped him. "No, you must make the calls from this phone. Make sure you destroy it after you've made the calls."

Uncle Sergey raised his tea cup and Sarah and Turgo joined him. "To nine eleven two!" He said with great satisfaction.

9. The Sting

All was not well for would-be terrorists in Newark. Agent Fred Lee had seen to that. Immediately after nine eleven he sent agents to hang out around the mosque and he put aside a special slush fund to pay off Arabic speaking immigrants to inform him of any new arrivals from Saudi Arabia or elsewhere in the Middle East. It didn't take long for him to discover that some of these "pee-ays" (petty agents) as he called them, were taking money from the NYPD as well. So he paid a visit to the NYPD police commissioner and they came to an understanding of sorts. He wanted to do a sting operation and the commissioner was against it. But since the NYPD had no jurisdiction over anything that happened in Newark, the commissioner had no choice but to go along with it or his cover would be blown and that would be a disaster. They parted cordially, both agreeing to share all intelligence they collected, both having no intention of doing so.

Lee was determined to carry out his sting operation. These stings never failed, always resulted in lots of arrests, the juries always convicted in spite of the usual entrapment defense put up by the government paid defense lawyers. Most important, though, a successful sting operation would get him noticed in D.C. and set him on a sure path out of this rat-hole they called Newark.

The day before, he picked up his vintage FBI style dark gray suit from the dry cleaners run by immigrants from Libya, or so they said. He gave them extra good tips and they gave him excellent service and any information they thought he might be able to use. In fact, he first met his future quarries in the dry cleaners. They had heavy accents and said they were from Iraq. They laughed and joked around and seemed like regular guys. But Fred Lee knew better. The dry cleaners gave him their addresses and he sent a couple of his agents to pal up with them. One of them worked as a security guard for a local private security outfit, the other drove a taxi. They went to the local mosque regularly so their heads were sure to be filled with the hate-America drivel spewed forth by the local mullah. It

101

didn't take long for his agents to rope them in. The hardest part of the operation was to get a hold of an old non-functioning shoulder-fired grenade launcher. He had contacts at the armory in Hoboken. It took several weeks, but finally they were able to smuggle one out of the armory and get it to him.

*

This morning, Fred Lee shaved with his best razor that he saved for special occasions. After each stroke, he ran his fingers over his skin behind the razor. It was beautifully smooth, as smooth as, well, let's not say it. He combed his short cropped sandy hair and admired his figure in the mirror, naked except for a tightly fitting undershirt and bikini style briefs. He carefully slid into his tailored white shirt perfectly pressed by his Libyans; each button he meticulously pressed through its button hole. He followed with his suit pants, slipping the elastic suspenders over his shoulders. Next was his gun holster, which fitted snuggly over his shoulder, the gun nestling close to his arm pit. The jacket fitted nicely over all, leaving just a slight bulge where his gun was. Exactly as he wanted it. He patted himself down. It was hard for him to leave the mirror. He released his phone from the charger and bounded down the stairs to the front door and out to the leafy streets of Ridgewood, his haven from Newark. Just around the corner he would stop off for his usual donut and coffee at Donut Queen where Agent Crosby would be waiting for him.

*

Take President Obama, add about a foot and, with a tweak or two, you have Agent Danforth Crosby. The tweaks are significant, though, mainly because of director Lee's insistence that Agent Crosby have his hair done in dread locks so he would look more authentic African American and blend in with the local culture. Crosby offered to grow a bushy beard as well, but for the director that would have been too much. "We blend, we don't become," the director liked to repeat in his most superior tone. Crosby pointed out that if he were Islamic, it would be part of his religion so he would be within his rights to have a bushy beard.

"But you're not Islamic, Crosby," said the director shaking his finger at him, "who do you think you are, the ACLU?" At which he simply turned away as if there were no possibility for Crosby to counter that perfect truth.

At 5.00 a.m. Agent Crosby was up feeding his one-year old. Now this was fortunate because it was the morning when he had to be out at

Ridgewood to pick up his boss in time to get back to Newark to conduct surveillance of the Newark mosque, monitor the crowds as they left after dawn prayer. This time of the morning it would be about a twenty minute drive and he would pick him up at the Donut Queen as usual. He got really annoyed with his boss because he had insisted that they had to do this operation for the dawn prayer session. There was no good reason that it be then. The midday Dhuhr, about 1.00 pm. in Newark, would do just as well. It was especially annoying given that his boss would oversleep as usual and he'd be left double parked outside the Donut Queen. He usually dropped the kids off at daycare on his way to pick up the director, but this morning he could not, so he had made a deal with his wife that she would take the kids to day care and that he would pick them up.

Agent Crosby managed to quiet the baby and as soon as he heard his wife moving about upstairs, he stepped out into the dirty street of Newark. The place was basically a slum, but again it was not his choice to live there. Director Lee had told him that he must live "in the hood" as he insultingly called it, as part of his blending into the culture. Then Lee added insult to injury by making him pick him up every morning in the company car, and some company car it was, a Honda Fit into which it was a miracle to be observed every morning that a person so tall, with limbs like Spiderman's, managed to get every part of himself inside that tiny car, let alone drive it.

Agent Crosby arrived at the Donut Queen at exactly 6.10 am, but as expected, the director was nowhere to be seen. So he double parked as usual and bought himself a long black coffee and three jelly donuts. He had read the entire local paper that lay on the counter by the time his boss showed up.

"Good morning, sir," Crosby said.

"I suppose that's your third?" remarked Lee, pointing to the donut.

"Well, I've been waiting for a while."

"You'll get fat and have a heart attack," he said and continued without waiting for Crosby to respond, "I'll take a large coffee, with three fingers of half-and-half, three sugars and a glazed donut."

"Hey let me get it, sir," offered Crosby.

"How many times have I told you, Crosby, that it's not ethical? We each pay for our own, no matter where or when. Are you eating jelly-filled again?"

"I am. I can't give them up," smiled Crosby.

"Danforth, how many times have I told you that the jelly will spurt out and drip down on your suit?"

"It's worth the risk, sir. And please don't call me Danforth. Only my wife calls me that, and I don't like her calling me that either."

"In any case, Crosby, listen to me. FBI men never take risks, not even with jelly donuts."

"OK. I'll try sir."

"We're doing a pickup today. How will it look if you show up and put cuffs on the suspects and there's red jelly all down your jacket?"

"Not too good, I guess."

"Then don't do it again, or next time I will put it in your evaluation."

Crosby tried changing the topic. "So how are we doing for time? Will the men be in place?"

"We're running a bit late, but I called up the mosque to find out when this morning's session ended. Won't be until 7.00 AM. They have some visiting mullah from Texas or somewhere. The ATF guys have been told. They'll be in their positions by the time we get there."

They both looked out the window to the street just in time to see a parking attendant about to write a ticket for double parking. Director Lee was by her side in a flash. He looked around, then showed his FBI badge and said, in his most serious tone, "Officer, FBI. We're on special assignment."

"So I see," replied the attendant, eyeing his donut. She put her docket book away and moved on. "Have a nice day," she called over her shoulder.

*

Most likely, Director Lee had misunderstood the prayer times he had been told over the phone. In any case, their quarries had still not appeared in front of the mosque, in spite of many comings and goings. Crosby had finally found a parking spot just across from the mosque, thanks to the little Honda that could fit in just about any little gap. Director Lee had long ago told the ATF guys to step down and be on call, await his signal. Midday prayer had come and should have been gone. Director Lee had settled down for a nap, having ordered Crosby to remain vigilant. Crosby, chronically short of sleep because of his kids not sleeping through, slept soundly too. It was only thanks to a sharp pain in both his legs, pins and needles of the most excruciating kind, that awoke him and he noticed a stream of people exiting the mosque. He combated his pins and needles by opening a power bar to munch. And just as he took the first bite, Director Lee awoke suddenly with a shiver.

"What's this? Crosby, you're eating on duty! You know that's against the rules! Only allowed when you are working undercover."

"We are undercover, aren't we?"

"Get rid of it or I'll write you up! This is the second time today!"

"Sorry, sir. It's gone." He crammed the entire bar into his mouth and chewed ferociously.

"They're coming out." Lee opened his phone and tapped out his instructions to the ATF. Agent Crosby stirred and opened his door. His legs would not move. "Aahh, my legs," he winced.

"Come on Crosby. Let's go. I think I see them."

"Sir, couldn't we use a larger car? This is really hard for me."

"I've told you many times. It's FBI policy to blend in with our communities. We don't want to turn them off by sporting a fancy big car. Hearts and minds, remember. Hearts and minds."

Lee sprinted across the road followed by Agent Crosby, limping badly. Suddenly Lee stopped almost in the center of the road and pointedly surveyed the rooftops above. He raised his hand with thumb thrust upwards. He rushed forward just in time to confront two men in western dress, wearing telltale black and white checkered scarves.

Director Lee stood tall, all five foot five inches of him, holding up his badge. "FBI! You are under arrest for conspiracy to commit a terrorist act. Cuff them Agent!"

A crowd of onlookers exiting the mosque began to gather as it watched Agent Crosby efficiently handcuff the suspects.

"Very good, Agent. At least they taught you something useful at Quantico. Read them their rights."

Agent Crosby pulled out a crumpled piece of paper and began to read them their rights.

"You can't say them by memory?" asked Lee incredulously.

"I don't want to mess up sir," Crosby responded.

The suspects stood petrified. The crowd of onlookers was getting larger and some were inching closer. Someone called out, "What did they do?" and another, "Leave them alone you bullies!"

Director Lee was trying to find his phone. "I'll call for the pickup," he said, "and you better pat them down. They might have knives or guns."

Crosby, however, had messed up reading their rights and had started over so now was trying to pat them down at the same time.

"You have the right to remain silent—"

"OK. Bring the van around. We've got them," ordered director Lee.

A black Escalade pulled up and the rear doors opened. The suspects still had not spoken. Now the small crowd was becoming an angry mob. Onlookers began to jeer and they were closing in. One spat at the feet of

Director Lee and moved as if to attack him, or at least that is what Lee later testified. Said he thought he had a knife. So he looked up to one of his spotters and gave the signal. There was a loud crack and a bullet whistled past Lee's ear, or so he thought. He dropped to the ground yelling, "Down! Down! We're under attack!" The bullet crashed harmlessly into the pavement, spraying small shards of concrete into the crowd which quickly dispersed, people running frantically in every direction.

Crosby, either unaware of events or completely calm, ushered the suspects into the Escalade. "Where are we taking them, sir? He asked.

Lee struggled to his feet, brushing down his best suit. "To my office of course!" he answered.

"But we can't hold them there sir. We don't have enough room."

"My office! I'll follow in the Honda." But Lee didn't follow, he led. He placed the blue flashing light on top of the Honda Fit and zipped forward, speeding through the traffic, squeezing through tight spaces, like a roller derby player. Of course, he went through the ten red lights between the mosque and the FBI headquarters which were located on Washington Street. He arrived well before the van which had been held up in the traffic snarls mostly caused by Lee running the red lights. He screeched to a halt right in front of the Grand Old Liberty Insurance building and parked illegally. He flashed his badge to the parking officer who stood, hands on hips, not at all pleased.

"FBI! Counter terrorism operation in progress! Make way! Make Way!" ordered Lee.

The Escalade pulled in. Agent Crosby stepped out, grinning. "Now this is my kind of car," he said to the director. The back doors opened and Crosby awkwardly grabbed at the suspects trying to help them down. They were now in leg chains so they half fell out of the van as Crosby pulled at them. He then prodded them towards the entrance.

The FBI office was on the top, fifteenth floor of the Old Liberty Insurance building, the oldest multi-story building in Newark, complete with beehive turret on the top. The suspects shuffled towards the grand brassy entrance, the revolving doors spinning as people came out. Agent Crosby pushed the suspects towards the doors and they fell down, unable to cope with the speed of the doors because of the chains on their legs. The door was jammed and someone else was trapped on the other side. Crosby tried to push the door around, but it would not budge. The person on the other side was yelling obscenities. Crosby looked to his boss for help.

"Pull them out Agent! Pull them out! Didn't they teach you anything at Quantico?"

The suspects were panic stricken. One began to scream. Director Lee ignored it all and continued with his orders. "And what about the rocket launcher? Bring it too!"

Agent Crosby left the suspects to their plight and returned to the Escalade, pulled out a large shoulder firing grenade launcher and carried it towards the revolving door. The crowd of onlookers reeled back in horror when they saw it. One of the onlookers, rather frightened, opened the side door and beckoned to Crosby. At that moment, a loud police siren sounded, immediately followed by the arrival of a Newark Police vehicle. It was Captain Buck Buick.

"You guys need a regular cop, that's what you need," called Buick. "Hey, Freddy! Why didn't you tell me you were doing your pick-up?"

Crosby, Lee, the crowd, all watched Buick in silence. "Just a minute," he said as he strode forward and wrenched the door back, dragging the suspects out. They cried out as their limbs were twisted and squashed against the door. "OK animals. Let's go!" Buick pulled them upright then roughly pushed them forward to the open side door.

The suspects were traumatized. The helpful citizen kept the door open, but tried to stand back as far as he could as though he were about to be infected with vermin.

"Are you gonna keep 'em over night?" asked Buick.

"We'll need longer than that."

"Then why didn't you call me? We can use the Newark lock-up. You don't have one, do you?"

"We don't. But rules are that I have to question them at official FBI headquarters. There's the U.S. flag and everything. You don't have one in your lock-up do you?"

"You guys are really dopey."

"What was that?"

"Hope it's gonna work. Reckon you've got a good case?"

"Watertight. We never lose with these stings. Juries always convict."

Buick and Lee stepped into the now functioning revolving door. They entered the old marble lobby which was laced with lots of shiny brass and indiscernible sculptures set into the ceiling and walls. Agent Crosby finally entered through the side door and placed the rocket launcher against the wall, beside the elevator, which he then held open.

Buick roughly pushed the suspects in. "Come on animals!" he growled. They all piled in and rode the elevator to the fifteenth floor.

"Captain Buick. They're suspects. Innocent until proved guilty. Treat them with respect," cautioned Lee.

"You want help with the interrogation?"

"Not from you. The FBI knows best how to question a terrorist suspect, especially when it's been a sting operation. Don't want to mess up our case."

"As you wish. But they won't break for you softies. Call me when you need me. It's more than just this one case, you know. We have to find out when it will be."

"When what will be?"

"You know, our special mission with the mayor."

"But that's the point. We have the terrorists. We've foiled the plot."

The elevator reached the fifteenth floor. As Buick pushed the suspects out the door he called, "Yeh, right! I'll await your call." He looked with amusement at Lee. The elevator doors closed and he hit the button for the lobby as and he chuckled to himself all the way down.

*

The FBI office took up a small corner of the fifteenth floor. It was one room in which were crammed a very large desk with an exotically leather padded desk chair, a very large U.S. Flag standing to the side, a small student sized desk with wooden chair in one corner for Agent Crosby, and one chair for visitors placed squarely in front of the Director's desk. Director Lee slipped quickly behind his desk. Agent Crosby, unsure what to do, left the suspects standing and went to sit at his desk.

"Agent Crosby, another chair for the suspects," ordered Lee, as he leafed through a folder on his desk. Crosby brought his chair to the suspects and they struggled to sit, unused to managing their chains and hand cuffs.

"Now gentlemen, let's talk civilly, shall we? Our undercover agent has you on video buying a rocket launcher. Before we picked you up, we paid a visit to your home and retrieved it."

Lee looked around the room. "Agent, where's the launcher?" he said with annoyance.

"Oh. I left it in the elevator," Crosby apologized. He made to leave but stopped, worried that he was leaving his boss alone with two terrorists.

"Go on, go get it!" ordered Lee, and Crosby obeyed.

Lee continued to address the suspects. "Of course, the launcher is non-functioning. You couldn't have done any damage." He looked at each of the suspects trying to make eye contact. They looked at the floor. "What are your names?" he asked. They did not answer. Of course, he had their names in the folder right in front of him, but he had to admit that he did not know which was which. They were both about the same height and build, both had lots of black wavy hair, both had black bushy beards, both had checkered scarves. "Your names?" he repeated, this time in a much louder voice. Still they remained silent. Lee drummed his fingers on his prized cherry wood desk that he had personally picked out at Raymore and Flannigan. "Alright, then, if that's the way you want it. I'll call you both Abdul. You," he pointed to the one on his left, "you're Abdul One, and your pal is Abdul Two."

"We are innocent. You tricked us!" blurted out Abdul One.

"We want a lawyer," complained Abdul Two, "this is America. We have a right to our lawyer."

"Of course you do. It's only right. Do you want to call one now?"

"Yes," replied Abdul Two, "this is wrong."

"We were just fooling around," said Abdul One.

"Buying a launcher isn't just fooling around."

Agent Crosby returned with the launcher.

"Is this the launcher?" asked Lee, pointing to the weapon.

"Might be," shrugged Abdul One.

"You were planning a terrorist attack. When were you planning to carry it out? Nine eleven?"

"We had no plans," said Abdul One. "We were just fooling around! Please, you must believe us!"

"You'll get for certain life in prison without parole, maybe the death penalty," Lee said, looking at them very seriously, but still getting no eye contact. "If you cooperate, I can try to get the U.S. Prosecutor to go easy on you."

"But there's nothing more to tell," complained Abdul Two with a whimper, "you know everything. You have it all on video, you said."

"We want to confirm the planned date of the attack, and the names of others involved. Just two people can't carry out an attack of this magnitude. Especially if the target is Ground Zero, and it is, right?"

Abdul One looked alarmed. "No! No! We know nothing of this."

"There are no others!" added Abdul Two.

"I want names and target confirmation," demanded Lee.

The suspects began to sob. They bowed their heads as far as they could.

"Please believe us. We are just ordinary men with families and jobs. I am a taxi driver. He is a security guard," pleaded Abdul One.

"We know," answered Lee calmly.

"We want our lawyer please," said Abdul Two, daring to lift his eyes just a little.

"As you wish. But I could make it much easier for you." Lee signaled to Crosby to hand Abdul Two the telephone.

"I want to call my wife," said Abdul Two.

"Wife or lawyer. Your choice," said Lee.

Abdul Two made his call and began an hysterical conversation with his wife. It was all in Arabic. Abdul One sat hunched rocking back and forth on the chair. He muttered to himself in Arabic.

Agent Crosby then leaned over the director's desk to speak to his boss. "Sir, this is the day I have to pick up my kids from day care. I have to leave in ten minutes."

Lee pushed back into his chair, and cranked the handle to raise the chair to its highest position. He shook his finger at Crosby. "God, Country, then Family. Wait till we're done," he lectured.

"But sir, we had an agreement."

"We're dealing with terrorism here, Agent Crosby! It's not just some common crime!"

"Please, sir! Let's call in Captain Buick then, to take my place. My wife's away. I can't put my kids at risk."

Director Lee stared at his underling and then at the suspects who were now conversing rapidly in Arabic. Suddenly, they appeared to him as impenetrable, hostile Al Qaeda operatives. But he had made an agreement. And it would be a good excuse to call in Buick. "All right. Then before you go, call Buick and arrange for him to pick up our friends here and transfer them to the Newark PD lock-up."

"Thank you. I won't forget this, sir."

Agent Crosby snatched the phone from the suspects and called Captain Buick.

10. Extraction

The front end of the Bangalore Five Star weapons factory didn't look like a factory at all. It rose to four stories, a gleaming glass and steel structure, with geometric shapes protruding here and there, set in an expanse of cleared fields ploughed and flattened, ready to plant a huge lawn. In contrast there were, nestled around the structure, a higgledy-piggledy array of shanties and makeshift tents of local workers and their families. Dr. Jamal squatted under a lean-to that was strung to the branch of the one sole tree left standing. Squatting next to him was a very dark skinned South Indian. They spoke in Telugu.

"And how are things in Vizag," asked Jamal.

"They are well. My father sends his regards. And I will be married late next month, if the planets are aligned properly, but everything looks good. You will come to the wedding?"

"Of course. And with the money you are getting, I expect a very big wedding!"

"It will be the greatest wedding ever held in Vizag."

"Your bride is also from Vizag?"

"Yes, but I don't think you would know her. Her family moved to Vizag after you went away to Oxford."

"Ah, my times in Vizag. We had such a fun time. Got up to lots of mischief!"

"Yes, we did, Jamal. But now we must be serious," he said half joking.

"All right then. So let's get down to business. The Nags are already disassembled?" asked Jamal.

"Yes, and packed in one compact crate."

"How big?"

"About the size of a Tata Nano."

"And the truck? Where is it?"

"We will use a Five Star truck."

"Really? But how?"

111

"It's easy. With the money you pay, it's easy."

"I am pleased to hear it. You must have paid out a lot?"

"Well, as a matter of fact, I do need another $500,000."

"What? But I already gave you a million for expenses, plus a million each for the missiles and launcher."

"I know, I know. But I had to reach the executive director — the top dog, you know — to smooth out the operation."

"But it's half a million more than we agreed!"

"The top dog drove a hard bargain. He could blow the whistle on the whole thing. He wants half a million to look the other way."

Jamal's legs were cramped. He was not used to squatting like this anymore. He stood, turned to face the factory and stretched his arms and legs. "The truck rolls out tonight?" he asked.

"Yes, for sure."

"It will be in Mumbai in two days max?"

"With a Five Star truck, it will be a smooth drive. No questions."

"OK. You win." Jamal handed over his cell phone. "Call this number for the money. Code name Zero."

The South Indian grinned broadly. "Thank you, thank you! You are a Sahib, a perfect gentleman!"

"Here is the paperwork for delivery to the ship in Mumbai. It's a freighter called the Maple Leaf, sailing under a Greek flag. Indian customs should already be taken care of."

"No worries Sahib. No worries!"

"If there's a problem at the Port, call the other number in the cell phone contact list."

"Yes, Sahib. Anything else?"

"When you're done with the job, you must destroy the phone," he said, "and that's enough of the Sahib. It's not funny anymore."

The South Indian turned towards the Five Star factory and walked towards the rear of the building, picking his way across the ploughed field. Jamal opened another cell phone and made a call.

*

Shalah Muhammad sat at his favorite table at his favorite hotel in the world, the Mumbai Taj Mahal. He sat outdoors, eating a large English breakfast of eggs and bacon, even though it was well into afternoon. He gazed at the Gate of India which threw a long shadow across the pavement over which tourists wandered here and there, taking photos of each other, trying to frame photos that caught everything, the languid cerulean sea lapping at the stone embankment, the arched Gate of India, the white frilled Taj. This was his idea of bliss.

He gulped down a mouthful of egg, licking the yellow yoke from the corners of his mouth, followed by a slurp of coffee. He looked around the restaurant and mused how awful it was that such an idyllic spot was recently the scene of an horrific terrorist attack. There was no sign of it now. Had he been in charge, this place would not have been a target. Anyway, he knew nothing of it. It was the stupid Pakistani ISI that did it. You couldn't trust them. He tried to have as little to do with them as possible. And he chose his Pakistani operatives with great care, making sure as far as possible that they had no links to the ISI. He had just lit a cigarette when his phone rang. It was Sarah.

"Kommie! Right on time! Where are you?"

"I'm out walking in this beautiful place overlooking a waterfall in the mountains of Kyrgyzstan."

"And how is your uncle?"

"He is fine, everything is fine, but I suspect that uncle does not want to do nuclear."

"What do you mean?" Muhammad was annoyed.

"He hasn't said no, but he and his scientist Turgo say that ricin would be a much more startling attack."

"I said I want nuclear."

"I know, I know. And he'll still do nuclear. It's just that he says that they can make it cheaply and easily in the U.S. Uncle says Turgo is an expert on ricin."

"And the delivery mechanism?" asked Muhammad aggressively.

"We didn't talk about that."

"This is bad. In fact I've a good mind to go elsewhere."

"Darling, that would not be wise, now that they know what we are planning.

"I've told you not to call me Darling."

"Sorry — Shali — is that all right?"

"It's better than Darling."

"They don't know what they are talking about. It's never been used successfully before. The Japs botched it on their subway."

"Uncle says he will do it for half the price of nuclear."

"I'm beginning not to trust your relatives."

"He also says that Turgo already has nuclear components stashed away in the U.S. So transporting would not be a problem."

"Then why are we talking about ricin?"

"Uncle thought, and I do too, that you should understand what options were available. Like buying an energy efficient car, you know?"

"I have another call. We shouldn't be talking about this by phone anyway. I hope you're using the scrambler phone. Tell him it must be nuclear, or no deal." Muhammad abruptly closed his phone and took a deep draw of his cigarette. His phone rang immediately, playing the first measure of "Stars and Stripes."

"Yes?"

"Is this Mr. Zero?" It was the dentist Dr. Jamal.

"Who is this?"

"You know who this is."

"OK. OK. I told you not to call me," answered Muhammad with considerable annoyance.

"I know. But I wanted to let you know that the extractions have gone very well and the X-rays revealed nothing out of place. However, you will be billed another $500,000 for additional X-rays that were required."

"My insurance paid you more than that amount up front," replied Muhammad clearly conveying a threat.

"Oh, there has been a misunderstanding. In the interest of customer satisfaction, I will not charge you for the additional amount."

"I should think so."

"I have made arrangements for Dr. Maple Leaf to contact you upon arrival in America for a follow-up appointment."

"Excellent. I am feeling much better already." Muhammad closed his phone and leaned back with satisfaction. The sun was inching towards the horizon. Soon the sea would take on its evening luminescence.

*

The large crane swung a container on to the deck of the freighter. Though it was late afternoon at the Port of Mumbai, the sun baked its heat into the pier. Dr. Jamal, standing in the shadow of the crane, watched nervously as a customs officer shouted to the crane operator to stop the loading and began to return the container to the pier. Jamal had thought everything was covered, but he knew from experience that last minute games to extract more bribes were likely. His dock worker through whom he had funneled his initial bribes gesticulated widely, and delivered a torrent of abuse at the customs officer. Jamal reached into his pocket and counted out five $100 notes. He signaled to the dock worker. An incident like this could draw in other officers whom he had not paid off. It could kill the whole project which Jamal knew full well would mean his demise. Shalah Muhammad took personal pleasure in punishing failure.

At last the dock worker saw his signal and let up with his abuse. Jamal's policy was never to hand a bribe directly to a government official. He always had others do it for him. Multiple layers of corruption were more difficult for investigators to uncover. And it made it easier to ensnare the investigators themselves into the web of corruption. It was not so much the fear of getting caught that concerned Jamal, but the delay it would cause, which would upset the finely organized plan of attack he knew Shalah Muhammad always had in motion.

The dock worker came across. The crane had stopped moving the cargo, and the container hung in midair, half way from the dock, half way to the freighter. Keeping his back to the customs officer, Jamal counted out five $100 bills to the dock worker, plus another for the worker himself who smiled broadly. The customs officer continued to order the container be returned to the dock, but not so forcefully. In fact, he struck up a friendly conversation with the crane operator. With a subtly cowed demeanor the dock worker approached the officer who immediately saw that a resolution was in the offing. He clicked his heels and came to attention. "May I be of service?" He asked politely.

"I just want to thank you for all your help," said the dock worker as he proffered a hand shake, "thank you very much for your excellent service."

They shook hands and in the dock worker's palm was $300 folded into the size of a strip of chewing gum.

"The Government of India at your service sir!" answered the officer as he saluted and clicked his heels once again.

As if on cue, the crane sprang to life and the container was reloaded on to the freighter. In no time at all, the freighter sounded its horn and Jamal watched with great satisfaction and relief as it slowly inched away from the pier.

*

After a brief diversion for an Asian breakfast, which he had missed greatly since leaving Mumbai, Manish Das approached 1 Police Plaza, NYPD HQ via the pedestrian walkway. He was nervous and uncertain about doing this because his boss Professor MacIver had told him that it would be a waste of time, though he had not forbade him from trying. The entire approach to 1 Police Plaza was a stark example of the effects of Nine Eleven. Park Row, once a four lane artery that linked the financial district to Chinatown had been closed off because NYPD feared a terrorist attack on its HQ. It was the direct outcome of his professor's campaign to get New York to harden its targets.

Das looked up at the squat thirteen story building. It seemed too small a building to house the nerve center of the NYPD, the largest police force in the world. After several checks of his ID, he made it into the lobby and was directed up to the sixth floor where he had an appointment to meet with the Assistant Commissioner in charge of crime prevention. He was immediately confronted by a desk sergeant. She sat bolt upright behind a large, elevated desk. Das showed his ID and was immediately directed to sit as if in a doctor's waiting room.

An hour went by. Das played with his cell phone. Finally, he lost patience and approached the desk.

"My appointment was for 8.00 AM. It's now 9.00 AM."

"Superintendent Askanazy is very busy. There's a lot of crime to prevent in this city, you know," she answered officiously.

"I'm here on behalf of Distinguished Professor MacIver. It is urgent. There is a lot to do and very little time left to do it."

"In this country we patiently wait our turn. Sit down and the commissioner will be here shortly."

Das paced back and forth in front of the window which looked out on lower Manhattan. He jangled the keys in his pocket, played with his iPhone, doing Google street view of the streets he saw below. At last, he was called.

"Mr. What's-your-name?" called the desk sergeant.

"Das. Manish Das."

"The commissioner will see you now."

Das entered the assistant commissioner's office, which was but a larger version of the desk sergeant's. Assistant commissioner Askanazy, a tall, overweight fellow with flushed puffy cheeks, stood in front of his desk, his sizeable rear end leaning against it, arms folded. "So what do you want now?" he asked.

"Professor MacIver asked me to personally hand you the risk assessment protocols that will help you decide what places need protection and what kind of target hardening would be appropriate."

"I already know the targets at risk. Everyone knows that."

"This is scientific sir. Not based on whimsy."

"Whims-what? Speak English for Christ sake!"

"Apologies commissioner. Risk assessment is a scientific way of doing it. Eliminates personal bias or anything else."

"It's bull shit, that's what it is."

"Science isn't bull, Sir."

"Look, I don't need any professor, least of all his student lackey to tell me how to do my job."

"Commissioner, we must act quickly. There could be an attack any day. We must know what to protect and how to mitigate the fallout of any attack."

"We do that by arresting terrorists and criminals and getting them off the streets. That's how we prevent crime around here."

"But sir, the mayor!"

"I work for the Commissioner, not the mayor, that hand-wringing liberal progressive!"

"Sir! This has nothing to do with politics! As my professor says, 'This is science, not politics'!"

"Yeh, sure. Just shows how you pointy headed academics know nothing of the real world."

"Here are the protocols, commissioner. I am available any time and as much as you want, to help in implementing them." Das dug into his briefcase and thrust a handful of papers towards Askanazy.

"Just leave them with the sergeant on your way out."

Das took out his iPhone and began dialing. "Maybe you would like to speak directly with Professor MacIver?"

Askanazy stared over Das's shoulder.

"Sir? This is Das, sir. I'm in assistant commissioner Askanazy's office. He says it's unnecessary to do a risk assessment, sir."

"I warned you not to go to him," answered MacIver.

"Would you speak with him sir?"

"No point. I'll speak with the mayor."

"OK, sir. OK. Bye, sir." Das looked to Askanazy. "He says he will speak with the mayor, sir."

Askanazy's face reddened. "Don't forget to leave the protocols with the sergeant on your way out," he directed, then turned his back, walked behind his desk and stood, looking out the window.

Das stumbled backwards, then turned and hurried out, stopping briefly to leave the protocol papers with the desk Sergeant.

"Thank you so much!" she said.

His iPhone rang. It was the sound of Jai Ho, the Slumdog Millionaire hit.

"Hello Professor, sir."

"The mayor will do it with her people. She's moving officers on to it from the traffic division. It will be better, anyway."

"Should I go to City Hall now sir?"

"Yes. Take the protocols and training materials. Do as much as you can."

Das reached on to the sergeant's desk and retrieved the protocols.

"Changed your mind?" asked the sergeant sarcastically.

Das left without a word.

11. Enhanced Interrogation

The Special Operations Division of the Newark Police Department on 472 Orange Street looked more like an auto body shop than a police bureau. It was a low box of a building, sitting on a small block that was concreted over like many such blocks in Newark, weeds, some of them thriving, growing up through cracks. A bunch of black trash bags bulging with who knows what contents leaned against one side of the building.

Monica Silenzio parked her 2012 Volvo wagon across the street from the PD in a lot encircled, in excellent security style, by an eight foot chain link fence, barbed wire at the top. Her Volvo looked out of place among the other Ford and Chevy SUVs and the occasional motor bike. She knew that for a single woman of her age, people disapproved of her driving such a vehicle. Only married women with the regulation two kids and a husband who drove a Toyota Camry were supposed to have one of those. "It's no wonder you're single when you drive a car like that," her women friends would say. "You should get a brightly colored sports car. The guys will be buzzing around you like bees to a honey pot," imagery she did not appreciate. She had been surprised that MacIver had not made such a comment. He didn't seem to notice her car at all. Not that it mattered. In any case, she liked her car because it showed what she was about, safe, secure and comfortable. Given her meager beginnings, growing up in Coalwood, West Virginia, the chances of her becoming who she was today were incredibly slim. Her dad, a wizened, always exhausted coal miner, who died before he was fifty, wanted nothing more than for her to marry a coal miner and have a bunch of kids. She left home as soon as she could and worked her way first through community college then transferred to John Jay College. Occasionally she saw her mom, now in her eighties, still living in Coalwood, now pretty much a ghost town. Her mom was happy enough. She had a few friends her age who had stayed in the small row of company town houses built for miners back in the fifties. "I probably should go see her more often," Silenzio thought as she crossed the street to the Special

Operations Division. She looked back at her Volvo and clicked the remote to lock it.

It took her some time to locate the interrogation room, such as it was. In fact, she had trouble finding the front door since the whole place seemed to be composed of garage doors, behind which, she presumed, were garages. When she finally did find her way in through one of the garages that was open, she found an empty holding cell. She asked a duty officer for directions to the interrogation room. There wasn't a permanent one, he said, they were using a makeshift section of one of the garages. Silenzio understood. So there would be no cameras, no one-way mirrors. It was through the next door to the right. Captain Buick was there with two suspects, the duty officer said.

Silenzio opened the door quietly and slipped in. The place smelled oily like a garage and there were tools and other vehicle paraphernalia pushed into one corner. The rocket launcher was lying among the tools. There were two chairs on which the suspects, Abdul One and Abdul Two sat, cuffed and chained, whimpering, looking pathetic. Buck Buick strutted around and around them. He barely noticed Silenzio enter.

"I know, I know. You want your lawyer. You already had her," he said in a sing-song voice.

"Please officer. We know nothing. We are just ordinary guys with jobs and a family," whimpered Abdul Two.

"Yeh, and a few extra wives to boot!"

"No, officer, no! We are just ordinary Americans, just like you!" exclaimed Abdul One.

"Oh, no you're not. Now, I'm going to give you a chance to get through this easily and friendly-like."

"Our lawyer said we should not say anything," said Abdul Two.

"Bad advice! Has your lawyer ever represented terrorists before?"

"She said say nothing. We have rights!" answered Abdul One.

"Rights? You say rights?"

Buick grabbed a large chain from the pile of tools and swung it so hard at the steel wall that the whole building shook and the noise was frightening. "These are my rights! And you'll feel them if you don't cooperate!" he yelled as he held up the chain and passed it from hand to hand.

"But we have nothing to say. We know nothing!" complained Abdul One.

"You were going to hit Ground Zero on nine eleven, right?"

"No! No!"

"We meant nothing!" whimpered Abdul One.

"So you had a plan but didn't mean it?"

"We had no plan. It was the undercover guy's plan."

Buick strode behind the chairs and grabbed each of them by their copious black hair. They screamed in pain. "What Al Qaeda cell are you with? Come on! Come on!"

"We don't know any Al Qaeda!"

Buick wrenched them up and they fell backwards over their chairs. "Stand up animals! Stand up!" They groveled and cried at his feet. He grabbed them by the hair again and was about to drag them around the garage when Silenzio intervened.

"Captain Buick, what are you doing? Are you crazy?

Buick paused, then let them go. "Oops, sorry. Just doing a bit of enhanced interrogation. Unfortunately, we don't have any water boarding equipment. At least not yet."

"Come on! They don't know anything. They were set up by the FBI," she said firmly.

"They already admitted that they planned something, but 'they didn't mean it.' I tell you, with thorough interrogation we'll find out what Al Qaeda cell is planning the attack, and whether it's on Ground Zero on nine eleven."

"Does anyone else know you are doing this interrogation?" asked Silenzio.

"Well, not exactly, though it was Lee who asked me to take them over."

There was a silence, broken only by the muttering and whimpering of the suspects. Silenzio was about to speak when the door opened and MacIver entered accompanied by the suspects' lawyer.

"You idiots!" screamed MacIver.

"Hey, I only just got here!" Silenzio complained.

The lawyer looked stern "OK. This is over. You had no right to do this. If there is anything on them, you have just ruined the case. And there's no need, in a local jail, to keep them in cuffs and leg chains."

Buick looked the lawyer up and down. "Just what the country needs. Another liberal lawyer."

And the lawyer retorted, "Just what the country needs, another cop who tramples on the constitution!"

MacIver looked to Silenzio. "Apologies Monica. I expected this would happen. I told the mayor it would. Can you call Lee and get him to release these two poor guys?"

"Not going to happen. Once the FBI gets its teeth into a sting, they won't let go."

"Well I'm going to the mayor about this. And I'm quitting this task force. I don't approve of torture and I'll bet neither does she."

"I haven't tortured anyone and have no plans to. It was just a tough interrogation. Gees, we do this pretty much every day!" complained Buick.

"Let's get these guys back to their cell, and then we can talk about your quitting, Larry," said Silenzio smoothly.

Buick looked at them both, puzzled, annoyed that they were on a first name basis.

MacIver looked back at him. "Maybe it's Buick who should quit."

"Say or do what you like. I'm no pansy quitter," pronounced Buick.

The lawyer stepped forward. "If you don't mind paying attention to the pitiable condition of my clients. Please take them back to their cell, and please gently un-cuff and un-chain them," she demanded.

All looked to Buick. He shrugged and shouted through the open door, "Duty officer! Undo these cuffs and chains, and then help the darlings to their cell."

"Can't you get them out?" the lawyer asked Silenzio.

"Not a chance. They're suspect terrorists."

Buick accompanied the duty officer and suspects out the door.

"Trouble is," said Silenzio, "if they do know something — and I admit it's very unlikely — then we'll never forgive ourselves if we could have stopped an attack."

"It's unscientific. It's not rational," said MacIver. "The probability is very tiny that they know something, even tinier that what they might know would be of any use to us."

"Look, I'll talk to some people I know in the state department. They're very experienced with terrorism cases. And they know how to stand up to the FBI," said Silenzio.

"You're talking rendition?"

"It will only take a few weeks, if that. It's mostly logistics and rule-following that takes the time."

"Say no more. I want nothing to do with it." MacIver turned to leave, hesitated at the door, then left.

Silenzio picked up one of the upturned chairs and sat on it, then made a phone call.

*

MacIver made his way out to Orange Street and was standing on the corner pondering the last several minutes. How could he have been so stupid to agree to this task force? Not noticing the traffic, he stepped on to the road, intending to walk back to his office. There was a slight screech of brakes and an old Dodge Caravan, dark black with black tinted windows pulled up within inches of him. It was Manish Das, driving his "Google van" as he called it. The van bristled with antennae, including a revolving camera on the roof. Das beeped the horn and lowered the window.

"Sir, hello sir, is everything all right sir?" he called.

"Das, that's you?"

"Yes sir. Just back from NYC sir. Can I give you a lift to the school?"

"Well, OK. I was going to walk to let off steam." MacIver climbed into the front seat, looking around the interior, amused. The van was chock full of computers, cameras and recording devices. There was a mattress on the floor at back.

"Welcome to my humble little retreat, sir."

"Wow! Even better than the FBI!"

"It's better than Google, sir!"

"Phew! So you're using this for your car theft dissertation?"

"Yes, sir. So what happened sir?"

"It's impossible, hopeless. Why can't they make decisions based on scientific data?"

"Sir?"

"They have all assumed that the attack is going to be on Ground Zero, by Al Qaeda, and on Nine Eleven. They're simply grasping at anything, in fact Buick will do anything to support his knee-jerk assumptions."

"Sir?"

"Sir what?"

"Maybe it's not a bad hunch? I mean, Ground Zero is an attractive target, especially given the spectacle of the last attack."

"Et tu, Das?"

"Ha! Ha! Like Caesar, sir!"

"What? Speak up Das."

"I mean, one thing we learned from nine eleven is how easy it was to hit a stationary target from the air."

"Are you serious?"

"Specially a target that stuck right out there. I mean it was only matched by the Statue of Liberty. And now there's the Freedom Tower, sticking out, just the same."

"You just defeated your own argument, didn't you? Why not the Statue of Liberty? That's why we have to assess all the attractive targets in NYC and assign risk values to each of them, and harden the targets accordingly. You should know better, Das."

"Very sorry sir. Very sorry. It's just that a missile fired from somewhere outside NYC could destroy it."

"All sorts of terrible things could happen, but it's very unlikely that they will. How would they get the missiles? Where would they hide them? I'm beginning to wonder whether you're really on board with forensic crime prevention."

"You're right sir, I am not thinking straight."

Das stopped in front of the Rutgers University School of Criminal Justice.

"I have a faculty meeting. I'll see you tomorrow, and by the way, we need to review where you are with your dissertation."

"Sir. That's very threatening sir!"

"And your data collection?"

"Google Street is great sir! But my humble van is even better! I know where most cars are stolen from —"

"OK, OK. We'll talk about it tomorrow. Thanks for the ride."

Das pulled into the car park on Washington Street and climbed into the back. He activated a number of switches, as well as laptop computers and three screens. He sat glued to his computer, watching Google Street in action on one screen and video footage that he had taken from his own patrols on another screen. And on yet another, there was live video of the car park and surrounding streets. He typed in a message to Google Street asking when the street views were last updated in Newark and all along the Hudson through Northern New Jersey.

12. Mafia Imports

Uncle Sergey first got into the mafia business through his brother Nicholas who operated a thriving business smuggling stolen cars out of the U.S. to Russia and Eastern Europe and the Middle East. Nicholas appointed him as his manager of the Eastern Division, as he called it. They operated a mostly legitimate export business, but its main purpose was to provide the cover for smuggling high end vehicles to the black market in Russia, Eastern Europe and the Middle East. It was a relatively simple business model. They stole the cars right off the streets of Newark, then reprocessed their documentation and shipped them out. They gave the cars a new identity, vehicle ID number and the works. Forging the new identities of cars was not difficult and not even risky. The authorities had gone to a lot of trouble to make sure the identities of individuals and organizations were authentic, so forging them was risky. But they remained pretty much ignorant of the process of falsifying the identities of cars. Besides, if there was a problem, the people working for the New Jersey Department of Motor Vehicles were poorly paid and easy to buy off.

So on this early September morning, a white box truck with the name "GREAT IMPORTS" in small black letters on a vinyl strip adhered to its side approached the Port of Newark container terminal on Calcutta Street. Turgo sat beside the truck driver. He was wishing they had used a forwarding agency, but uncle Sergey had warned against it because they would lose time and they did not want the container sitting for any time within the terminal. Turgo had followed the progress of the Maple Leaf on the web, and knew that it had arrived and that the container had been unloaded. Since nine eleven, trucker and Sea Link IDs were hard to come by and forgeries were risky, so Nicholas had insisted that they both get legitimate ones. As it was, because they both had Green Cards, getting the IDs was not that difficult, especially as Nicholas with his contacts was able to get the applications on a fast track. Even so, Turgo was nervous as the truck pulled up to the entry gate and they were both asked to step out of the truck and show their IDs.

The officer on duty examined the documents carefully. "Looks OK. You're here for container C12?"

"Yes, that is right," said Turgo. "These the papers you need?"

"Let me see. Yeh, looks OK. Picking up a Mercedes are you?" he asked, joking.

"Oh, yes officer. They bring such good price here."

"Really? I wouldn't buy one myself. I'd rather have a Chevy."

"Ah! Good American car!" exclaimed Turgo.

The officer handed the papers back and raised the boom. "OK. It's Lot C, second on left. Pull up there and they'll help you load."

"We don't want the whole container, just the crate inside. Can we do that here?"

"Don't see why not. Better ask the boys down there. They have the forklifts to do it."

The truck rolled forward and Turgo smiled as they passed by. They found Lot C and were directed to container C12. "Can we open it?" Turgo asked the dock worker. "We just want to pick up the crate that's inside."

"No problem. This is from the Maple Leaf, just in from Mumbai, right?"

"Right."

"Our biggest fork lift should do it." The worker whistled loudly and received a whistle back. "He's on his way."

The container was opened and they loaded the crate, the only item in the container, into the truck. They drove slowly to the exit of the lot and once again had to get out to show their IDs, and as well, the officer on duty briefly looked inside the truck.

"You're taking this to Indian Point? So they're finally upgrading it huh?"

"Cooling pumps, I think, officer," said Turgo.

They left the facility and joined the permanent traffic jam of trucks and cars as they slowly inched their way towards the New Jersey turnpike north, from which they eventually exited and found their way to Skyline Drive. Nicholas had even gone to the trouble to get them a permit to drive the truck on Skyline Drive, because it was illegal to do it without one. Turgo had thought that was unnecessary until they were pulled over soon after they entered Skyline Drive and asked for their permit. The narrow curving road was dangerous for trucks, the officer said, so they should drive carefully and keep well within the speed limit.

The truck passed through beautiful parks and pricey suburbs and every now and again offered a glimpse of the fabulous skyline of New York City. "It would be a shame to destroy it," mused Turgo. It took a good half hour to get to the safe house, now identifiable by a blue tarpaulin draped over its roof. They had difficulty maneuvering the truck on the narrow road, and blocked traffic as they tried to back it into the driveway. The garage door of the house opened, and a large fork lift emerged. The crate was deposited in the garage.

*

Another envelope had arrived. This time postmarked in Newark, New Jersey. It did not contain money, but what appeared to be a debit card issued by HSBC. Shouldn't they take it to the New York State Police? Mrs. Kohmsky asked herself. She knew immediately Mr. Kohmsky would not want to, especially as it had one small post-it note attached, which simply said "Nicholas." They left it sit on the kitchen table for several days until finally Mrs. Kohmsky could not contain herself any longer and snatched it up right after they had breakfast one morning and went off to the nearest HSBC ATM.

She pushed the card into the slot and withdrew it as directed. But then it asked for her pin and of course she did not have it. She stepped back, embarrassed, to let the person behind her use the machine. She immediately thought of Nicholas as the PIN, but it was too many letters. And the PIN had to be a number anyway. She walked home, feeling rather silly. She had just put the key in her door when it dawned on her. It must be Sarah! She turned and hurried back to the bank, got half way, then stopped. S-A-R-A-H are letters, which was no good. What numbers could SARAH stand for? She turned around again and went back home. Mr. Kohmsky sat in his usual place in the corner of the living room, reading and took no notice of her. She went straight to their telephone and looked at the dial. This had to be it! With a shaking hand she wrote down the letters and their numbers from the phone key pad: 7-2-7-2-4.

Excited, Mrs. Kohmsky rushed out the door and back to the bank. She pushed in the card, retrieved it, punched in 7-2-7-2-4 and it worked! She selected BALANCE and it showed $100,000! Stunned, she stepped back, then stepped forward again to log out of the machine. Could Sarah have sent this money? And why, if she did? Or was Nicholas, from whom they had heard nothing for some thirty years, trying to establish contact? And if so, why use money instead of a letter or even a phone call? And more puzzling, what was he doing in Newark?

13. Barriers

Ruth Newberg, first ever woman mayor of New York City, was a very determined woman. To have become mayor was clear evidence of that. Her inherited wealth, on its own, was of little use in getting her elected, and to a considerable extent, a liability. Now, after three years in office, with the media pretty much turned against her, and daily, street protests of one sort or another, any other person would have been rattled. As she walked under the fabulous rotunda of City Hall, where Abraham Lincoln had lain in state, where all manner of historic events had occurred, she steeled herself for the press conference she was about to hold on the City Hall steps. She would stay the course, would not be jostled by the media or anyone else into a panic response just for the sake of media satisfaction. The media didn't give two hoots about public safety. They thirsted for 'news,' that is spectacle and sensation. The media obviously stood to benefit a great deal from a terrorist attack in New York City. She would have to be careful not to say that to them this morning.

Trouble was, the traffic snarls caused by the proliferation of street closures, barriers and altered street patterns that MacIver had engineered, had pushed the people of Manhattan to breaking point. She had to admit it. To herself, that is. Not to *them*.

Foster led the way out to the steps and guided Mayor Newberg over to the rostrum that was crowded with microphones. He ushered MacIver to her side.

"Professor, are you sure you want to do this?" Madam Mayor asked MacIver.

"You need my support."

"Just be careful what you say. You know what they are like." She tapped the microphone and looked out over a small group of reporters and a noisy mob of protestors. There were signs saying UNCLOG OUR STREETS, TEAR DOWN THE WALLS, and SURVEILLANCE NO! She addressed the audience.

"Let me begin by saying that I greatly appreciate your concerns and thank you for coming here today. I know we have created some inconvenience for you, what with the street closures and barriers and so forth, but I assure you that our best researchers think that hardening targets is the wise thing to do."

A reporter interjected. "Madam Mayor, why isn't your Police Department involved in this? Is it true that you fired the Assistant Police Commissioner for crime prevention?"

"No it is not true. We just thought that the traffic division had more expertise in handling street closures and traffic, obviously."

"Could have fooled us! You've made life hell for New Yorkers," yelled a protestor.

"To explain in more detail why we are doing what we are, I'd like to introduce you to Professor MacIver from Rutgers University, world expert on terrorism and crime prevention. Prof. MacIver?"

There were boos, cat-calls a-plenty. But MacIver stepped up, undaunted.

"We are faced with the prospect of another attack on the scale of nine eleven." The crowd shuffled nervously, then went silent. MacIver continued, "I hasten to add. Such an attack is very unlikely, but we must be prepared for it, just in case."

"Can't you do it without making our lives so miserable? It takes me two hours to make a half hour commute these days!" called another protestor.

"We are only hardening those targets we assess as most likely to be attacked."

"But it's so unpredictable," responded a reporter, "streets are closed, barriers appear almost magically overnight."

"But that's the point," MacIver responded, "they must be unpredictable, that's how we stopped suicide bombing in Israel."

Another reporter saw an opportunity, "But this isn't Israel," she called.

"Not yet. But our borders are just as porous as Israel's used to be before they built their fences."

"Build your freaking fences in Texas, not here!" yelled another protestor.

"We have to control our borders. The problem goes beyond NYC!" replied MacIver.

The crowd became restless, people calling out, loud arguments starting among various factions.

Madam Mayor intervened. "Of course, Professor MacIver is not advocating that we close our borders. That's a discussion for another day.

We are not planning a 'ring of steel' around New York. This is not Belfast. We are just taking small, cautious steps."

"Are you expecting another nine eleven style attack any time soon — on nine eleven maybe?" asked another reporter.

"We've heard some vague chatter but nothing specific. We just want to make sure."

"Is it true you have Islamic community centers, including in Newark, under twenty four hour surveillance?"

"The NYPD as far as I know does not put innocent people under surveillance. If they are, there'll be hell to pay."

"But didn't the FBI just arrest two Al Qaeda suspects at the Newark mosque?"

"I know nothing about that. You had better ask the Mayor of Newark."

At that moment, Foster received a phone call. He listened attentively, then moved to get attention from the Mayor, whispering something to her. In response, the Mayor stepped back and Foster stepped forward. "Thank you all. This news conference is now over," he announced.

Mayor Newberg, turning to Foster, asked, "You're sure of this?"

"That's what Buick said."

"Uh Oh. What's he done now?" asked MacIver.

"It seems they sent the two Al Qaeda suspects for rendition to Saudi Arabia. And they talked."

"Said what?" asked MacIver.

"There's a plan to attack Ground Zero. That's all he would tell me. Says Silenzio wants a meeting of our task force."

"She arranged the rendition?" Mayor Newberg asked.

"Yes, she did. Or at least, I guessed she would when we confronted Buick at the Newark PD lock-up," said MacIver.

"Seems I'm the last to know what's going on," said the mayor.

"If you don't mind a political neophyte saying so, you're better off not knowing, and certainly better off not knowing what Buick was up to," said MacIver with a smile.

Foster's phone rang again. "It's Silenzio," he said.

"Foster, can you put me on to the mayor?" Foster handed the phone to Mayor Newberg.

"Monica?

"Yes, Ruth. We have full confessions. They are part of an Al Qaeda cell that is planning to use a drone to bomb Ground Zero. Supposedly, launched from the roof top of a Newark Hotel. I think we need another meeting of our task force."

"I'm not sure what can be accomplished by such a meeting. We have put a lot of protections in place."

"But not in anticipation of a drone attack —"

The mayor looked at MacIver. "Can you make it to a meeting of our task force, Skyline Restaurant, in two hours?"

"I doubt it will achieve anything. But if it's so urgent, OK. I'll need to pick up Das on the way."

"Agent Silenzio, you got that?

"Good, Skyline Restaurant in two hours," replied Silenzio.

"May I speak with Silenzio? asked MacIver. The mayor passed the phone.

"Monica?"

"Yes, Larry."

"This rendition. You made it happen? Were you there?"

"Yes, and no. Couldn't stand to watch one of those."

"They don't produce reliable information."

"I know. But as I said before, we have to cover all bases. Got to go."

"See you soon."

MacIver handed the phone back to Foster, then called Das on his own phone.

Manish answered immediately. "Hello sir! What can I do for you, sir?"

"I'll pick you up in an hour. There's an urgent meeting of our counter terrorism task force. I'd like you to do a brief presentation on how you have hardened targets in NYC."

"Yes sir! No problem sir! There's no need to pick me up. I will meet you at the restaurant, sir. It will give me more time to prepare, sir."

"OK. That's fine."

"You should see my Google data, sir!"

"Yes, yes. We'll get to that."

*

One hundred and nine Skyline Drive, Ringwood New Jersey was a rare find, a single-story suburban house on the edge of a commercial development, a few hundred yards down the road from Wells Fargo bank. For a single-story New Jersey house, its roof was unusually high, built to mimic an old English house with big timber beams and white stucco walls. Viewed from Google Earth, the house sat square in the middle of a large lot of about an acre, all trees completely removed. On the commercial side the lot was lined with elms planted in orderly rows and on the other two sides by a dense forest of the heavy leafed trees of New Jersey: maples and oaks, with a sprinkling of dogwoods, silver bell, serviceberry and spicebush. Nicholas had done well to find a house close enough to the road with a drive wide enough to allow a large truck to enter, one that was not buried in one of the occasional suburban enclaves that were slotted in between the several nature reserves and parks along this Passaic county road. The large blue tarpaulin now stretched over the complete eastern side of the roof. Nicholas had even gone to the trouble to erect a small contractor's sign to allay any suspicions the neighbors might have. They were converting a residential house into some kind of commercial establishment.

The large expanse of lawn at front was freshly mowed and the remains of an English garden lining the front of the lawn just back from the road showed signs of neglect. The house had been empty for some time, but by at least mowing the lawn, the new owners were showing that they were going to take care of their property.

Inside, Turgo and his assistants were hard at work. The walls had been knocked out to make room for tools, the launcher and a bench for the missiles while they were being assembled. The two missiles, about five feet in length and a diameter of a foot tapering down to about six inches at each end sat open on the work bench set up in the dining room. They were mostly reassembled, the covers at the nose open revealing a maze of wires and switches and computer chips and circuit boards. LED lights flashed intermittently, accompanied by occasional beeps in response to Turgo's manipulations. The scene was not unlike that of a hospital emergency room, Turgo's assistants running back and forth, providing him with various instruments and parts.

"Cannot fit payload in tip. Have to remove some fuel to make room," Turgo muttered in half English and half Russian.

"Why we not use drone? Much better and easier," asked an assistant.

"Agree. But have to work with what they give us," answered Turgo, then after some thought added, "need much bigger space to launch drone with this size payload."

"We make deadline?"

"Nine-eleven is one week away. Have plenty time. Only problem is payloads. Not enough explosive for two missiles."

"Where you get explosive?"

"Sergey's little brother arranged it."

"What you do?"

"What Sergey and I planned from the beginning. We put ricin in one missile which will weigh much less than explosive so will use less fuel."

"Where you get ricin?

"We make it right here in kitchen."

"But how?"

"Have equipment in kitchen. Basic ingredient is protein from the waste left over from castor oil manufacture. That in garage. We start make it now and let it dry overnight."

"How deliver payload?"

"I program detonate one hundred meters up from ground. Will spray toxin over many kilometers," said Turgo with confidence and considerable satisfaction.

"How it kill?"

"Ingestion, breathing, or through skin. Will be first major use of bio toxin terrorist attack. Spectacular!"

*

Time was running out for the task force. It was obvious that the members could not work together. They just did their own thing. Days had slipped by, MacIver had managed with Das's assistance to harden most of the likely targets in New York City. The mayor had managed so far to fend off protests and attacks from the media. MacIver had kept out of the way there, though he did give a long interview for '60 Minutes' which had not aired as yet, but he suspected would air tonight, the eve of the nine eleven anniversary. The task force had, in the end, not met in response to the last so-called emergency precipitated by the rendition of the two suspects. But as the anniversary of nine eleven loomed, the mayor had insisted that they should meet and review the situation. Some had already charged that she had not responded to the information obtained from the rendition, even though those same critics complained about their lives being messed up by street closures and unpredictably changed traffic patterns.

They met in the Skyline restaurant, same room as before. Foster, alone, arrived early to place pads and pencils around the table.

Mayor Ruth Newberg entered. "We need water, could you see to it?" she asked.

"Haven't been able to find the waiters. Their supervisor says they called in sick. I'll see what I can do," replied Foster.

MacIver and Das entered. "Where is the projector?" asked Das.

"Sorry, I couldn't find their I-T guy," answered Foster, a little frustrated.

"Don't bother with slides Das." said MacIver, "anyway, you brought handouts, didn't you?"

"Sir, yes sir." Das busily trotted around the table leaving copies of notes and graphics, carefully straightening everything up at each place.

Mayor Newberg, turned from a pensive moment gazing at the view of New York City, and asked MacIver, "What are you planning to do?"

"Das will present an overview of how we predict targets most likely to be attacked, the talk he was going to do before. He'll outline the method of identifying attractive targets, how to harden them, and briefly show the results of our efforts to stop suicide terrorism in Israel."

"Is that really necessary?" asked the mayor.

"From the events of the last weeks, I think that people do not really understand what we are trying to do."

At this moment, the door opened and Monica Silenzio quietly entered. MacIver nodded.

"I think they do," observed Silenzio as she sat down, "but they don't appreciate the cost to the comfort of their daily routines that it entails."

"Good afternoon Agent Silenzio," smiled MacIver.

"Fact is, they want us to do everything unseen, unnoticed," Silenzio continued.

Mayor Newberg quickly added, "and when something happens, they blame us for not having done anything."

Manish Das, sitting in his corner seat raised his hand. "Sir, Professor, shall I start? Or should we wait for Captain Buick?"

"It's Buick who needs to be made to understand it all. But I've really given up on him as a hopeless case," answered MacIver.

Right then, the door flew open and in walked Buick. "Who's a hopeless case?" he grinned.

Silenzio spoke up quickly. "I think we should really get down to deciding what to do about the information we got from the rendition."

"That's what the meeting's for, isn't it? Or have I missed something?" said Buick.

"I think Agent Silenzio is right," said Mayor Newberg, "let's get the rendition business out of the way first."

"I give up," sighed MacIver.

"Perhaps you can take the materials I have put out, and we can discuss them at a later time?" offered Das helpfully.

Silenzio answered, "OK. Let's get on with it. The suspects have talked under rendition. They say there is a plan by an Al Qaeda cell to launch a drone from the top of a Newark hotel with a payload of ricin."

"What's ricin?" asked Buick.

"It's a bio toxin that attacks the nerves, a small speck can kill in a few seconds. It's cheap and easy to make from the widely available castor plant."

"And how is it spread?" asked Mayor Newberg.

"We can go into all that later. For now, we have to decide what to do," said Silenzio, one eye on MacIver.

Buick spoke up. "Are the two suspects part of the Al Qaeda cell?"

"They say not. But it doesn't matter." Silenzio looked around the table, puzzled. "Where's Agent Lee?" she asked Foster.

"I think I forgot to invite him," he answered with a slight smirk.

"It doesn't matter. Once it goes to CIA, the FBI washes it hands of the case," said Silenzio.

MacIver got up from his chair and looked out the window.

"We have to search every Newark Hotel," continued Silenzio, "you must clear a wide space around Ground Zero. At least a radius of one mile, and that may not even be enough. We don't know how they will deliver the ricin, should it turn out to be a ricin tipped payload."

MacIver turned from the window, cheeks flushed under his closely cropped beard. "This is ridiculous," he complained, his voice a little too loud for the room, "we have no evidence — zero — that there is going to be any kind of attack, let alone a bio attack. Besides, how do you launch a drone with a payload big enough to drop on Ground Zero from a hotel roof top? It's all fantasy. You people watch too many movies."

Mayor Newberg responded quickly. "The professor is right. Anyway, I'm not going to act upon information that was obtained under torture. I can't justify it morally, let alone politically."

Buick fidgeted with his pencil, snapping it into pieces, then pushed his hands against the table, pushing back on his chair.

Silenzio, in a measured voice turned to the mayor and said, "Madam Mayor. That's a foolish policy. You have to act to protect the people of New York. You may or may not approve of so-called torture, but if it has produced information, you are duty bound to act on it."

"She is acting on it. I am acting on it. 'It' being the scientific estimate of the probability of when and where an attack may occur. That's why we are putting up barriers and closures," countered MacIver.

Buck Buick could contain himself no longer. "You pointy headed idiot!" he yelled, breaking his pencil into even more pieces and throwing them across the table at MacIver.

"Careful now!" warned MacIver, adopting a superior tone, at the same time, grabbing up the pieces of pencil and squeezing them tightly into his fist which he then raised as if to retaliate.

"Captain Buick. Control yourself. You're not in Iraq now!" lectured the mayor, looking first to Buick then to MacIver.

"Control myself, you puny bastard!" growled Buick in consternation. "An attack is imminent, and the professor's got you putting up fences and barriers around city hall, stopping people from visiting the statue of Liberty, causing massive traffic snarls, protestors amassing in front of city hall. And you just want us to wait around until we are attacked!"

Silenzio firmly gripped Buick's arm. "Buck, this isn't helping —"

"Can't you see?" he pleaded. "If we don't act now, take out the animals, people are going to get hurt, and you, Madam Mayor, will be blamed!"

Das, squirming in his corner, timidly raised his hand, looking across to MacIver. "Sir, er, Madam Mayor, Madam, I've been thinking about drones, Madam. I mean, it might not be a drone, but surely it's obvious that the easiest, perhaps the only way, to reach a well-protected stationary target like Ground Zero, is from the air."

They all fell silent, awaiting MacIver's reaction. He did not disappoint. "For the last time Das, I've had enough of this. You're either on board with target hardening or you can pack up and go back to Mumbai." Das cringed in his seat, staring hard at the floor.

Buick grabbed the opportunity. "You see, even your own bum-boy thinks you're wrong!"

"Sir!' cried Das in consternation and embarrassment.

MacIver threw the pieces of pencil in Buick's face. Buick laughed, stood up quickly, knocking his chair backwards, hands on his hips. "Now Professor. My fist is bigger than yours," he grinned as he frowned.

"Boys! Please!" pleaded Silenzio.

MacIver, embarrassed, but certainly not sorry, sat down, head in hands. "We're leaving. Come on Das."

Das remained in his seat, still cringing. "Sir, I'm sorry, sir. I was just trying to find a compromise. Sir?"

"Perhaps we should disband the meeting, Madam Mayor," suggested Silenzio.

Mayor Newberg said, "Captain Buick. If you want to go after them — whoever 'them' are — I can't stop whatever you do in Newark. That's for you to work out with your Chief and the Mayor of Newark. But I'm sticking with MacIver's strategy."

"The blood, and there will be blood, will be on your hands," warned Buick.

All were about to rise when Foster, his phone in hand, turned to the Mayor, then whispered something. He then turned on the TV. "Before you leave, I think we had better watch this," he said.

The TV flickered and Foster tuned to Fox News. The news commentator spoke:

"Exclusive to Fox news, this just in. The FBI has arrested six individuals it says are members of a terrorist cell that is planning to attack Ground Zero on nine eleven. The FBI made this announcement at a press conference a half hour ago. I think we have some video of that now."

Agent Fred Lee stands center screen, flanked on one side by the NYPD Police Commissioner John Ryan and on the other by Agent Crosby. Lee addresses the group of journalists who hang on his every word:

"I know that many of you have been very concerned about the rumors of these past few weeks of an impending attack by Al Qaeda on Ground Zero on nine eleven. That rumor was true. But, thanks to the close coordination between the FBI and the NYPD, we have had the Al Qaeda cell that was working out of the Newark Community Mosque under surveillance for some time. Earlier this evening, we arrested all six of them, and they are even now on their way to Guantanamo Bay where they will be held and processed, in anticipation of trial by a military tribunal. I will now take a few quick questions."

"What kind of attack was it?"

"It was to be a drone set off from somewhere in Newark, we still don't know where, carrying a nuclear tip."

A buzz of excitement ran through the crowd.

"Just to be sure. You said nuclear???!!"

"That's right. But we believe that part of the rumor to be false. In fact we believe that the drone does not exist either."

"Wait a minute. How do you know?"

"From our preliminary questioning."

"But how do you know they're telling the truth?"

Agent Lee turned to Commissioner Ryan.

"Because we've had the Islamic community under surveillance for over a year and are certain that if drones or bombs, especially nuclear bombs were present, we would know about it," answered Ryan confidently.

"NYPD has had the local Newark Islamic community under surveillance for over a year?" asked a reporter.

"That's right."

"Does Mayor Newberg know about this?"

"She probably does now."

"And the Newark mayor?"

Agent Lee interjects. "We had to do this completely under cover. Could not let either of the mayors know." The reporters murmured their surprise.

Lee continued, "Thank you for your attendance. You can rest easily that we have this operation entirely under control and that there is no threat of a nuclear or any other type of attack from Al Qaeda."

The reporters pushed forward, hands raised, calling out questions. Lee waved his hand as he turned away and said, "I'm sorry, but as you can imagine, we are very busy and have no time for any more questions."

The Fox News Announcer returned to the screen and continued:

"There you have it. We understand that Governor Christie will be making an announcement soon in response to this incredible news conference."

Foster turned off the TV. The Mayor was flabbergasted. "I guess I am estranged from my Commissioner, rather than he from me," she said, "hopefully, as far as our task force is concerned, this changes nothing."

"Buick, you didn't even know about this?" asked MacIver, having calmed down.

"Got to hand it to the assholes. They pulled it off right under my nose. I'm as stunned as the mayor."

Foster's phone rang again. It was the sound of 'I Love New York.' "It's the Governor," he said, passing the phone to his boss.

"Which one?" she asked.

"Yours."

"Governor?"

"What the blazes is going on?"

"You tell me! I've been broadsided."

"I want you in my office in one hour. I want to know everything."

"Pardon me, Governor. But I answer to the people of New York City first, and it is to them that I will speak just as soon as I am in Manhattan which will be in a half hour."

"Where are you now?"

"I am consulting with my special counter terrorism task force."

She handed the phone back to Foster who looked at the phone, then said to it, "Governor Cuomo, er, the mayor had to rush to her helicopter. Good-bye, and thank you for your concern, Governor."

Mayor Newberg rose to leave just as Foster received another call. He looked for the TV remote, and switched the TV on again, waving to his boss to watch it. The old TV flickered once again, and Governor Christie came into view, speaking to an animated group of reporters:

"It has come to my knowledge that the New York City Police Department has been conducting undercover surveillance of our fellow citizens of the Islamic community of Newark. This has been going on for an extended period of time. This was done without authorization or consultation with either the Mayor of Newark, or my own Justice Department. I apologize to our Muslim friends for this unconstitutional invasion of their privacy rights as free citizens of New Jersey. I promise a full investigation to get to the bottom of this travesty, both at the federal and state levels. Thank you. That's all I have to say at this time."

Foster switched off the TV. Mayor Newberg turned to the group and said, "We should continue on our current strategy. Looks like MacIver has been right all along."

"No it doesn't!" countered Buick.

"Captain Buick. This makes you look even sillier than me. You're the one who is supposed to be protecting Newark. You'll do well to bow to MacIver's strategy." And then she left, Foster right behind her, talking on his cell phone.

But just as they reached the door, Das called out, "Madam, if I may say so Madam Mayor! I am still not convinced there's no attack. One from the air, a missile or two, would demolish Ground Zero and the Freedom Tower."

Mayor Newberg hesitated, then resignedly gesticulated to MacIver, and left.

"Das, that's enough," scorned MacIver, "get out of here and get back to your work."

"Sorry, sir! But, OK. Sorry sir, Sorree! Sorree!" Das rushed out of the room, followed by Buick.

"Perhaps I can drive the professor to his office?" offered Silenzio solicitously. MacIver said nothing, but followed her to the parking lot.

*

Manish Das slowly walked to his van, deeply chastened. Buick caught up with him. "You upset your boss, not a good idea!" he said, trying to make light of it.

"So did you!" said Das.

"But he's not my boss!"

"Can I show you my van?" asked Das with a faint smile.

"What?

"My van, my surveillance van. I call it my Google van."

"You have a surveillance van?"

"Yes, captain. I use it to study car theft in Newark and Northern New Jersey. It's for my dissertation."

"Car theft?"

"Yes, I monitor the coming and going of parked cars. Do you use Google Street?"

"What's that?"

"You must have seen the Google vans patrolling the streets, taking video."

"So that's what they're doing."

"It's a kind of surveillance, except that they only update theirs once a year. I do mine weekly, sometimes even more frequently."

"You do that? Don't you have anything else to do?"

"Er, I suppose not. It's for my dissertation. I must get finished, so I can go back to Mumbai and get married."

"You have time for a girlfriend?"

"Oh, no. I haven't met her yet. My parents are arranging the marriage. A very good one too."

Buick was lost for words. He grinned and frowned at the same time.

"Come, let me show you," said Das.

14. Ricin

Nicholas had kept in touch with his brother Sergey over the years. He had tried to get him to migrate to the USA but he wouldn't hear of it. He was making too much money where he was, he said, and could not imagine that there could possibly be more opportunities in America than in Kirghizstan, what with the Afghan war, the Middle East loaded with money, drug and arms smuggling galore, you name it. Nicholas had migrated to America when he was fifteen. He got a job on a Russian freighter and jumped ship when it docked in Newark. That was in 1980. And he had stayed there ever since. In those days it wasn't hard to get the right documentation. In fact the people he met in the Salvation Army hostel where he stayed until he found a job helped him apply for a social security card, and he had it in a couple of weeks. Otherwise he had no documentation, no birth certificate, nothing. It didn't matter. There was plenty for a young teenager looking for adventure to do. He hung around the bars and street corners across from the Newark railway station and in no time had found work in a chop shop that received stolen cars and chopped them up for parts. He started out doing the mechanical stuff and learned a lot, but it was too boring for him. He wanted excitement and pretty soon he was stealing cars on his own and bringing them into the shop for processing.

Now, he owned several chop shops, though he preferred to call them remanufacturing facilities. His clients came to him for specific car models and he had his gangs steal them off the Newark streets, bring them to one of his shops, where he would replace the Vehicle Identification Number (VIN) and re-register it with the New Jersey DMV. He paid his operative inside the DMV to process the registration papers and also to supply him with old VIN numbers he could use on his remanufactured cars. These days he rarely sold them for parts. His best clients were in Eastern Europe and Saudi Arabia. And the Port of Newark was very convenient, again, with willing contacts, who, for a little extra money, would make sure his cars had a smooth passage through the port. So importing the package from Mumbai that Sergey sent him was a simple matter, though his contacts were a bit surprised that he was importing rather than exporting.

But the problem was the ricin and Sergey had called him about it. He did not like Sergey to call him at all, even on a stolen or supposedly secure phone. He had never once been picked up by the cops in his thirty years in the business. This was because he was very careful, but also because he had many good friends in the Newark PD. There were times he had to close down operations for a period when he was tipped off that the FBI was sniffing around. Usually, that only lasted for a few months when they lost interest. This was especially so since nine eleven, now that they were obsessed with the terrorism thing and had little interest in stolen cars.

The money Sergey offered him to smooth the way for the missiles from Mumbai through the Port of Newark, to find a safe house and install a ricin lab in it was just too good to pass up. But he was apprehensive. It did mean that he had to do things right under the nose of the FBI and he knew they were running a sting operation. He had decided to take the risk when he discovered that the FBI and the NYPD were conducting a combined sting operation but it was focused entirely on the Muslim community around the local mosque. So as long as he kept away from Muslims, which he did anyway, he was probably OK.

When he complained to Sergey that he knew nothing about the manufacture of ricin, Sergey passed it off saying that it was a simple process, and said he'd have his nuclear wizard Turgo call him with the instructions. "Anyway, you can get the recipe off the web," Sergey said. Trouble was, when Turgo called as promised, his knowledge was not much better. "You get it from the beans of the castor plant," Turgo said. When Nicholas complained that this was not much help, Turgo responded haughtily, "I'm a nuclear scientist, not a chemist who mixes up witches' potions." So there he was, searching the web for ricin recipes. There were lots of them and as soon as he saw them, he knew he had a problem. It was not so simple a recipe, at least not good enough to produce enough for a missile payload. The first recipe he found on the web was at http://www.zoklet.net. It advised as follows:

1. Get some castor beans from a garden supply store.
2. Put about 2 ounces of hot water into a glass jar and add a teaspoon full of lye. Mix it thoroughly.
3. Wait for the lye/water mixture to cool

4. Place 2 ounces of the beans into the liquid and let them soak for one hour.
5. Pour out the liquid being careful not to get any on exposed skin.
6. Rinse the beans off with cool water and then remove the outer husks with tweezers.
7. Put the bean pulp into a blender or coffee grinder with 4 ounces of acetone for every 1 oz. of beans.
8. Blend the pulp until it looks like milk.
9. Place the milky substance in a glass jar with an airtight lid for three days.
10. At the end of three days shake the jar to remix everything that's started to settle then pour it into a coffee filter. Discard the liquid.
11. When no more liquid is dripping through the filter, squeeze the last of the acetone out of it without losing any of the bean pulp.
12. Spread the filter out on a pan covered with newspaper and let it stand until it is dry.
13. The final product must be as free of acetone and other contaminants as possible. If it is not powdery but still moist and pulpy it must be combined with the appropriate amount of acetone again and let sit for one day.
14. Then repeat steps 9-12 again until a nice dry powder is produced.

Given the dire warnings of ricin's toxicity, there was no way Nicholas was going to attempt any of this and he could see that there was no way that Turgo and his pals would be able to manufacture enough powder in time, even if he supplied them with the beans and other ingredients. So he switched his web search to manufacturing plants that made cosmetics and pharmaceutical products including castor oil and its derivatives. And he found one right in Fairfield New Jersey, just around the corner! It was an easy matter to purchase a large quantity of castor mash and then to purchase a chromatographic lab which he installed in the kitchen of the safe house on Skyline Drive. According to the instructions, he'd need enough mash which, once processed would produce 10% of its initial weight in ricin paste. He made a quick call to Turgo and described his purchases. Turgo this time was more amenable and seemed to understand what was needed. Just one last item was necessary: a dehydrator to dry out the paste from which the lethal powder could be produced. Nicholas ended the call, and immediately saw that he had a new voicemail. It must have come while he was talking to Turgo. He immediately checked the message. It was from someone who said, "Hi, this is Sarah, your niece." He was perplexed and disturbed, not that it was she, but how she had got his number. He knew of her existence of course, but had never met or spoken to her. He did not return the call.

*

Turgo had rearranged the chromatographic equipment on the kitchen counter and placed the dehydrator on top of the oven. After a few trials, Turgo had figured out the process and began manufacture of the ricin. He had made three batches so far and figured that one more batch would be enough. The dehydrator was hard at work on the last batch. It was the dehydration stage that took all the time.

Turgo stepped back from one of the missiles. He and his collaborators were encased in anti-bio toxin suits, helmets and the works. Nicholas had overlooked nothing. He was certainly very good. "OK, careful now. Bring ricin," he ordered, "You need syringe to insert toxin in the tube container in the tip right here." Turgo pointed to the spot inside the bare insides of the missile. His assistant stepped forward carefully, syringe in gloved hand. He could not insert the syringe into the opening of the container.

"Visor foggy. Cannot see properly, gloves too big," complained the assistant. He opened the visor of his helmet, but the gloved hand holding the syringe got caught on one of the wires inside the missile. The syringe slipped from his gloved fingers and in his effort to grasp it before it fell through into the internal workings of the payload, pressed the syringe plunger and ricin powder squirted out into his face as he leaned over the missile.

"Watch out you fool! Don't breathe!" yelled Turgo as he stepped quickly away from the missile. But it was too late. The assistant choked, had spectacular convulsions and dropped down, writhing like a beetle on its back. In minutes, the movement stopped and he lay there in a coma.

Turgo was pleased. His manufacture of the ricin had been successful. It worked! He proceeded, unperturbed and inserted the ricin into the payload, and closed down the door, giving it a friendly tap. "You're all set, my beauty! You will spread your wings over New York!"

"What do we do about him? Do we have to clean up the ricin? What about the nuclear tip?" asked the other assistant, also suited up.

"I have already taken care of the nuclear. It's ready to go, just needs the navigation to be set to the target," said Turgo ignoring the question.

"But the ricin?"

"There is one last batch cooking in the dehydrator. We'll add that tomorrow."

"I mean the ricin he spilled."

"Oh, yes, I forgot. Just spray everything with ordinary soap detergent and water. Detergent under sink, in kitchen."

"That is all?"

"Conditions have to be exactly right for it to spread and to attach itself to humans. Here, spray my bio toxin suit so I can get out of it."

*

Das had entered his enclave in the back of the old Dodge Caravan, while Buick kneeled looking over the back of the front seat. Das was suddenly transformed from the meek student sitting in the corner of the meeting room, to some kind of animated robot, moving swiftly from one apparatus to another, tweaking dials, pressing buttons, using voice activation with others. "This kid's a little mad," Buick thought.

"You see, I have a revolving camera on the roof, and it is all recorded on this computer. And unlike Google, I don't have to block out the license plate numbers," said Das with pride as he darted to and fro.

"Impressive. But I'm more impressed by the well-used mattress. This hi-tech stuff attracts the babes?"

Das was shocked. "Oh, no Captain Buick. I told you, I am pledged to be married in Mumbai."

"Yeh, right. So why the mattress?"

"Well, Captain Buick, you see —"

"Oh no. Don't tell me. You live here?"

Das did not answer immediately. He was too busy. Then he said, "you know, if I were a terrorist I would choose a place somewhere near where we are right now and use a short range missile. There are many available."

"Your boss has already told you not to go that way. You're already in trouble. He'll send you back to Mumbai, if you're not careful.

"Not if I am right. And I will prove I am right if I have to work all day and all night to do so." He stopped briefly and turned to face Buick. "Please Captain, stay with me a while and I will show you what I can do with my video data bases. You know, the database of stolen cars that the Newark PD uses owes its existence to me," he boasted.

"You're kidding. Really?"

"Not kidding. I merged the police reports with my video databases and produced a very useful source for you. That's why when you check out a license plate, if the car was stolen, or the plate was stolen, you get back not only the information of the car, but a video of it wherever it was last seen in my database. Pretty amazing, if I may say so, captain."

"I haven't used it much, I have to admit. Anyway, car theft doesn't have much to do with terrorist attacks."

"Really, captain? I am surprised, since it is a very effective way for a terrorist to use a vehicle without divulging his identity."

"They usually rent them, don't they?"

"I don't know much about terrorists, but if I were one I would not rent because it leaves a trail and requires that I produce some identification which exposes me to risk, even if the document ID itself is stolen or forged. Stealing is much cleaner."

"So have you searched your database for a stolen truck that would carry missiles?"

"Not yet. But I am about to."

"But your boss is right, isn't he? I mean you're obsessed with this missile idea because you're in love with your database. You don't have any evidence."

"It's a hunch, sir," Das answered, reverting to his submissive role. "You know what the U.S. Nine Eleven Commission said in 2004, when it criticized America's failure to anticipate the attack?"

"No, what?"

Das turned to face Buick squarely, and he recited, taking on the demeanor of a kid spelling the winning word in a spelling contest, "The most important failure was one of imagination."

*

"Don't know what I am doing here," said Silenzio, "it's late at night. In fact, it looks like even you hardly come here." She surveyed MacIver's office. It was sparse, lined with book cases that contained few books. There was one computer, obviously never used. In fact the whole office looked hardly used. There was a shiny leather couch placed opposite the desk.

MacIver stood beside her, just inside the door. He made no effort to sit down at his desk. "I try to stay away from the school," he said, "most of what they do here is useless, in my opinion."

"And that goes for the books you don't have on your shelves?"

"Pretty much."

"Interesting. So you are unappreciated and unloved?"

"Pretty much."

"So there's no one back home who loves you?"

"What is this, enhanced interrogation?"

"Pretty much."

"So far, I think I can cope with it. And no, I'm divorced for quite a while. Never felt like subjecting myself to it again. Let me guess. You're a career girl. Always single."

"Hmm. He can do enhanced interrogation too, except that he answers the questions he doesn't ask."

"Yeh. I guess it's *Jeopardy* all round."

Silenzio turned to face MacIver, looking in amusement and anticipation. She elicited the desired response.

"You are a very beautiful woman," observed MacIver, almost embarrassed.

"From a professor I was expecting something a bit more poetic," answered Silenzio grinning.

"As a scientist, best I can do is mumble something about birds and bees."

"And a shy scientist at that, even though you love the spotlight of TV cameras."

"I see it as career advancement, in contrast to this," said MacIver as he waved his hand at his desk and bookshelves, "which is career interference." He slid his arm softly around Silenzio's waist and guided her to the couch. But she was already moving towards it. He kicked the door closed behind him.

*

The door to MacIver's office burst open. Das and Buick rushed in. MacIver and Silenzio were straightening their clothes, MacIver behind his desk, Silenzio standing by the couch.

"Sir! Sir! We know where the terrorists are! You wouldn't believe it!" yelled Das, oblivious to everything around him.

"No I wouldn't," replied MacIver, staring at Das with annoyance.

"Listen to him MacIver. I made him come to you. He didn't want to," said Buick looking over Das's shoulder.

MacIver looked to Silenzio.

"Larry?" she said.

"OK. This better be good. What do you have?" said MacIver trying to stand tall and unruffled.

"You see," said Buick, "he was showing me Google Street view and comparing it to the street surveillance he does and —"

MacIver interrupted. "Das, you tell it please."

"Well, as he said sir, I was doing my street view —"

"OK. OK. We know that. Where are the freaking terrorists?"

"They're on Skyline Drive, sir. Not far from the restaurant."

"So you drove right by the terrorists to come and tell me that? Why didn't you call me?"

"Because we can't be absolutely certain it is them. Captain Buick is having his men run the license plate of the truck."

"What truck?"

"The truck they used to pick up the missiles from the warehouse at Port of Newark, sir."

"And how do you know that?"

"Because, sir, with my street surveillance I do for my car theft research, I noticed it show up in several places between the warehouse and Skyline drive. And trucks aren't allowed on Skyline Drive."

"That's it?"

"Sir, well sir, we also noticed when we drove past the house where the truck was parked, that there was a big blue tarpaulin spread over the roof of the house that faces the NYC skyline."

"And?"

"Sir, I know sir, it's just supposition. But I just know that the terrorists are in there. And there is a way —"

Buick cut in. "Once we find the truck, we'll have a better idea."

"And?" asked the skeptical MacIver.

"It didn't come up stolen. I'm guessing it's a rental. I should get a call any minute on what company. Trouble is it's too early, no one in their offices yet."

"It's not enough. And it's all suspect because Das, here, having thrown science out the window, 'just knows' the terrorists are there."

"Of course there is another way," suggested Buick.

"Your way?" said Silenzio.

"Right. I get my boys together, form a strike force, and we go in there and take them out."

"Sure. And we kill a bunch of innocent suburban citizens who are renovating their house."

"Sir, I was going to say, sir, that there might be a way to verify that the missiles, sorry, the hypothesized missiles, are in there, sir."

"Go on."

"Well, it's thanks to you sir."

"Das, get on with it!"

"Long ago, sir, you advocated the installation of Wi-Fi ID chips on all new weapons. Many armories have adopted that, including the U.S. Military which uses it to track weapons for logistical purposes. I may have a transponder that can read the Wi-Fi signals. All we need to do is drive by the house and see if we get any signals. Also, sir, I do have in my office a data base of stolen or missing weapons, worldwide. There are thousands lost every year. I'll search for anything that would be ideal for firing at NYC from New Jersey. That's why we came back to my office, sir, but then we saw the light on in your office."

Das started to back out of the office. Silenzio suddenly felt she had to explain why she was there. "Professor MacIver was teaching me about hardening targets," she blurted. Das did not hear. He was already running to his office. And at that moment, Buick got a phone call.

"Hey, what's up?" said Buick. "No kidding? Great, thanks a lot." He closed the phone. "It was a rental truck. Whoever rented it paid cash up front. The guy who rented it had a heavy accent, probably Russian. Used a false address and ID. That's enough for me. I'm getting my strike force together. There's too much at stake here."

"Buck, take it easy," cautioned Silenzio. "Let's wait and see what Das comes up with. Can we find out where the shipment that they picked up at the warehouse came from? Customs is supposed to keep a detailed database of incoming and outgoing cargo."

"I don't know any of the feds," said Buick, looking for help.

"Let me make a couple of calls," responded Silenzio, "I may be able to get access to the customs database." Silenzio opened her phone.

"Come to Das's office," said MacIver, "he will access the database."

MacIver and Silenzio pushed past Buick who muttered, "while you're screwing around, me and my team will take them out," then left without waiting for a response.

*

In any ordinary student's office, there would have been enough room for MacIver and Silenzio. But Das had so much equipment crammed in there, a plethora of computers, video screens, cables and other hi-tech paraphernalia that Silenzio had to remain at the door, peering in. Besides, Das needed to be able to scoot around on his desk chair from one terminal to another.

"It's amazing how many weapons are reported lost or stolen here and around the world!" said Das as he crouched over his computer.

"I'd be amazed if you found anything," said MacIver, excited in spite of himself.

"What date do you think the truck was at the warehouse?" asked Silenzio.

"Up to three weeks ago," came the answer.

"OK. Then here's the password to the U.S. Customs data base of incoming cargo." Silenzio passed her phone to Das.

"Trouble is I'm not quite sure what I'm looking for," said Das as he scooted to another computer, almost running over MacIver's toes. "Come on! Come on! Do your work," he said affectionately to his computer. He quickly scooted back to the Customs database. A few more key strokes, then, "hey, what do you know! A shipment from Mumbai was picked up on the day in question. Says they are cooling pumps bound for Indian Point nuclear power plant." Back to the other computer. "That gives me an idea! You know the perfect missiles for this job? The brand new Indian mini Nags! Just a minute, let me search the missing weapons data base."

MacIver and Silenzio watched, amused and captivated. The genius was at work!

"Here it is! Two mini Nags reported lost around the time of the shipment. There are two mini Nag missiles in that house!"

It was time for MacIver to pour cold water on the speculation. "It's just supposition, Das."

"But sir, enough to justify at least knocking on their door. Sir?"

"If you could fit your laptop with a transponder we could sit outside the house and see what ID chips responded to our signal, I suppose," said MacIver without enthusiasm.

"Sir, as a matter of fact, sir. I have one. I use it at the supermarket."

"At the supermarket? What on earth for?"

"Sir, you don't want to know, sir."

Das rummaged through the drawers of one of his desks, looking for the transponder.

"Don't tell me," said MacIver amused, still thinking about the supermarket, "you were changing the prices on the items that had Wi-Fi ID chips."

"Sir, here it is! I will need to install it on my laptop. May have to write some quick code to allow it to access the missile IDs. With some luck, I could even find a gateway into their control systems. Sir, would that be OK sir?"

"What do you think, Agent Silenzio?" asked MacIver with a smile.

"Entirely justified. But we have to hurry, get there before Buick and his big guns."

"Sir, if you can drive my Google van while I work on the code, sir? I know it's a bit unusual."

"I can manage. Used to have one in another life, to drive my kids around."

"You have kids?" asked Silenzio, surprised.

"Now's not the time. Let's get out to Skyline drive."

*

Rage, it's all in the hands, thought Buick as he rode the elevator down from MacIver's fifth floor office. It was a slow elevator and as it moved in response to his way too hard hit on the LOBBY button, he stood impatiently, pushing the fist of his left hand into the open palm of his right. He pulled his phone out and started to thumb through his contact list to pick his team. But his thumb wasn't ready for it. It wanted to stay clenched. He could squash the little phone in his hand.

He reached Washington Street and got into his cop car, which he had left idling in a no standing zone. He sat trying to calm down. He thought of those movies and comic books he used to read in the seventies. It wasn't the super heroes who fascinated him. It was the bad, really evil guys, who used their super powers to destroy any object or person at will. That scene in one of the Star Wars movies. The old guy who was obviously full of rage, pointed his finger at Luke and caused him all sorts of pain. He nearly killed the poor kid! Buick never had a rage problem until that horrible day of the nine eleven attack. One of his mates from NYPD whom he knew from police academy, was killed. But it wasn't only that. He just got so mad watching the TV channels, all of them, show the plane hitting the tower over and over again that he got up and — with his hands — picked up the whole TV, carried it outside into the little front yard of his little house in Hoboken, and beat the hell out of it with a snow shovel. Now *that* was rage, he smiled to himself.

The very next day he had enlisted in the services, with the ambition to become a Navy SEAL. And that is how he ended up in Iraq where he saw more violence, but up close and personal. Not like the nine eleven disaster which was horrendous enough to look at over and over again on TV, but in Iraq he saw it up close and in full color, as they say. It was possible, using the mind control techniques his navy counselor taught him, to close off the nine eleven imagery, get it out of his mind. But he couldn't close off the scenes of carnage he saw in Iraq. There it was different. Besides, he had to admit that he caused some of the carnage, most times coincidentally, but sometimes intentionally. He had to watch while his buddies were maimed. What would they do when they had their hands blown off, he would ask himself. How would the rage find its way out?

Buick wheeled the car out into the traffic. He was thinking of his little two year old nephew. He knew how to express his rage and he didn't need his hands to do it. He just opened his mouth wide like an opera singer and bellowed. It had an immediate effect. Anyone within earshot would stop as if to say, "Shut that kid up!" And once he learned to shut up, his rage would quickly find another way out, through his hands. That's why, for his last birthday, Buck had bought him a hammering set so he could bang wooden pegs with a wooden hammer. It took him forever to find it. He'd had one when he was a little kid. They didn't make them anymore, but he found one in a specialty toy shop in Ridgewood. Buick looked at his watch. Maybe he could pay a visit since his nephew and his single mom lived just around the corner on Central Avenue. A visit there would work wonders. But it was too late. Way past midnight.

He had calmed down. Now he could call his guys and put together an awesome strike force and take those bastards out.

15. Transponder

The journey up Skyline Drive was dark and quiet. The road wound through nature reserves that covered most of the roadway, so the only source of light was that provided by the old Dodge van. MacIver kept the lights on dim. Occasionally they passed through commercial districts or residential enclaves whose spotty lights broke open the darkness, but not enough to stimulate MacIver or Silenzio to speak. Das muttered to himself as he worked feverishly at his lap top. As time went by, MacIver started driving more and more slowly, trying to guess at what point he would need to stop. Das looked up and said, "Keep going, keep going. It's about another five miles, I think. You'll see it on your right, back from the road, an open lot surrounded by forest. And there's a small commercial center just the other side of it. So you should see those lights in time for you to turn off your lights and pull up in front of the house." Das enjoyed giving instructions to his boss. He turned back to his lap top and reached to the roof to adjust an antenna.

*

MacIver allowed the van to roll slowly to a stop, lights and engine switched off. They could just make out the tarpaulin flapping lightly in the breeze. There were lights on inside, the shades pulled well down. "I'm going to knock on the door," said MacIver.

"I wouldn't do that," whispered Silenzio.

"Wait, sir. I'm getting signals," said Das, "several signals. Probably several parts inside the missiles have ID chips."

"Probably a TV or stereo system," said MacIver with a hint of "I told you so."

"No, sir, there is a match at least with one of the chips with an ID in my lost or stolen data base."

"I'm going in!" announced MacIver in a loud whisper.

"No you're not!" commanded Silenzio.

155

"I'll just knock on the door. That's harmless enough."

"At five in the morning? And a black van out front bristling with antennae? Better to wait for Buick."

"That's why I want to go in now. To avoid unnecessary bloodshed."

"You're so sweet, but really naive. If you knock on their door, they'll welcome you with a bullet."

"I'll be ready. I've got my own, you know." MacIver patted a bulge under his jacket.

Das noted the pat. "Sir! You pack a gun, sir? You're a Rambo sir!"

"And you need to come with me. Can you disarm the missiles?"

"Sir! I'm no Rambo sir! I can do what I need to do from here."

"And you can disarm the missiles?"

"Sir, I don't know sir! Reading the ID Wi-Fi chips was easy. Getting into the device manager is very hard."

"I'm going in. They are most likely preparing the attack right now. The original nine eleven was at exactly 8.46 AM."

"So that gives us 24 hours at least," said Silenzio as she gripped MacIver's hand. "You're no Buick. Keep that trigger finger in your pants!"

"You underestimate me. I'm one of the best in my gun club, you know."

"Shooting clay pigeons, or whatever, is different from shooting terrorists. Besides, there's nobody shooting at you in your club."

MacIver pulled his hand away from Silenzio. "I know what I'm doing," he said.

"No you don't!" Silenzio used all her considerable strength to restrain him. "Look," she said, "let's call Buick to see where he is."

"Sir, it would be helpful if we knew what the payloads were, sir," said Das.

Silenzio answered, "I am assuming the worst. Nuclear." She was about to open her phone when it rang. "Buick?" she asked, "where are you?"

"Had a hard time rounding up enough guys this time of night. There are six of us. That should be enough to take on these Al Qaeda animals."

"Can you get a hold of a Geiger counter and any other equipment that could detect payloads, including bio-toxins like anthrax or ricin?"

"Already thought of that. We have a remote nuclear detector. But there's nothing for anthrax or ricin. Have to physically collect samples. But we're bringing what we have."

"Better bring protective gear too."

"Will bring a few for you guys. My guys don't wear that stuff. We draw the line at bullet proof vests."

"And you call me Rambo!" whispered MacIver to Das.

"So where are you?" asked Silenzio.

"Be there in ten minutes."

"Tell him no sirens!" pleaded MacIver.

"Buick? No sirens!" She looked at her phone. There was no response. "Don't know if he got it," she said, closing the phone.

*

Turgo had achieved everything he wanted on that day. Now, he lay on a cot in the corner of the room, napping, his eyes covered by a sleep mask, Shostakovich playing quietly in the background. The near dead Russian had been dragged to the opposite corner. The technicians had already placed the two missiles on the launcher. Two technicians were tinkering with the missiles, painting labels in roughly drawn letters. One had so far written, IN LOVING MEMORY, BIN — and still had the payload door open. The other was just putting the finishing touches to, HAPPY BIRTHDAY FROM AL QAEDA.

Two guards, dressed in old jeans and jackets, stood by the front and back doors respectively, handling their automatic weapons. "Getting light outside," said one. "Should check."

"Not open curtains! Stay away from window," called the one remaining technician.

"But heard car pull up."

"You want let know we here?"

"But if raining not pull back tarp."

"You're paid to guard. Not give advice. Take up posts by the two doors. We'll hear the rain anyway, fool," said the technician derisively. Turgo stirred. "Look now, you woke him up."

"Could slip out back while still dark. Check for spies," persisted the guard.

Turgo removed his eye mask.

"Spies? What spies, you fool. The Americans have no idea we are here! How could they know?" mocked the technician.

Turgo sat up on the cot. "They know nothing!" he said, clearing his throat, hoarse from sleeping with his mouth open. "They fear everything. But we not take chances. Go out, take trash can to front."

The guard went to the back door.

"Leave your gun, fool!" ordered the technician.

"But, what if spies there?"

"You as bad as Americans. Go on, get out there! Trash can just outside door. Must get all that ricin and crap out anyway," said the technician as he pointed to a large black trash bag in the kitchen. The guard grabbed the trash bag and pulled it through the doorway. He heaved it into the bin and wheeled it to street. It was then that he noticed the Das van. Being without his weapon, he began to retreat, but then changed his mind. He would find out who they were.

MacIver was the first to see him. "Someone's coming! I'll talk to him," he said excitedly.

"And say what?" asked Silenzio.

"You'd rather I shot him?"

"I'm beginning to doubt your reputation as a cool, rational scientist."

Suddenly, Das climbed out of the van, holding up a magnetic sign in one hand and an ID in the other.

"Das! What the —" exclaimed MacIver.

Das slapped the sign on the car door as he climbed out. He waved to the "hypothesized terrorist," a term MacIver had insisted on, who walked cautiously towards him. Das remained standing by the van, waiting until the hypothesized terrorist was close enough to see the sign, which read GOOGLE STREET. "Good morning sir!" said Das politely, "sorry to disturb you. I am the Google man, recording video for Google's wonderful Street View web service." He flashed his Google ID. "I'm sure you have seen the Google van driving around. Have you tried Google Street view on the web?"

"Yes. No. Don't like this here," said the hypothesized terrorist. "You go soon?"

"In no more than twenty minutes. We're having some trouble with one of our hard drives."

"You invade privacy, no?"

"Oh no sir! We video only public streets."

"You go soon please."

The hypothesized terrorist walked slowly backwards, stumbling near the trash can. He then turned and walked briskly to the back of the house.

"So who's Rambo now?" asked MacIver as Das climbed back into the van.

"No big deal, sir. In my car theft research a lot of people ask me what I am doing. I just tell them I'm the Google man, show my ID, and they go away."

"Where'd you get the Google ID?"

"Best you don't know, sir."

Silenzio's phone rang. "Buck?" she answered.

"Five minutes away. Sirens off. Tell MacIver and Das to stay in the van. You too."

*

The guard tramped into the kitchen, slamming the door behind him. "A van, antennas all over it. Indian, say he Google man."

"What color is the van?" asked Turgo.

"Black, all black, windows all."

"It's not Google. It's CIA!"

"We take care of them. Just one surveillance van, not many inside."

"Yes, better you take gun this time," said the technician.

"No, not yet" ordered Turgo, "we must bring forward the launch. We do it now! Just one payload to finish."

"But can easily kill them!"

"Yes, Yes. But we don't know what backup they have. And once we start shooting, we have to launch immediately. I will get both missiles at the ready first. Better keep guns at the ready though."

"You want the payload for the other missile?"

Turgo detached the open payload door. "Yes, ready now. Careful!"

"Is small bomb, no?" asked the technician.

"Looks small, but very big explosion. Will be felt for twenty miles around. Even here." Turgo deftly placed the payload in the missile, attached different colored wires and flicked switches to set the launch code. Then he went to his lap top and began programming.

"How long?" asked the technician.

"About three minutes. I set to launch one minute apart.

*

"Patience and perseverance," said Silenzio, once again holding MacIver back, "those are the most desirable characteristics of the scientist, aren't they?"

"Where the hell is Buick?" asked MacIver pulling himself away from her. "If these terrorists have any sense at all, they will figure out that this is not a Google van. It looks more like a CIA or FBI van. We need to be ready. They could attack us any time. In fact, I think we should get out of this van. It's a death trap."

"But sir," pleaded Das as he worked feverishly at his lap top, "I have all my computers here and the databases too. I'm making headway into the missile launch manager. Someone in there is programming the launch right now. I'm monitoring his keystrokes. I just need a minute or two."

"I'm going in there," announced MacIver as he opened the van door.

"No you're not!" Silenzio lunged at MacIver and grabbed him tightly around the waist, hugging him to her.

"Feels like high school," quipped MacIver as he allowed himself to fall back into Silenzio's lap. At the same moment, the lights of an approaching car appeared in the distance, and as they came closer, they suddenly switched off. It had to be Buick.

In the glimmer of dawn, MacIver could just make out two police vans pulling up about fifty yards down the road. Darkly clad strike force officers slipped out, crouching, coming towards him. Buick was signaling orders. The squad split up, some creeping to the back of the safe house, the others dispersing to the front and sides.

Silenzio slackened her bear hug as MacIver stepped down from the van. She followed him out.

"You guys, stay in the car. This is man's work," whispered Buick very much the commander.

"Don't kill! Capture!" called MacIver in defiance. "We have to be able to stop the launch. We can't do it without their help."

"What do you mean? We just shoot up the missiles and that will stop the launch."

"And risk blowing us and everyone around here to smithereens," said MacIver derisively. "Manish is trying to crack the code so he can switch off the launcher."

Das poked his head out the van window. "I think I disarmed one," he said with satisfaction. "Trouble is they are set to fire one minute apart. And I don't know which one I have disarmed!"

"We're going in! Now get back in the van," ordered Buick, but MacIver had already darted up to the front window of the house. Buick sprinted up to him. "OK. Professor," he whispered, "if you must play Rambo. Let me do the assault. There's always a chance something unexpected will happen. You stay out by the door ready to save me if I'm cornered, right?"

MacIver nodded.

16. Countdown

Turgo was barking orders. They had the missiles at the ready and were in their final countdown phase. The technician and one of the guards were having difficulty pulling down the tarpaulin from the inside. In the end they cut it around the edges of the hole they had made in the roof, revealing the dim light of a fresh dawn sky.

"We are ready? Must get away from the launcher, or we may be incinerated. When I say to, run for the garage outside." Turgo placed his lap top on the kitchen bench. He tapped one button. "OK! Go!" he barked. The launcher clock began counting down from 60 seconds.

Buick and his force burst through both doors and side windows. The earsplitting crash and din of Buick's men as they broke in stunned Turgo and his technician. They froze.

"Not the old guy!" shouted Buick.

The two guards, however, were at the ready. The main guard had waited just inside the front door and when Buick broke through, he grabbed him in a vice-like neck hold, forcing him to drop his weapon. The other guard was killed by Buick's men, along with the unarmed technician. But now there was a stand-off. Buick eyed Turgo, who stood, poised over his lap top at the kitchen counter, a superior smile on his face.

Buick tried to point at Turgo. "Kill him! Kill him!" he commanded.

"I kill you!" threatened the guard, jamming the barrel of his weapon into Buick's back. Buick's men hesitated.

"Too late anyway!" said Turgo mockingly.

"Kill them, kill them all, including this asshole! We are minutes away from the destruction of New York!" cried Buick.

Suddenly, MacIver appeared at the doorway, his revolver raised in both hands. The guard was surprised, just enough to make him pause for a fraction of a second. That was all MacIver needed. Buick saw the gun recoil in MacIver's hand, and immediately his captor's body slumped to the floor. MacIver had shot him clean through the temple, the bullet coming out the other side of his head and grazing Buick's cheek, spattering it with bits of bone, blood and brain. Without a 'thank you' to MacIver, Buick reached for his weapon and leaped towards Turgo.

"This one's mine!" shouted Buick, pushing Turgo with the butt of his weapon.

"You are too late. When will you Americans ever learn?" mocked Turgo.

"Is that right?" retorted Buick as he casually shot Turgo in the foot. Turgo screamed.

"Stop the fucking launch!" yelled Buick.

Turgo groaned, but did not answer. The counter was at ten seconds.

Buick yelled again. "OK. Asshole. Maybe this will help." He shot Turgo again, this time in the upper leg.

More screams of agony, but Turgo refused to answer. Instead, he glanced quickly over at his laptop on the kitchen bench. MacIver followed his gaze and stepped over to the bench, grabbed the lap top and ran towards the door. Das may be able to use it, he hoped, and then almost collided with him at the door.

"Watch out!" Das cried. "The first missile was programmed to launch in 60 seconds, which must be nearly up!"

The orange LED counted down relentlessly. Five, four, three, two, one, zero!

No launch!

MacIver breathed a sigh of relief. "You picked it Manish! You're a genius! You saved us!"

Das was happy that he had pleased his boss. But he had bad news. "Unfortunately," he said, "I haven't been able to crack the code for the second missile."

"Here's his lap top. Will that help you?" asked MacIver.

"It would take me more than 60 seconds to learn how the laptop is set up. Besides, it's probably in Russian," answered Das, "I'll keep trying with my own."

The launch counter started again at 60 seconds.

"Officer. Cuff the suspect," ordered Buick, "no, not like that. To the bottom of the launcher."

"Buick! You can't!" said MacIver with consternation.

"It's him, or several million innocent people dead. An easy choice, don't you think?" retorted Buick.

The counter reached 30.

"You mean it's nuclear?" asked MacIver.

"Come on you Russian asshole. What's the code?" Buick bashed Turgo's bleeding leg with the butt of his weapon. Turgo responded with the desired scream of agony. "Give it up, or you'll be with Allah in just a few seconds."

Counter reached 15.

"Allah? Who cares about Allah?" mocked Turgo, still convinced of his own superiority. "If you paid me a million dollars, then I'd give it up —"

"Sure, I can get you a million. But I don't have any money on me right now. The code or burn!"

Counter is at 10.

Das shouted hysterically, "I think I did it!"

"You stopped it?" asked his boss.

"Not exactly. I diverted it."

Counter is at 5, 4 —

"Get out of here all of you, or we'll be badly burned!" ordered Buick.

The countdown continued relentlessly: 3, 2, 1, zero!

Lift off!

The missile launched and the heat from its propulsion incinerated the screaming Turgo.

*

Hearing such awful screams, Silenzio ran from the van to find MacIver. Everyone shaded their eyes, trying to follow the streak of the missile as it flashed across the dawn sky. But it had already disappeared from view.

"God! If it's nuclear," cried MacIver squeezing Silenzio's hand. "Manish, where is it going? This is a catastrophe!"

"Sir, I'm sorry sir. But I think that it's going to hit the biggest —" Das stopped in mid-sentence. There was a muffled explosion and a huge black cloud appeared over the New York City skyline in the direction of Ground Zero. Later, he would tell others that he felt the ground shake beneath him.

"It's not a mushroom cloud," observed Silenzio. "I've never seen anything like it."

"No, it wasn't nuclear," said Buick, "at least it didn't register on any of our instruments."

"Thank goodness. But it was a huge bomb, that's for sure. God knows where it has hit," said MacIver.

"Sir, as I was saying, sir. I think I diverted it to the biggest rubbish dump in the world, even bigger than the one in Mumbai!"

"What? Where?" interrupted MacIver.

"The Staten Island dump, sir!"

*

Police sirens sounded and a host of cars descended on the site.

"You saved us all, Manish. I'm so proud of you!" said MacIver as he made an attempt to put his arm around Das's shoulders and to hug him.

"Oh no sir! It is thanks to your excellence. You are my Guru, sir!" replied a proud Das, wriggling away from the hug as politely as he could.

Buick finished giving orders to his men and sidled up to MacIver.

"You saved my life," he said, "thank you."

"Just a scientist doing what he had to do," replied MacIver, "you also saved our lives."

"Still, I have to hand it to you. Where'd you learn to shoot like that?"

"At my gun club."

"I told him it would be harder for him killing real people," said Silenzio who was standing by, listening in, "boy, was I wrong!"

"I have to admit," said MacIver with some hesitation, "I found it pretty easy and very satisfying. It gets a bit boring shooting clay pigeons, especially when you hardly ever miss."

Buick turned to him and grinned. "We'll make a real cop out of you yet!" Then, as though this had reminded him of who he was, he said, "I better call my chief." He had suddenly realized that his own position was a little precarious. "He's not going to be pleased. I never told him anything."

A helicopter appeared and landed right in the middle of Skyline Drive. Mayor Newberg stepped down, followed by Foster. They hurried forward, bent over by the noise and wind of the helicopter. The Mayor was obviously very pleased.

"I can't stay long," she said, "just wanted to thank you all. You saved many lives."

"Was anyone killed at the dump?" asked MacIver.

"None reported so far."

The Mayor called to Buick who was again issuing instructions to his men for clean-up and securing the site. "Captain Buick. I want you to know that I will do what I can to protect you. There's going to be fallout from his, and you will be an easy target."

"No problem Madam Mayor," replied Buick, smiling and clearly unperturbed. "You forget. I used to defuse bombs. Politicians don't scare me."

"No doubt," she said, "trouble is, though, that politicians can sometimes be more destructive than bombs."

A TV crew approached. Foster tugged at Mayor Newberg's arm and whispered to Buick, "watch your back."

Avoiding the cameras, Mayor Newberg darted back to her helicopter, just as another appeared a few houses away.

Silenzio tugged at MacIver's arm. "I need to hide," she said, "coming?"

Das intervened. "Yes, please. Come and I will drive you both in my van. Or if you would prefer, sir, my Guru, why don't you and Agent Silenzio take my van, and I'll find my way back with captain Buick, sir."

MacIver had already walked towards the TV crew. Das turned to Silenzio and shrugged.

"Could you give me a lift, Manish?" asked Silenzio. Manish opened the door with a flourish and a bow. Silenzio was about to enter, when she heard Buck Buick shouting orders again. She stopped to listen. He came bounding across the lawn.

"I need to hide real quick. I expect you feel the same. Want a lift in a sexy not-so-undercover police car?" asked Buick.

Silenzio looked across to MacIver then back to Buick.

"Let's get out of here," she said.

*

It's hard to believe, but Mr. and Mrs. Kohmsky had their truly first and only big argument the day Mrs. Kohmsky returned from the bank with the incredible news that the debit card had an account of $100,000. They had never had a real argument. It was in fact impossible, or so thought Mrs. Kohmsky, to have an argument with her husband for the simple reason that he did not talk, or talked hardly at all. Having an argument with him was like having an argument with oneself. But this time Mr. Kohmsky spoke up, not only that, he kicked the furniture a couple of times too. The argument was over what to do with the money. Mrs. Kohmsky wanted to go to the FBI and give them the card and access to the account so they could use the information to track the origin of the account, and maybe that would lead them to Sarah. Mr. Kohmsky was adamantly opposed. The FBI would take the money and do nothing, he insisted, and could not be shaken from this position. Mrs. Kohmsky persisted, and every day at breakfast raised the issue. And every day for some days, Mr. Kohmsky had either ignored her, or grunted out through those pursed lips of his that they were not going to hand the money over to those liars. Mrs. Kohmsky cried, at first putting it on in an attempt to soften him up, but of course after so many years, she should have known better. There was no softness there. So the breakfasts soon became more authentic — she was crying because she really was upset. And through the tears she tried to get her immovable husband to just give a bit. Didn't he care about finding their daughter? The money had to have something to do with Sarah. What about the password that spelled her name? And it was evidence, wasn't it, that she was not dead? They both agreed about that, didn't they?" Finally, at the last breakfast they had together, Mr. Kohmsky could stand it no longer. He threw his book across the room, jumped up, his tall frame almost reaching to the ceiling, and kicked the chair over. Mrs. Kohmsky cringed and sank into her chair. He then righted his chair, sat down, pulled off his shoe and, yelling obscenities, he banged it on the table, just like Khrushchev did.

Sobbing, Mrs. Kohmsky ran to the bedroom and sobbed some more. She heard Mr. Kohmsky walking back and forth, back and forth like a caged animal. "He must have put his shoe back on," she mused as she fell into a fitful sleep.

*

It was still light when Mrs. Kohmsky woke. She had no idea what time it was, and the apartment was silent. Her eyes stung from the salt of her tears. She slipped into her old slippers and shuffled out to the kitchen intending to make herself a cup of Russian tea. Maybe that would perk her up. Mr. Kohmsky was seated at the kitchen table, reading his book. He never looked up as she passed him on her way to fill the electric kettle. Things were normal as far as he was concerned. She clanged the cups and saucers while she waited for the water to boil. Finally, she asked querulously, "Want a cup of tea?"

"Good," he said, not looking up from his book.

She poured the tea and brought the cups to the table, and as a special offering, added a couple of plain sugar cookies, the one indulgence that he accepted. She sat across from him and sipped her tea. It was too hot so she had to slurp it to cool it down as she sipped. Then Mr. Kohmsky reached for a cookie, dipped it lightly in his tea and took the soaked part into his mouth, slipping it between his tight lips. After he swallowed — the movement of his Adam's apple that Mrs. Kohmsky had come to loathe — he spoke, not looking up from his book.

"We will go to the State Department," he said.

"What is that?" asked Mrs. Kohmsky.

"The United States Embassy. The State Department."

"Do you mean the CIA again?"

"Perhaps. But we should try the State Department. Tell them that our daughter disappeared from Oxford and we suspect she is held hostage somewhere, probably in Russia since that is where the previous packets of money came from."

"But how would we explain the money? Hostage takers ask for money. They don't give it away to the victims," Mrs. Kohmsky argued, forcing Mr. Kohmsky to acknowledge the absurdity of his position.

"Of course you are right. Then we will not show them the debit card. Just the envelope it came in.

"But the debit card with its bank account is the first time there is a chance of following the trail of the money. Someone had to open that bank account and put the money in it." Mrs. Kohmsky was on the verge of tears again. She realized that their conversation was beginning to escalate into a repeat of their last argument.

Mr. Kohmsky sat, still looking at his book, silent. Mrs. Kohmsky dabbed at her eyes with a Kleenex. Minutes went by. Mrs. Kohmsky could see that he was staring at his book, but was not reading it. She shifted on her seat.

"We will go to the State Department and tell them everything we know," he said.

Mrs. Kohmsky looked up, a small glint in her eye. "We could spend the money first," she said, almost apologetically.

"On a trip to Russia," answered Mr. Kohmsky.

Mrs. Kohmsky thought she detected just a tiny hint of a smile. It made her happy. And then he continued:

"Go back for good."

17. Droned

The Hamas section leader droned on. The dozen or so operatives sat on the floor, impatient to have their say. Shalah Muhammad was in a foul mood. He always was after meeting with Hamas, an organization run by a verbally aggressive people who never listened, who spoke to others as if delivering a lecture on every topic, whether something simple or pedestrian such as brushing one's teeth, or something dreadful like sending a teenage suicide bomber into a coffee shop. Their bodies and their minds, were infected by what Shalah Muhammad called a psychosis of liberation theology that was transmitted from generation to generation of peoples who had known no other reality but one of repeated rape and plunder of their property and their loved ones. Certainly an understandable psychosis, but that didn't make dealing with them any easier, especially with their top strategists and leaders. It narrowed their outlook. As he had always argued, they were no different than the PLO, except that they were much smarter. But, as they demonstrated even after he got rid of Arafat for them, they were unable to examine all options as he could, to do it dispassionately, to anticipate the outcomes of terrorist attacks; to plan the long range strategies needed to establish an independent Palestinian state. No matter what they said, and they said a lot, they could not exist without the financial and ideological support of the West. Talk about false consciousness! This was it! The result was that they brought on themselves the ire of the Israelis that simply added to their consternation and suffering. They clung to old ways of doing things, and their enemies benefitted by it. Their persistence with suicide bombing was a good example. The Israelis were on to them, had been for a few years now. Yet, in the face of repeated failure, they kept at it, wasting lives and money.

Several people were now talking at once. He looked at his watch and was relieved to see that it was time to leave. He grasped Sarah's hand and nodded to the door. They quietly let themselves out, unnoticed by the speakers or their audience.

169

*

Sarah held Shalah Muhammad's hand, stroking it lightly, as they sat in the back of the BMW. She could see that Shalah was fed up. She would calm him. They had just departed what was left of the town of Abed Rabbo in Gaza. Their Hamas contacts had insisted on meeting with them there, again, Shalah was sure, in order to make an obvious point: it was the town that was bombed out of existence by Israel's 'Operation Cast Lead' in 2009. Hamas had driven Israel to distraction and the destruction of Abed Rabbo was the predictable result. So he was seething with anger. Anger at what the Israelis had done to the men, women and children of Abed Rabbo, anger at the Hamas operatives and their insufferable psychoses, and now, anger at Sarah, whose stroking of his hand was really annoying him. She was like a leech, he thought to himself. A blood sucking leech.

Shalah pulled his hand free from Sarah's caresses to look at his watch again. It was getting late in the day. He leaned forward to tell the driver to go faster. He did not want to be late. Seeing the spectacle of the second bombing of Ground Zero would make up for the annoyances of the day.

Sarah remained silent. She had learned from her parents that this was the way to deal with the anger of others. Well, not exactly, since her dad remained silent regardless. And her mom, poor old mom, had learned to cope with the silence and so replicated it, if that was the right word. Sarah allowed herself to drift back to those times. She thought now that her mom had tried very hard to communicate with her, but she had not responded. Why did I do that? She asked herself. There just seemed to be something missing inside her. Maybe she was born without something that made her want to get attached to her mom and dad. The very strange thing was that she felt 'closer' relatively speaking, to her dad than to her mom. People used to say that she was like him. And it was obvious that he had no feelings at all for anyone. Or if he did, he didn't show them. It had been a long time. Maybe she should try contacting them, just to let them know she was all right. The idea had been floating around in her head for the past month or so. Actually, since she met up with Uncle Sergey. It was why she disobeyed him and tried to call Nicholas. She found herself biting at her lower lip. What would Shalah say if she said she wanted to go home? Or even just call home? If only he would return her affections. She loved him so.

A feeling of grief or maybe loneliness, she was not sure what it was, welled up within, her eyes watering up. And just as a small tear was forming at the edge of her eye, the driver swore and stamped on the brakes.

"Checkpoint! Where in Allah did that come from? There has never been one on this road before." They stopped some forty yards from the checkpoint. Two officers appeared, Uzis raised at the ready, one came cautiously forward.

"This is suspicious. They're acting like they knew we were coming and that they know who is inside. Have to assume they may be looking for me," said Shalah.

"And me?" asked Sarah.

"Of course not," said Shalah, "why would they be looking for you? You're a good American Jew."

"You better get into the trunk," warned the driver.

"How can I without them seeing me?"

"They think BMWs don't have access to the trunk through the back seat, and they're right. Except for this one. Pull the lever at the top of the seat back."

"This is really humiliating. They will pay for this, whoever it was who fingered us," growled Shalah. He quickly lowered the back half of the seat, roughly pushing Sarah out of the way, then crawled into the trunk. "Close it!" he called to Sarah.

Sarah closed the seat back and without difficulty spread herself out across the entire back seat. "OK. Go!" she called to the driver.

The driver approached the officer slowly, and lowered his window. He could see there would be no conversation. The officer had his Uzi at the ready, pointing at him and ready to fire at anyone else in the car.

Sarah lowered her window. "Is there a problem officer?" she asked in as broad an American accent as she could.

The officer moved to her window as she lowered it; he could see that she was the only occupant, and a large one at that. He asked for her ID and she gave him her American passport. He looked at it carefully and scanned it into his iPhone. There was no match. "OK, looks good," he said and passed it back. "I just need to check the trunk. Could you flip it for me please driver?"

Sarah did all she could to hold back a gasp. She was terrified and hoped he could not see it in her face.

"This model does not flip from the cabin. It's not locked, though. You can open it from the outside," said the driver trying his best not to offend.

The officer moved to the rear of the car and lowered his Uzi to the side while with the other hand he felt for the pressure latch. The lid did not pop right open as do the Mercedes trunks, but remained just a few inches open. He began to lift it when Shalah Muhammad swiftly thrust it full open, knocking the officer momentarily off balance, giving Shalah time to grab him by his collar and pull him down to the trunk, banging his head on the way down, then in a well-practiced flash of his right hand, he slit the officer's carotid artery with his box cutter.

"Go! Go!" he yelled and fell back into the trunk, trying to pull the lid closed behind him. But the driver took off with great speed, the BMW 328xi sport responding beautifully. The car hurtled forward, speeding past the remaining officer who managed to get off a few rounds of his Uzi, most of which missed, though some ricocheted loudly off the wildly flapping trunk lid. With Sarah's help Shalah struggled into the back seat. But the car began to swerve crazily and only then did Shalah notice the blood streaming out of the driver's ear as he fell forward either unconscious or dead. Shalah quickly reach over to steer the car.

"Kommie! Grab his leg, pull it off the accelerator!" he yelled.

Sarah struggled forward, her bulk making it very difficult to reach the driver's leg. She managed to get a handful of his trousers and pull it up. The car slowed. She shoved the gear stick into ONE and it lurched drunkenly to a halt. Shalah climbed into the front seat and steered the car to the side of the road. There was no vehicle chasing them, but it would not be long before there was. He grabbed the driver's cell phone and brought up its GPS. They were on the edge of Jerusalem, an area where there were few houses and light traffic, and quite a few pedestrians who were keeping well away from them.

"Are you OK?" he asked Sarah.

"Just. Not hit or anything."

"We need to get away from here. It's not that far to the safe house. I'll call for a car." Shalah was about to make the call with the driver's cell phone when Sarah leaned over and snatched it from him.

"This phone. The IDF is tracking us with it. That's how they knew we were approaching," she said.

"You're right. Let's get out of here."

They got out of the car and hurried across the street and into an alleyway. Sarah hurled the phone as far away as she could. Shalah was already calling for a car and it arrived in no time, an old 1979 Peugeot diesel 504 in poor condition. Trouble was that it was such an exceptional car that people stared at it, which is not what Shalah and Sarah wanted right now.

"Did you have to bring this car?" Shalah asked.

"Only one we had. Sorry."

They climbed in and Shalah issued directions. They would go by a circuitous route and get dropped off a few streets away from their destination. Later, the driver would bring their luggage, always shipped separately in case something like this happened.

*

At last they arrived at the safe house. Sarah had been looking forward to this visit for some weeks now. Maybe Shalah would let go just this once, and give himself to her. Despite their recent adventure, he was in good spirits, bounded up the steps to the house and thrust open the door. Halid the handler had left it unlocked and had pinned a note on the door bidding them welcome, saying he was attending the celebration of his son's tenth birthday. He had done well. There was a big screen TV in the video area, just as Shalah had requested. He walked immediately to the kitchen and saw that the refrigerator was well stocked, then checked the bedroom to find that Halid had installed a bed, not much of a bed, but a bed just the same. He returned to the kitchen and called to Sarah to turn on the TV. Then his eyes lit up when he saw the bottle of Johnny Walker blue label on the bench. The Handler had done well! He would try to find him a new job in Iraq. Pouring himself a double shot, he returned to the front room to watch the TV.

"Naughty, naughty! Allah is watching," kidded Sarah as she sidled up behind him, put her arms around his waist, and planted little kisses on the back of his neck. He's even handsome from behind, she thought. Shalah tossed down the shot and strained forward against her weight to grab the remote.

"It's a special occasion," he replied.

Sarah convinced herself that she heard a gentle purr in his voice.

"Allah will be elated when He sees what's coming," he said.

"Shouldn't He already know what's going to happen?" quipped Sarah. Shalah ignored the remark.

The TV came to life with CNN World News. A newscaster prattled on, against the amateur video showing a missile hitting a huge rubbish dump, the news ticker at bottom identifying the place as New York's Staten Island. Shalah Muhammad's eyes widened and he roughly shook himself free from Sarah's hug. The commentator, clearly with a smirk on his face as far as Muhammad was concerned, revealed the awful details:

"At approximately 7.00 AM. Sept. 10, a missile of some kind struck New York's Staten Island. At this time, five people are reported killed, but the number could go higher. There are reports that it came from the direction of Northern New Jersey —"

"We hit them! There'll be dancing in the streets again!" cried Sarah.

"Shut up! Listen!" growled Muhammad. "It's a day too early! Idiots!"

The Newscaster continued:

"There are unconfirmed reports that traces of the bio weapon ricin have been found."

Muhammad threw his arms up, furious. "No nuclear! Those assholes! They dumped ricin in my missiles!" He turned to look at Sarah. His anger was beyond furious.

"What do you mean Shali?" asked Sarah solicitously.

"I mean that your Russian uncle has fucked us over. What did you pay them?"

"Ten million, and promise of five million after the target is hit with both missiles."

Muhammad looked into her eyes, his carefully clipped beard bristling. Little twitches appeared in his cheeks. He smiled grimly, coldly. He reached forward with a hooked finger and pulled at the V of her shirt where her football sized breasts strained at the buttons. He was repulsed by her fatness yet at the same time found her disgustingly ripe. "They're not getting the five million," he said as he drew her towards him.

Sarah could hardly believe what was happening. She allowed him, no, helped him, draw her to him. She had at last found the way in! The key was anger! Make him angry and he wants her! She had dreamed that he would give himself to her. Dreamed of it so often she responded as if the dream were reality. She pecked his cheeks with kisses and quickly they became big sloppy kisses. And now, to her surprise, the dream came true: he voraciously returned the kisses, right on her lips, almost biting them, his tongue looking for more. He pulled her towards the bedroom, and they struggled as if in a one-legged race to get there. The bed stood high, a solitary mattress on a box spring, American style. They propelled themselves as one on to the bed. Ecstasy was near. Sarah ripped open her shirt and pants with tugs and tears, helped by the violent thrusts of Muhammad. Now she was naked and now Muhammad wanted to insert himself in her body as though he were diving into a huge open wound. He allowed her to open his pants and push them down. She was frantic. He was full of the most disgusting lust one could imagine. With great effort, he managed, by grabbing and pulling handfuls of fatty flesh to communicate to her that he wanted her turned over and finally, when this contortion was accomplished, he pushed her forward and had her bent over the edge of the bed. He thrust himself into her, and, feeling for his jacket, peeled it off and threw it across the bed. With his left hand, he clasped her chin from behind and pulled her head back and kissed the nape of her neck. He felt a noise rise up from deep inside of him, a barbaric cry of ecstasy, or a cry of anger, no matter which. Then in a flash, his right hand shot forward and, pulling her chin even higher, he slashed at her throat with his box cutter and swiftly leapt back. He did not want to get blood on his carefully tailored pants.

"She got what she wanted," Muhammad muttered to himself with satisfaction, "she died in total fulfillment. What more could anyone want?"

Sarah's limp body slid off the bed and onto the floor, parts of her flinching like jelly. Muhammad rearranged his trousers and walked to the other side of the bed to get his jacket. He coughed to clear his throat and spat on the body.

"White trash!" he snarled and walked to the bathroom to wash up and clean his box cutter.

*

Shalah Muhammad too was fulfilled. Even though the mission was a failure, a terrible failure in his eyes, he felt greatly satisfied with himself. The feeling of failure had been partly erased by his brief outpouring of rage, the spilling of Sarah's blood, his deep satisfaction that she met her death in ecstasy. Surely that moment was her time in Heaven, he smiled to himself. And he had let himself go for just a few minutes and now he felt that a huge weight had been lifted from his body and his mind. He went back to the bedroom and looked at the scene with satisfaction. He rummaged through Sarah's clothes for her cell phone and flipped it open to her contacts list. He would enjoy dispatching them all, especially her uncle.

He returned to the kitchen and poured himself another shot of Johnny Walker. "Allahu Akbar!" he said as he raised his glass and tossed down the shot. He sat down in front of the TV and lit one of his special cigarillos. The newscaster was still at it:

"This report just handed to me. There were apparently two missiles, one of which was not fired. All the terrorists were killed when a special counter terrorist team, orchestrated by Mayor Newberg of New York, raided their headquarters in a suburban house in northern New Jersey. We go now to one of the counter terrorism team that caught the terrorists red handed."

MacIver appeared on the screen.

"So it was he," muttered Muhammad to himself, "who would have thought?"

"Yes, that's right," said MacIver, responding to the interviewer, "the forensic scientist tries to prevent crime or terrorism from happening. Prevention is better than cure, as they say."

"And it was this approach that led to the killing of these terrorists?" asked the interviewer.

"Not completely, but it certainly helped us find their operational HQ. We used cutting edge techniques originally developed by my student Manish Das for preventing car theft."

"You killed the terrorists rather than captured them. One of them was pretty burned up I'm told. Is this part of the forensic science approach?"

"It was a team effort," answered MacIver, annoyed.

"Some criminologists say you do science with a gun. Is that a fair observation?"

"It's completely wrong."

"But you do carry a gun, I hear?"

The newscast cut back to the commentator who announced, "We have to leave it there. And in other news —"

Shalah Muhammad switched off the TV, looked around the room as though he had forgotten something, and then stepped out of the safe house. He stood at the top of the steps and took a deep draw of his cigarillo, enjoying the crisp evening air.

*

Across the street and around the corner from the safe house, Halid the Handler sat on his moped. His smart phone was open and as soon as he saw Shalah Muhammad appear at the door of the safe house he began tapping out a quick text message. He pressed SEND, waited for confirmation that the text had been sent, then started his moped and sped away down the alley.

Shalah Muhammad looked at his watch. He had not sent for a car, preferring this time to take an evening stroll. He took a deep draw of his cigarillo and looked up at the deepening sky with considerable satisfaction. It was then that he heard a faint, familiar sound. The sound of a drone, and just as he realized what it was, the safe house exploded and Shalah Muhammad was first transformed into fire and brimstone, then all that was left of him on this earth was a very big hole in the ground.

18. Loose Ends

In November, Larry MacIver was awarded the Stockholm prize in criminology in recognition of his contributions to the science of criminology and his brave acts that saved the lives of many. MacIver declined the award and did so publicly by doing the rounds of all the talk shows. This was not a good experience for him because he had great difficulty explaining his decision to his interviewers, all of whom thirsted for public adoration and recognition, and did not hide their obvious resentment and scorn of one who rejected the acclamation of his peers. How could he explain to them that he did not need the adoration of his peers to tell him how good he was? That he himself was the only judge of that. It sounded so arrogant.

Unfortunately, the future was not all roses for MacIver. His knees had given out on him, so he could no longer run his five miles a day. His right knee was so painful he had to get around with a walking stick. What with that and the depression he suffered from not being able to run, he turned into an insufferable oaf, becoming more like the obnoxious TV personality 'House' every day. To make things worse, in order to fend off his depression he had taken to working in his office and attending all faculty meetings assiduously. He drove his colleagues half-crazy with his outlandish behavior and one rather plain looking female colleague lodged a sexual harassment complaint against him. Around that time, MacIver decided to renew contact with his two kids. His daughter would be in college and his son still in high school. There's another long story here and quite frankly a pretty boring one. So we will not go there.

Manish Das, the true hero of our story, at MacIver's urging, turned himself into the University health center to see if anything could be done about his Asperger's disorder, a disorder that someone at that very same health center had diagnosed. The trouble had been -- at least as far as MacIver could fathom -- that Das was unable to get down to writing his dissertation because his disorder kept him collecting data and tinkering

177

with his gadgetry. So MacIver was a bit miffed when Das returned from the health center all smiles, to report that that they had misdiagnosed his Asperger's and that in fact he really had ADD or perhaps OCD, or maybe a bit of both. Whatever it was, this seemed to please Das, and he soon settled down to write his dissertation and to defend it that summer. He returned to Mumbai the following fall to marry as arranged, and MacIver, who made a practice of never attending social occasions when invited by his students, made an exception and went to the wedding. It was a lavish affair, the photos taken at the gate of India, the food on one of the days of celebration consumed in the Taj Mahal Hotel. The following year, Manish brought his bride to the United States and took up his new position as assistant professor at Texas Christian University, where he taught criminology in the department of religious studies.

The following year, Mayor Newberg was re-elected to a second term in a very close contest. Although the campaign was down and dirty as any proper New York City campaign should be, this one was particularly nasty because the deputy police commissioner for crime prevention, Askanazy, ran against her. This was unexpected, since all had assumed that her estranged Police Chief Ryan would run. And he was poised to run too, but unfortunately on the day he announced he was running, he choked to death on a piece of ice he swallowed while drinking a 16 ounce soda.

Mayor Newberg used Askanazy's Russian sounding name against him, reminding New Yorkers that it was Russians who fired the missile at the Freedom Tower, which was now completed. She also cleverly played with the pronunciation of his name, suggesting that it was an appropriate one for a police chief of his overbearing demeanor.

She was also successful in garnering the Islamic vote, even managing to arrange for a mosque to be built, inconspicuously around the corner from the Freedom Tower. Pundits enjoyed insinuating that it was the Islamic vote that tipped the scales in her favor.

Within three months of Mayor Newberg's re-election, the following legislation was issued by the New York City Council, bowing to her demands: all tea and coffee sold in restaurants and fast food outlets was to be decaffeinated; the caffeine in all sodas was to be replaced by the equivalent amounts of Demerol; sugar was banned in all supermarkets and restaurants; cameras were installed in all restrooms that were open to the public and those not washing their hands after they went were issued a "dirty ticket" as it became known; the smoking of cigarettes was now only permitted on Staten Island. She tried, unsuccessfully, to have subway tokens reintroduced so that her likeness could be etched on both sides, but on this the City Council would not budge. Instead, she had to settle for all Metro Cards used for mass transit to be printed with a touched up photograph of Mayor Newberg on one side and on the obverse a statue of a boy from Brooklyn wearing the Roman cap of Liberty.

Buck Buick was placed on paid leave while a special prosecutor appointed by the Mayor of Newark, who was pretty pissed off at having been left in the dark, investigated the charge of his having used excessive force in killing all the terrorists, including torturing and burning one of them to death. He turned to Mayor Newberg for help in finding a good defense lawyer, but she of course did not respond. Help came from an unexpected source. Fred Lee, Director of the Newark Branch of the FBI was promoted to the position of Director of the FBI national counter terrorism special branch, a position that gave him considerable power. He moved quickly to classify all evidence and documents related to the attack on the Staten Island dump as crucial to national security so the special prosecutor was unable to proceed with the case. During his forced paid leave, Buick started watching movies and came across *Hurt Locker*. The very next day he re-enlisted in the marines and went back to defusing bombs and killing terrorists.

The local Newark mosque sued the Newark Police Department and the City of Newark for unspecified damages, for false arrest of its constituents, invasion of privacy of its worshippers, and infringement of their First amendment rights. The mayor settled for an undisclosed amount and to pay for it legalized marijuana in the city, allowing only city owned distribution centers to sell it. This business became so successful that the Newark city council passed a resolution to reduce the property tax by 5% a year until the levy was reduced to zero.

Agent Fred Lee's appointment as director of the FBI Special Counter Terrorism Branch caused Agent Crosby considerable distress. Lee insisted that Crosby move with him to be his assistant in his office that was located at the FBI special training center in Quantico, Virginia. Crosby's wife was pregnant with their third child and did not want to move. Lee could not see the difficulty. "It's a simple choice," he said to Crosby. "You come with me or you stay with your wife." Crosby stayed with his wife and got a job as the security boss at the local supermarket chain. Lee was very upset with Crosby's choice, so he made sure that the Honda Fit went with him to Virginia. Crosby did OK though. He got a company car with his new position, a 2001 black Ford Lincoln town car.

Monica Silenzio's role in orchestrating the rendition of the FBI sting suspects could have come under scrutiny but thanks to Lee's classification of all the documents as top security, nothing ever came to light. In fact, she went on secret assignment for CIA operations in Beijing where she met her current husband, multi billionaire real estate developer, Li Wan Lei. Silenzio quickly learned how to spend huge amounts of money, tastefully, and became a frequent visitor to Sotheby's in New York and London. They celebrated their wedding in the stylish Tribecca Tower in Manhattan, just around the corner from Freedom Tower. She invited both Buick and MacIver to the wedding and both showed up, surprising her, but nevertheless she was most flattered that they bothered. Unfortunately, she had only a few moments with them and was whisked away to meet the many other rich and fawning guests. It ended up rather badly for Buick and MacIver who, seeing an open bar with endless drinks and fabulous appetizers, made pigs of themselves while they regaled each other with stories of adventure and bravery. They stayed by the bar and never quite made it into the wedding ceremony. A large security person, dressed to look like a waiter, white jacket, black bow tie and the rest, hovered around them, and when it became apparent that they were unable to stand up without each other's support, he guided them firmly to the elevator and saw them down to a taxi.

The dental profession lost an outstanding practitioner when Dr. Kumar Jamal decided to retire from the profession and moved to Mumbai to become a Bollywood actor. He had played so many different roles as an ISI double agent, he reasoned, that acting would come naturally to him. With the considerable stash of money he had reaped from the Newark caper, he still had enough to support him for life and even longer, and perhaps, even to bribe whoever it was necessary to work his way into the Bollywood elite. Maybe even invest in his own movie! So he packed his belongings, sold off his dental practice, and took a train, top first class air conditioned of course, to Mumbai. It was during a brief stop at an out of the way station where one of his informers told him that the Americans had droned Shalah Muhammad. He had heard that the Newark adventure was an incomplete success, and should have been relieved by the news of Muhammad's demise. But he knew that Iranian bigots would pick up where he left off, and track him down to extract a portion of their revenge, even though he had done everything on his side perfectly. He gave his informer a much bigger tip than usual and chose to ignore, for the time being, the worrying fact that his extremely reliable network of informers was his Achilles heel. The train slowly pulled out of the station and chugged towards its final destination. Kumar reached into the inside pocket of his jacket and retrieved his ticket for the Enoma International

Film Festival. He looked forward to sitting back in one of the plush theater seats, ordering samosas, sipping on fresh lemonade.

Halid the Handler took early retirement. He explained to his wife and ten year old that they were in danger of being targeted by a drone, so it would be best to go where the Americans could not find him, which was the United States. His wife, in full compliance, did not ask where they would get the money to make the trip, but she could not help but notice that suddenly they had a lot more money to spend. They packed up all their worldly belongings and shipped them to an address in Nogales, Texas where they arrived some months later after a leisurely trip sightseeing in Greece, Italy and France. The Handler even had a job waiting for him, working as a customs and immigration officer at the border entry to Mexico. His son had much trouble adjusting to his new life, and took to yelling abuse at his father who had to constantly remind him that he had a new name, in fact the whole family had new names.

After his brother Nicholas showed up at his house unannounced, Uncle Sergey gave up the terrorism business and joined him in a lucrative trade selling women from Eastern Europe and the more impoverished parts of Russia, which was most of it. At first they began kidnapping these women, but then quickly found that most of them wanted to migrate to America or various parts of the West, so all they had to do was to arrange their forged documents and travel and charge a heavy price. The ones who couldn't raise the money, if they still wanted to migrate, Sergey arranged to send off to brothels or to sell them directly to men who were looking for wives. The business was so successful that they planned to expand into China where there was a well-known shortage of women.

The droning of Shalah Muhammad was the true beginning of his misfortunes. It turned out that Heaven was divided into sectors just like Jerusalem and because of a bureaucratic snafu, or perhaps it was Divine Providence, we will never know, Shalah turned up at the gate to the Christian sector. There he was confronted by St. Peter, who sat before the pearly gates, flanked on each side by two huge muscle bound eunuchs, each with their arms crossed. St. Peter shone so brightly that Shalah had to squint to see past him through the bars of the gates. And the more he squinted, the larger the eunuchs grew because St. Peter knew what he was up to, trying to get a glimpse of any virgin that he reckoned was his due. Most unimpressed by this lasciviousness St. Peter scolded him severely, and, when Shalah argued that he was not a Christian but a Muslim, St. Peter got really mad, checked his ledger, and accused him of being a communist and an atheist. The eunuchs edged forward, the muscles in their arms bulging in anticipation, their huge hands ready to grab him. St. Peter, his long white beard flowing like clouds, his white robes reflecting the glow of the wings of angels, pointed a gnarled finger, its nail uncut for eons, forcing Shalah to cringe at its point. You are sentenced to the deepest circle of hell, said St. Peter–well he didn't say it, he didn't have to, because up there everyone knows what everyone else is thinking–and the eunuchs leaped forward, grabbed him by the throat and testicles and threw him down to hell. There, nasty little demons with pointy tails and pitch forks implemented the specifics of the sentence which were that he must, for all eternity, keep his beard beautifully groomed by clipping it with red hot nail scissors. This may not seem like a punishment that was bad enough, except that in this circle of hell, his beard grew at the rate of an earth-month in one day.

If only Sarah Kohmsky, through some amazing miracle, did not really die at the hands of Shalah Muhammad! But she did die that violent death, even though it seemed unfair that she should meet such a horrible end. Is there not a way that she could live on? The mystery of her life will one day be known. In our story there was a gap of some eight years in her life about which we were told very little. Maybe something really did happen that night she got drunk and woke up in Shalah's bed? Wouldn't it be wonderful if poor Mr. and Mrs. Kohmsky had a grandchild living somewhere, even if it was in Cairo?

Mr. and Mrs. Kohmsky after repeated requests to the U.S. State Department to investigate the whereabouts of their missing daughter, migrated back to Russia. With the money they had received from Nicholas — they were convinced that it was he who sent it — they bought a modest but pleasant apartment in Tulgovichi, the town they had left so many years ago. Mr. Kohmsky, in celebration of his change in life circumstance, gave up reading 19th century Russian literature, and began a systematic reading of the Russian authors of the 20th century, including those who had migrated from Russia to other countries. Mrs. Kohmsky saw no reason to change. She just wanted her daughter back. She sent letters to the return address that was on the envelope they were certain came from Nicholas, but the letters were returned, address unknown. There was just one small matter that kept her busy, though, and that added a little adventure to her life. The CIA had recruited her to collect all kinds of information from the local Russian newspapers and to send it to them on a regular basis. For this, money showed up in their account at the Promsvyazbank in Tulgovichi.

Then one day a small, unmarked package appeared at the door of her apartment. It was rather heavy and at first she was a little apprehensive about opening it. She consulted with Mr. Kohmsky who lifted it slowly up and down and pronounced it safe. So she opened it and found a small burial urn. Inside the urn were ashes, or more accurately a substance that looked like a mixture of sand, small bits of rock, and ashes of some kind. She knew that it was Sarah.

In spite of political wrangling within Israel and condemnation by the United Nations, the fences in Israel and the Palestinian territories continued to be built and thwarted many suicide bombings every year. Unfortunately an astute politician noticed that some of his neighbors were sporting chicken coops that were far more elegant than the chickens they contained. He happened to joke about this during an interview with a journalist for *Haaretz* who instantly smelled corruption. Upon investigation he exposed an extensive network in stolen fencing wire that looked suspiciously like that used in the fences erected in the Palestinian territories. The government defended its actions by pointing to the fact that there were a number of Palestinian houses that also had similar chicken coops, which proved that, contrary to the naysayers, Israel and Palestine were able to achieve much when working together.

THE END

About the Author

Colin Heston is the pen name of a criminologist of international repute, so he knows something about the world of crime and terrorism. As a criminologist Heston has written nonfiction books on the history of punishment and torture, edited a four volume encyclopedia on *Crime and Punishment around the World* and many other nonfiction books, including the controversial *Just and Painful: A Case for the Corporal Punishment of Criminals* (Macmillan/Harrow). He contributes regularly to a variety of criminology and criminal justice journals. His next novel, *Murder Aborted* will be released early in 2017, and his collection of short stories, *The Tommie Felon Show*, will be available in paperback in the fall of 2016.

Read other books on Crime and Punishment published by Harrow and Heston, available on line on Amazon and most other e-book publishing outlets.

Migration, Culture Conflict and Crime edited by Joshua D. Freilich, Graeme R. Newman, S. Giora Shoham, Moshe Addad.

A Primer in Private Security by Mahesh Nalla and Graeme Newman.

Who Pays? Casino Gambling and Organized Crime by Craig A. Zendzian.

Representing O.J.- Murder, Criminal Justice and Mass Culture by Gregg Barak

A Primer in the Sociology of Crime by John P. Hoffmann and Shlomo Shoham.

A Primer in the Psychology of Crime by Mark Seis and Shlomo Shoham.

From Gangs to Gangsters by Marylee Reynolds.

Corporate Crime, Corporate Violence by Michael J. Lynch.

Race and Criminal Justice edited by Michael J. Lynch and E. Britt Patterson.

Close Control: Managing a Maximum Security Prison by Nathan Kantrowitz.

Vengeance: The Fight against Injustice by Pietro Marongiu and Graeme R. Newman.

Vendetta (Italian) by Graeme R. Newman and Pietro Marongiu.

The Mark of Cain by S. Giora Shoham

Salvation through the Gutters by S. Giora Shoham

Sex as Bait by S.Giora Shoham

Discovering Criminology from W. Byron Groves edited by Graeme R. Newman, Michael J. Lunch.

Punishment and Privilege edited by Graeme R. Newman and W. Byron Groves.

Personality and Deviance by S.Giora Shoham.

Crime and Social Deviation by Shlomo Shoham.

HARROW AND HESTON
Publishers

NEW YORK

Made in the USA
Middletown, DE
27 May 2018